R.D. VILLAM

The Great English Mess: The Queen Who Dances on Thrones

Copyright © 2024 by R.D. Villam

All rights reserved. No part of this publication may be reproduced, stored or transmitted in any form or by any means, electronic, mechanical, photocopying, recording, scanning, or otherwise without written permission from the publisher. It is illegal to copy this book, post it to a website, or distribute it by any other means without permission.

This novel is entirely a work of fiction. The names, characters and incidents portrayed in it are the work of the author's imagination. Any resemblance to actual persons, living or dead, events or localities is entirely coincidental.

R.D. Villam asserts the moral right to be identified as the author of this work.

R.D. Villam has no responsibility for the persistence or accuracy of URLs for external or third-party Internet Websites referred to in this publication and does not guarantee that any content on such Websites is, or will remain, accurate or appropriate.

First edition

This book was professionally typeset on Reedsy.
Find out more at reedsy.com

Contents

I   When Conquest Goes Wrong

The Day William Didn't Conquer	3
The Not-So-Merry Band of Conquerors	6
Dinner, Diplomacy, and a Double-Cross	9
Edgar's Last Stand (Or So He Hoped)	13
The Great Royal Rumble (and the Art of the Quick Exit)	17
The Throne Nobody Really Wants	21
The Throne's Final Joke	26
The Final Backstab (With a Side of Carnage)	30
The Crown Nobody Wanted (Except Everyone)	36
The Common Man's Crown (or: How Not to Start a Revolution)	41
Edgar's (Final?) Comeback and the Curse of the Crown	46

II   When the Crown is Cursed

The Prophecy of Doom	53
The Curse That Just Won't Quit	57
Crypts and the King Who Wasn't	61
The Crown and the Council Conundrum	66
Crusaders and the Pope's Problem	71
It's Always the King	77
The Cursed Relic Below	82
Normans, Scots, and the Pope's New Pet	87
Prophecies and the Perils of Ancient Enemies	92

The Pope and the King Who Fell	99
The Queen of England	104

III   When It's England vs the World

Suitors and the Pope's Latest Ploy	113
Knights, Lords, and the Papal Sword	119
Unholy Alliances and Unruly Lords	123
Vikings, Vows, and Vatican Vipers	127
Rebellion and Retaliation	132
Feast and False Foes	137
Daggers in the Dark	142
Celtic Complications	147
Allies and Ambushes	153
Deals, Deceits, and Dangerous Waters	158
The Queen's Conquest	163

IV   When Kingdoms Clash

French Fury and the Imperial Favor	169
The Emperor's Tribute and the Scottish Demand	173
The French Counterstrike	177
The Gathering Storm	181
The Sicilian Offer and the Merchant Plot	185
How to Break a Kingdom (And Make It Look Like an Accident)	189
The Best Laid Plans...	196
Of Kings, Popes, and Rebellious Bretons	200
The Long Game	205
The Breaking of Paris	210
The Queen Who Dances on Thrones	214

I

When Conquest Goes Wrong

The Day William Didn't Conquer

It was the morning of October 14, 1066, and William of Normandy was feeling exceptionally confident. Too confident, perhaps. As he mounted his horse, he glanced at his men, who were also busy polishing their helmets, sharpening swords, and double-checking whether they had packed enough arrogance for the day.

"Well, lads," William announced, with the kind of smugness only a man wearing chainmail that glistened just a bit too much could muster, "by tonight, we'll be dining on English pie!"

His men cheered, though one or two in the back quietly wondered if they even liked pie. But no one dared question William. After all, he was the man who had survived countless battles, conquered territories, and spent a small fortune on a banner that showed him striking a heroic pose.

The battlefield of Hastings stretched out before them, an expanse of gently rolling hills, thick forests, and what seemed like an unusually high number of rocks. Across the way, Harold Godwinson's forces stood ready, looking less glamorous but perhaps a bit more grounded in reality.

"Nice weather for an invasion," William's squire remarked, squinting up at the uncharacteristically clear English sky.

"Indeed," William replied, missing the squire's subtle jab. "Even the heavens favor us."

And with that, the Battle of Hastings began. Arrows flew, swords clashed, and the air filled with the sounds of men grunting, yelling, and occasionally making bad puns about hitting rock-bottom. William led the charge, his horse thundering forward as if it had somewhere far more important to be.

But as fate would have it, the same fate that had brought William to the shores of England and gifted him with dreams of a crown, had a different plan for the day. One of those inconvenient rocks happened to be in just the right place—or rather, the wrong place, depending on one's perspective.

William's horse, usually a model of equine grace, suddenly tripped over that very rock, sending the would-be Conqueror flying in a less-than-majestic arc. For a brief moment, William soared through the air, arms flailing, his helmet tilting dangerously over his eyes. Time seemed to slow down as he had a fleeting thought about whether his victory banner would need editing.

And then, with an unceremonious thud, William of Normandy, Duke of Normandy, the man who would be king, landed headfirst in a very muddy puddle.

His men, seeing their leader in a compromising position, quickly rushed to his side. The sight was, to put it mildly, less than inspiring.

"Lord William!" one of his knights gasped, trying to pull him from the muck. "Are you alright?"

William, now wearing more mud than armor, grunted as he tried to stand. "Never... been better," he wheezed. "This... is just a tactical... puddle."

But as he attempted to rise, the fates, ever the comedians, decided that this was William's grand finale. The sudden movement combined with the impact and the rather inconveniently placed rock had done more damage than anyone realized. William's breath caught in his throat, his vision swam, and with one last defiant gasp, he slumped back into the mud, his dreams of conquest slipping away with him.

Silence fell on the battlefield as the Normans stared in disbelief.

"Well, that wasn't in the script," one soldier muttered.

Across the field, Harold Godwinson, who had been bracing for the fight of his life, lowered his sword in confusion. "Did... did he just—?"

"Fall off his horse and die in a puddle?" his brother Gyrth chimed in, blinking. "Looks like it."

There was an awkward pause before Harold cleared his throat. "Well, that's... convenient."

The English forces, not entirely sure what to make of the situation, slowly began to cheer. The Normans, on the other hand, stood dumbfounded, their leader now nothing more than a muddy heap.

Back in Normandy, they would later call it the Battle of Hastings: The Wet Conquest That Never Was. As for William, well, his name would be remembered, though not quite in the way he had hoped.

The Not-So-Merry Band of Conquerors

As the Normans stumbled back to their camp, still reeling from the unfortunate demise of their leader, Harold Godwinson found himself in an unusual position. He had just won a battle by essentially doing nothing.

"So," Harold said, trying to keep a straight face, "what now?"

"Maybe a celebratory feast?" his brother Gyrth suggested, "Nothing too fancy—just enough to say 'we won because the other guy tripped'."

Harold nodded. "Right. But first, let's make sure the Normans know we're still here, and, oh, that we're taking Normandy next. You know, for good measure."

Meanwhile, across the channel in Normandy, news of William's untimely demise spread like wildfire. The Norman nobles, who had been eagerly awaiting tales of victory and riches, were instead greeted by the grim reality that their glorious leader had met his end in a puddle. And with no one clearly in charge, they did what any self-respecting noble would do: they started bickering like children over who got to sit on the biggest throne.

"If anyone should lead us, it's me!" Robert of Mortain declared, pounding his fist on the table. "I'm his half-brother, after all!"

"You mean the *half* that was always in the shadows," Odo of Bayeux shot back, "No offense, but you couldn't conquer a vegetable garden, let alone England."

"And you could?" Robert sneered. "You're a bishop, for heaven's sake! What are you going to do—bore them to death with a sermon?"

"Better than drowning in a puddle, Robert," Odo snapped.

As the argument grew louder, Matilda, William's widow, watched from the sidelines, sipping her wine with the resigned air of someone who had seen this coming a mile away. She leaned over to her maid, whispering, "You know, I've always wondered what it would be like to run a country without a man getting in the way. Might be time to find out."

Meanwhile, back in England, Harold was already setting his sights on Normandy. After all, if they had defeated the Normans once by simply standing there, why not take their homeland? It was practically an invitation.

"Think about it, Gyrth," Harold said as they stood on the cliffs overlooking the Channel. "They're in chaos. No leader, no direction—just a bunch of nobles tripping over themselves, and they've got even more puddles over there!"

Gyrth squinted across the water. "What's our plan? Send them a note asking if they'd like to surrender?"

"Not quite," Harold grinned. "We invade, offer them pie, and if that doesn't work, we let them argue themselves into submission."

And so, within weeks, Harold and his forces set sail for Normandy, armed with swords, shields, and an overwhelming sense of déjà vu. As they landed on Norman shores, they were met not with resistance but with confusion. The Norman nobles, still caught up in their squabbles, hadn't even noticed the English arriving.

"What's this?" Odo said, squinting at the horizon. "Are those... sails?"

Robert, who was already three goblets of wine deep, blinked. "Did we invite the English?"

"No, you fool, they're invading!" Matilda, who had taken command of her own forces in the absence of any competent men, stepped forward, a wicked grin on her face. "But don't worry, boys. I've got this."

Meanwhile, in London, a different kind of chaos was brewing. With Harold off to Normandy, the English nobles back home had started to wonder if perhaps Harold's leadership wasn't exactly inspiring. Sure, he had won a battle, but mostly due to William's unfortunate slip. Was this really the guy they wanted running the show?

Enter Edgar the Ætheling, the last male member of the royal House of Wessex and a man who had spent his entire life being the runner-up in every political race he entered.

"Now's our chance, lads!" one noble whispered to another. "Harold's off playing conqueror. Let's put Edgar on the throne before he gets back."

Edgar, who had all the ambition of a damp sponge, found himself being hoisted onto a makeshift throne in the middle of London with a crown that barely fit his head.

"Do I have to?" Edgar asked, glancing nervously at the crown-bearer.

"Yes," the nobles chorused, practically shoving the crown onto his head.

"Alright, but if Harold gets back and isn't too happy about this, I'm blaming all of you," Edgar muttered.

Back in Normandy, Harold's forces had successfully landed and were making quick work of the disorganized Norman resistance. The English soldiers marched into town after town, met mostly with indifference or, in some cases, pies. Matilda, however, wasn't about to let her husband's legacy—or what was left of it—be trampled by the English.

As Harold's forces approached her stronghold, she stood on the battlements, surveying the incoming troops. "They want to play conqueror, do they?" she muttered to herself. "Well, two can play at that game."

And so, as Harold's forces reached the gates, they were met not with resistance but with an invitation.

Harold frowned as he read the parchment handed to him by a nervous-looking messenger. "A dinner invitation? From Matilda?"

Gyrth leaned over to peek at the note. "Do you think it's a trap?"

"Probably," Harold shrugged. "But it's not like she has an army to back it up. What's the worst that could happen?"

Dinner, Diplomacy, and a Double-Cross

The moon hung low over Normandy as Harold Godwinson, recently rebranded as Harold the Conqueror of the Conquerors, approached the grand hall of Matilda's castle. Inside, the Duchess of Normandy had orchestrated a feast worthy of a king—or at least a future king who might need a little persuasion.

As Harold stepped into the hall, the first thing that struck him was the overwhelming smell of roasted meats, fresh bread, and... was that pie again?

"Either she's really into hospitality," Gyrth whispered beside him, "or she's trying to fatten us up."

Harold, who was never one to turn down a good meal, smiled diplomatically. "Well, let's hope it's the former, or we might need a bigger boat for the trip back."

At the head of the table, Matilda sat like a queen in waiting. Her eyes sparkled with mischief as she raised a goblet in greeting. "Welcome, Harold! I trust your journey was pleasant, though it must have been exhausting—invading and all."

Harold chuckled, taking a seat across from her. "Just a little jaunt across the Channel. You know how it is. One minute you're defending your country, the next you're thinking, 'Why not take Normandy too?'"

Matilda smiled sweetly, though there was something dangerous in her eyes. "Indeed. Normandy is such a prize. But wouldn't it be easier if we simply... joined forces?"

Harold paused, the pie halfway to his mouth. "Joined forces? You mean, you and me... together?"

"Oh, don't look so shocked," Matilda said, rolling her eyes. "William's gone, and I'd rather not see his legacy reduced to a muddle of squabbling nobles. With you as my husband, we could rule England and Normandy as one. A true power couple."

Gyrth, who had been busy sampling the wine, choked. "Power couple? Is that what they're calling it these days?"

Harold, ever the pragmatist, considered the offer. "And what's in it for me?"

Matilda leaned in, her voice silky smooth. "You'd gain control of Normandy without spilling any more blood, and you'd have a partner who knows how to keep these nobles in line. Think of the alliance we could build—no more fighting, just ruling."

It was a tempting offer, and Harold knew it. But before he could respond, the doors to the hall burst open, and a breathless messenger stumbled in, clutching a parchment with shaking hands.

"Sire! Urgent news from London!"

Harold frowned, taking the letter. As he read, his expression darkened. "Edgar the Ætheling... crowned king in my absence? The nerve!"

Gyrth leaned over his shoulder, scanning the letter. "Looks like the nobles back home decided you were taking too long and put Edgar on the throne. Can't say I blame them—what with you vacationing in Normandy and all."

Harold scowled, crumpling the parchment in his hand. "I leave for five minutes, and they give my crown to a man who couldn't even lead a parade. Looks like we'll need to head back to England sooner than planned."

Matilda, sensing her window of opportunity closing, swiftly changed tactics. "You don't have to choose, Harold. Take Normandy and England. Marry me, and we can deal with Edgar together. After all, a crown is only as strong as the head that wears it."

Harold hesitated, weighing his options. On one hand, securing Normandy through marriage would solidify his power in Europe. On the other hand, England was already slipping through his fingers, and Edgar wasn't exactly a worthy adversary—more like a walking, talking placeholder.

Just as he was about to respond, the door creaked open once more, and a new figure stepped into the room—a tall, broad-shouldered man with a thick, fur-lined cloak and an unmistakable air of menace.

"Harold," the man's voice boomed, his accent unmistakably Scandinavian, "I hear you've been making quite a mess of things."

Harold turned, recognizing the man instantly. "Harald Hardrada? I thought you were dead!"

Harald Hardrada, the King of Norway, grinned, his teeth flashing like a wolf's. "Rumors of my death were greatly exaggerated. Thought I'd let you two fight it out first before I made my move. Smart, right?"

Gyrth groaned, rubbing his temples. "Oh, great. Now we've got a Viking. Could this get any worse?"

Matilda, ever the strategist, sized up the newcomer. "So, you've come to claim England as well?"

Harald nodded, his eyes gleaming with ambition. "England, Normandy— why stop there? I could use a little more real estate in my portfolio."

The hall suddenly felt much smaller as three rulers—or would-be rulers— found themselves caught in a tangled web of alliances, betrayals, and overcooked ambitions.

Harold, who by now was getting quite fed up with all the interruptions to his dinner, stood up, looking between Matilda and Harald. "Alright, here's how this is going to work. Matilda, you get Normandy, but I'm not marrying anyone tonight—I have a crown to reclaim. Harald, if you want England, you're going to have to go through me. And Edgar? Well, he's about to have the shortest reign in history."

"Bold words," Harald growled, "but I've got an army waiting for me on the coast. And I don't think they're here to chat."

"Same," Harold shot back, "but mine actually know how to follow orders."

Matilda, sensing that the dinner party was rapidly turning into a battlefield, decided to make her own move. "Gentlemen, perhaps we can all agree that fighting each other to the death isn't the most efficient way to resolve this. Why not work together—just long enough to get what we each want?"

Harald raised an eyebrow. "And what's in it for me?"

"Simple," Matilda said, with a smirk. "We take England together, split it up like a pie, and leave Edgar with the crumbs."

Harold and Harald exchanged glances, each weighing the offer. Then Harold, ever the pragmatist, nodded. "Fine. We'll work together—for now. But once Edgar's dealt with, we settle this between us."

Harald grinned. "Deal. I've always wanted to see how you English fight up close."

An uneasy alliance was formed, with Harold, Harald, and Matilda setting their sights on England and the crown that sat, ever so uneasily, on Edgar the Ætheling's head.

Edgar's Last Stand (Or So He Hoped)

London had never looked more chaotic. The city's streets buzzed with rumors, as commoners and nobles alike tried to wrap their heads around the fact that there were now three—not one, but three—armies marching toward the capital.

In the heart of the city, Edgar the Ætheling, King-for-the-moment, paced nervously in what he was still trying to convince himself was his throne room. The crown on his head felt heavy—not with the weight of responsibility, but with the sheer absurdity of the situation.

"Well," Edgar muttered, glancing at the nervous cluster of advisors around him, "this has escalated quickly."

"Majesty," one of the more optimistic advisors stammered, "maybe it's time to consider our options? Negotiation, perhaps?"

Edgar snorted. "With Harold, the man who probably thinks I stole his crown? Or with Matilda, who likely wants to use me as a footstool? Not to mention Harald Hardrada, who I'm fairly sure eats people like me for breakfast."

There was a brief, awkward silence before another advisor spoke up. "We could... uh... ask the Welsh for help?"

Edgar blinked. "The Welsh? Are you serious?"

"It's either that or we try to win them over with pie," the advisor said with a shrug. "But I'm told the Welsh aren't big on pastry diplomacy."

With a deep sigh and the resignation of a man who has run out of both good and bad ideas, Edgar finally nodded. "Fine. Send word to the Welsh. Tell them we'll pay them handsomely—assuming we win and actually have anything left to pay them with."

Meanwhile, just outside London, the uneasy alliance of Harold, Matilda, and Harald Hardrada was making its way toward the city gates. The tension between the three leaders was as thick as the morning fog, and every step closer to London felt like one step closer to a dagger in the back—or the front, depending on who decided to betray whom first.

"So," Harald said casually, as his army of fierce Norsemen marched behind him, "what's our plan once we get inside? Kill Edgar and fight over the scraps?"

Matilda shot him a sly look. "You're so predictable, Harald. We're not savages, you know. We simply remove Edgar from power, divvy up the land, and leave it at that."

Harold raised an eyebrow. "And we're just supposed to trust each other?"

Harald grinned wolfishly. "Of course not. But isn't that half the fun?"

As they approached the outskirts of London, their combined forces spotted something unusual—a ragtag band of warriors gathered just outside the city walls, looking like they'd rather be anywhere else. At the front stood a short, stout man in armor that didn't quite fit, holding a banner that flapped pitifully in the wind.

"Who on earth is that?" Gyrth asked, squinting at the strange sight.

Harold narrowed his eyes. "Is that... Edgar?"

Indeed, it was Edgar, looking as regal as a man can look when surrounded by what could generously be described as the least threatening army in history.

"He must be joking," Matilda said with a smirk. "Is this his idea of a last stand?"

Before anyone could respond, a loud horn sounded from behind Edgar's pitiful force, and from the treeline emerged an unexpected—and equally ragtag—reinforcement: the Welsh. Their arrival was greeted with mixed reactions from the Londoners, who had heard of the Welsh but never imagined they'd see them coming to Edgar's aid.

Harold sighed, rubbing his temples. "Great. Now it's a comedy."

"Or a tragedy," Matilda added dryly.

Harald, however, seemed more amused than anything. "So, the little king has some friends after all. How cute."

As the three leaders weighed their options, Edgar took a deep breath and did what no one expected: he stepped forward, holding up his hands in a gesture of peace.

"Harold!" he called out, his voice shaking slightly. "Matilda! Harald! Can we not resolve this without bloodshed?"

There was a moment of stunned silence as everyone processed the fact that Edgar was actually trying to negotiate.

"Is he serious?" Harald muttered under his breath.

"Apparently," Harold replied, though he didn't seem convinced.

Matilda, always the diplomat, decided to play along. "And what exactly do you propose, Edgar?"

Edgar swallowed hard, clearly stalling for time. "I... I propose that we—"

But before he could finish, a horn sounded in the distance—one that didn't belong to any of the armies currently in the field. Everyone turned to see a fourth force emerging on the horizon, their banners unfamiliar and their armor gleaming in the afternoon sun.

"Now what?" Gyrth groaned.

As the fourth army approached, the figure at its head became clear: it was none other than *Tostig Godwinson*, Harold's estranged brother, who had apparently decided that now was the perfect time to make his own play for the throne.

"You've got to be kidding me," Harold muttered, his hand tightening around his sword.

"Tostig?" Matilda asked, arching an eyebrow. "Wasn't he supposed to be dead?"

Harald laughed, a deep, booming sound that echoed across the field. "This just keeps getting better and better. Who else wants to claim the crown today? Anyone? Going once, going twice?"

As Tostig's forces came to a halt just outside the reach of the other armies, he raised his voice to address the gathered leaders. "I hear there's a crown up for grabs! Mind if I throw my hat into the ring?"

Harold groaned audibly. "Of course, you would show up now, Tostig."

Tostig grinned. "Brother, it's been too long. I see you've made some interesting friends."

The field was now a tangled mess of alliances, betrayals, and more crowns than anyone knew what to do with. Edgar, for his part, was just trying to keep his knees from buckling under the pressure.

"So," Edgar said, his voice cracking slightly, "anyone else want to make a dramatic entrance, or can we figure out how to get out of this alive?"

The other leaders exchanged glances, each one silently calculating the odds and considering their next move. It was clear that the battle for England's crown had become far more complicated than any of them had anticipated—and that the only certainty was that nothing was certain anymore.

The Great Royal Rumble (and the Art of the Quick Exit)

The battlefield outside London was a scene straight out of the most confusing tapestry ever woven. On one side, Harold Godwinson stood with his battle-hardened English forces. Beside him, Matilda of Normandy surveyed the chaos with a calculating gleam in her eye. Across from them, Harald Hardrada grinned, his Norse warriors eager for blood. And finally, there was Tostig, Harold's estranged brother, leading a group of opportunistic mercenaries with the confidence of a man who has nothing to lose.

And then there was Edgar the Ætheling, who was trying very hard not to wet himself.

"Right," Harold said, trying to maintain some semblance of order. "We can still settle this like—"

Before he could finish, Harald Hardrada let out a war cry that could have frightened a mountain. "Enough talk! Let's see who really deserves this crown!"

With that, the Norwegian king charged forward, his men following with the kind of enthusiasm reserved for people who genuinely enjoyed the smell of battle. The English forces braced themselves, shields raised, swords drawn, while Tostig's mercenaries—clearly inspired by the prospect of a good fight and maybe a bit of loot—joined in.

"Here we go," Harold muttered, raising his sword. "Gyrth, stick close to me. And for heaven's sake, keep an eye on Tostig. I don't trust him as far as I can throw him."

"Considering he's your brother," Gyrth replied, "you might want to rethink that strategy."

The two sides clashed in a cacophony of steel, shouts, and what sounded suspiciously like someone singing a Viking drinking song. The battlefield became a swirling mass of chaos, with everyone swinging swords at anything that moved—and some things that didn't.

In the middle of it all, Matilda found herself ducking and weaving with surprising agility. "This wasn't quite what I had in mind," she grumbled, deftly dodging a particularly wild swing from a Norseman. "I was hoping for more negotiation and less decapitation."

"Join the club," Harold called out, parrying a blow from one of Tostig's mercenaries. "But it's a little late for that now."

As the battle raged on, Edgar the Ætheling stood frozen at the back, gripping his sword with the white-knuckled terror of someone who has never actually used one. The Welsh, who had been his last hope, looked just as eager to avoid the fray.

"Uh, Sire?" one of the Welsh leaders whispered, glancing nervously at the carnage. "Maybe it's time to consider a strategic retreat?"

Edgar blinked, the gears in his mind turning slowly. "Retreat? But... wouldn't that make me look like a coward?"

The Welshman gave him a look that clearly said, *Do you really need to ask that question right now?*

"Better a live coward than a dead king," the Welshman pointed out. "Besides, you can always come back later. When they've all killed each other."

Edgar, finally seeing the logic, nodded quickly. "Right. Yes. A strategic retreat. That's exactly what I was about to suggest."

And so, while the rest of the armies hacked and slashed their way through what was rapidly turning into a bloodbath, Edgar and his Welsh allies quietly slipped away, leaving behind the mayhem and the distinct possibility of reclaiming the crown later—preferably when there were fewer people trying to wear it.

Meanwhile, back on the battlefield, things had taken a decidedly more brutal turn. Harold and Harald Hardrada had found themselves in a vicious one-on-one, their swords clashing with the kind of intensity that only comes when two men are equally stubborn and equally angry.

"You know," Harald grunted as he swung his massive axe, "if you'd just given me the crown, we could have avoided all this mess."

"If you'd stayed in Norway," Harold shot back, dodging the blow, "we wouldn't be having this conversation!"

They continued their deadly dance, neither gaining the upper hand, while nearby, Tostig and Matilda had found themselves in an equally tense standoff.

"So, brother," Tostig sneered, circling Harold with a predatory grin, "are you finally ready to admit you should've treated me better?"

Harold, who was starting to feel the strain of battle, didn't bother with a reply. Instead, he lunged at Tostig with renewed fury, their swords meeting with a sharp clang. Matilda, watching the brothers' fight with a mixture of interest and disdain, decided to pick her moment carefully.

"Men and their petty grudges," she muttered, sidestepping a fallen soldier. "Honestly, if they put half as much effort into ruling as they do into killing each other, we wouldn't be in this mess."

But just as it seemed the battle might never end, fate—or perhaps irony— decided to intervene. As Harold and Harald Hardrada locked eyes in what could only be described as mutual murderous intent, a stray arrow, loosed by some hapless soldier in the thick of the fray, arced through the air and found its mark with unerring precision.

Harald Hardrada's eyes widened as the arrow struck him square in the throat. For a brief moment, he stood there, almost surprised by the turn of events, before crumpling to the ground in a lifeless heap.

Harold, covered in sweat and blood that wasn't all his own, stared at the fallen king. "Well, that was... unexpected."

Tostig, seeing his chance, lunged at Harold with a triumphant roar. But before he could land a blow, another arrow—this one loosed by a different soldier, who clearly had no idea what side he was on—whizzed through the air and buried itself in Tostig's chest.

Tostig's triumphant grin faltered as he looked down at the arrow, then back up at Harold. "You... lucky... bastard," he gasped before collapsing beside

Harald.

Harold, now thoroughly exhausted and wondering if he was the only one left standing, looked around the battlefield. What remained of the armies were either retreating or lying on the ground, dead or dying. Matilda, ever the pragmatist, had already started making her way to the nearest exit, clearly deciding that this was no longer worth her time.

"Well," Gyrth said, stepping up beside Harold and surveying the carnage, "that's one way to settle a dispute."

"More like the worst possible way," Harold muttered, wiping blood from his brow. "Is anyone left alive?"

Gyrth looked around, then shook his head. "Doesn't look like it. I think Edgar ran off with the Welsh."

"Of course he did," Harold sighed, staring down at the bodies of Harald and Tostig. "And here I thought I might actually get to rule England in peace."

As the dust settled and the crows began to circle, Harold took a deep breath, feeling the weight of the crown pressing down on him more heavily than ever before. He had survived the Great Royal Rumble, but at what cost? The throne was his—for now—but it seemed that in the end, the crown was more of a curse than a prize.

"Come on, Gyrth," Harold said, turning away from the battlefield. "Let's go find Edgar. I have a feeling this isn't over yet."

The Throne Nobody Really Wants

As the sun set over the blood-soaked fields outside London, Harold Godwinson trudged back to the city, his armor dented, his sword dull, and his patience worn thinner than a beggar's cloak. He had outlasted two rival kings and his own treacherous brother, but somehow, the crown felt heavier than ever.

"What now?" Gyrth asked, limping alongside him. "You've got the throne, the army's mostly intact, and the enemies are mostly dead. Isn't it time to relax?"

Harold groaned. "I'd love to, Gyrth, but I'm not foolish enough to believe this is over. Edgar's still out there, probably rallying the Welsh and trying to figure out how to hold a sword the right way up. And if Matilda isn't plotting something, I'll eat my helmet."

Gyrth chuckled. "You'd think after all this, they'd give it a rest."

"They will," Harold replied grimly, "when they're dead. Or I am. Whichever comes first."

Meanwhile, in a shadowy corner of a Welsh forest, Edgar the Ætheling sat huddled with what remained of his loyalists. The Welsh had offered him refuge, though it was less out of respect and more out of sheer pity.

"We need a plan," Edgar mumbled, trying to sound confident. "Something bold. Something... unexpected."

"How about we let Harold keep the throne and go live in a nice monastery?" one of his more pragmatic supporters suggested.

"No!" Edgar snapped, desperate to maintain at least a shred of dignity. "I'll reclaim my crown, even if it means... uh... finding some new allies."

At that moment, a grizzled Welsh warrior stepped forward, a sly grin on his face. "There might be a way to turn the tide, lad. Heard a rumor about some treasure hidden by Harald Hardrada. Word is, it's more than just gold—there's a secret plan, something that could topple Harold and anyone else who gets in the way."

Edgar's eyes lit up. "A secret plan? Why didn't you mention this before?"

The warrior shrugged. "You seemed more interested in not dying. But if you're serious about making a comeback, we could use that treasure to buy ourselves an army—and maybe even bribe a few Normans."

"Brilliant!" Edgar exclaimed, his confidence inflating like a cheap balloon. "We'll find the treasure, rally the Welsh, and launch a surprise attack on London. Harold won't know what hit him!"

As Edgar set off on his treasure hunt, Harold, back in London, was already trying to get ahead of the next disaster. He had barely cleaned the blood from his armor when a messenger burst into the throne room, out of breath and looking like he'd seen a ghost—or worse, Matilda.

"Sire! Urgent news!" the messenger gasped. "Matilda has sent word—she wants to meet in secret. Says it's about Edgar."

Harold sighed, rubbing his temples. "Of course she does. Fine. Arrange the meeting. But let's be clear—if this is another trap, I'm not in the mood to survive it."

The next evening, under the cover of darkness, Harold met Matilda in a small, abandoned chapel on the outskirts of London. She arrived with a handful of guards and an air of someone who had seen far too many plots unravel.

"Harold," she began, her voice low and serious, "we're both tired of this game. Edgar's out there, and if we don't deal with him now, we'll never have peace."

Harold crossed his arms. "And you're proposing... what, exactly? Another alliance? Because the last one ended with a lot of people dying and me doing all the hard work."

Matilda smirked. "I'll admit, you've surprised me. But this time, I'm not suggesting a partnership—I'm offering information. My spies tell me Edgar's after a treasure Harald Hardrada left behind, one that could spell disaster for both of us."

"Harald Hardrada? The guy who died because someone couldn't aim properly?" Harold scoffed. "What kind of treasure could he have that's worth worrying about?"

Matilda's expression darkened. "It's not just gold. Harald had a contingency plan, something he cooked up in case he didn't survive. A plan to destabilize England using mercenaries, bribes, and a lot of very angry Norsemen."

Harold blinked. "You're serious?"

"Deadly," Matilda replied. "And if Edgar gets his hands on it, he could use it to gather an army that would make our last battle look like a tavern brawl."

Harold considered this, his mind racing. "So, what do you propose?"

"We join forces," Matilda said, leaning in. "Hunt down Edgar, stop him from finding that treasure, and then... we settle our differences. Once and for all."

Harold nodded slowly, his eyes narrowing. "Fine. But if you double-cross me, Matilda, I won't hesitate to make you regret it."

"I'd expect nothing less," she replied, her smile as sharp as her dagger.

And so, a new and even more precarious alliance was formed. With Matilda's spies leading the way, Harold's forces set out to find Edgar before he could unlock whatever chaotic surprise Harald Hardrada had left behind. The chase led them through dense forests, across misty moors, and into the heart of Wales, where Edgar was making surprisingly good progress for a man with no real sense of direction.

Meanwhile, Edgar, blissfully unaware that he was being hunted, stumbled upon the fabled treasure—hidden in a cave behind a waterfall, because where else would a Viking king stash his secret plans?

"Finally!" Edgar exclaimed as his men hauled out chests filled with gold, weapons, and a scroll sealed with Harald's distinctive mark. "With this, we can—"

But before he could finish, an arrow whizzed past his head, narrowly missing his ear. Edgar yelped and ducked, realizing with a sinking heart that he was surrounded. Harold, Matilda, and their combined forces emerged from the trees, weapons drawn, and eyes locked on the prize.

"Drop the treasure, Edgar," Harold called out, his voice echoing off the cave walls. "You're outnumbered and out of your league."

Edgar, who was quickly running out of ideas, looked at the treasure, then at his men, then back at the treasure. "You know," he said, trying to sound brave, "maybe I don't need to be king after all. How about we split the gold and call it a day?"

"Not a chance," Matilda replied, stepping forward. "Give up now, and maybe we'll let you live."

Edgar hesitated, then sighed deeply, finally accepting that his brief flirtation with power was well and truly over. "Alright, alright," he muttered, dropping his sword with a clatter. "But for the record, this whole 'being king' thing is highly overrated."

Harold couldn't help but chuckle as he approached. "You've got that right. Now, let's see what Harald Hardrada left behind, shall we?"

With the treasure now safely in Harold's hands, the uneasy alliance was finally dissolved. Matilda took her share of the spoils and returned to Normandy, content to rule in peace—at least for now. Edgar, stripped of any claim to the throne, was quietly shipped off to a monastery where he could contemplate his life choices in solitude.

As for Harold, he returned to London, the undisputed King of England, but with a gnawing sense that the crown he had fought so hard to keep was more trouble than it was worth. The secret plan Harald Hardrada had left behind turned out to be little more than a list of names and some rather vague threats—enough to cause some headaches, but nothing that couldn't be dealt with.

"Looks like we've got some cleaning up to do," Gyrth remarked as they rode back to the city.

Harold nodded, the weight of the crown pressing down harder than ever. "Let's just hope there aren't any more surprise claimants. I don't think I can handle another Royal Rumble."

With the field cleared of rivals, Harold finally took his place on the throne—

though whether it was a victory or a curse remained to be seen.

The Throne's Final Joke

It had been a few months since Harold had finally settled on the English throne, and for the first time in what felt like forever, things were... well, not peaceful, but at least not actively on fire. Yet.

In the grand hall of the newly restored Westminster Palace, Harold sat on his throne, trying to get comfortable in what could only be described as the most uncomfortable seat in all of Christendom. He adjusted his position for the umpteenth time and grumbled, "You'd think after all this, the least they could do is cushion the damn thing."

Gyrth, ever the faithful brother, stood nearby, holding a stack of increasingly boring documents. "Cheer up, brother. You're the king now. You get to decide who cushions what."

"Maybe," Harold sighed, rubbing his temples, "but I can't shake the feeling that this crown is more trouble than it's worth. Everyone's either plotting to steal it or waiting for me to trip over my own robes."

"Speaking of plots," Gyrth said, his voice lowering to a conspiratorial whisper, "I've been hearing rumors. Some of the nobles are unhappy with the way things turned out. They think you're... vulnerable."

Harold rolled his eyes. "Of course they do. They're nobles. If they're not plotting something, they're probably dead. Who's behind it this time?"

Gyrth hesitated. "It's... complicated. But there's one name that keeps coming up: Matilda."

Harold let out a groan that could have shaken the rafters. "I should've known she wouldn't just take her spoils and go home. What's she up to now?"

"Word is she's been quietly gathering support among the Norman lords," Gyrth explained. "They're not too thrilled with how things ended either, and some of them think she's the rightful ruler of England—especially after your little stunt with the whole 'Royal Rumble' thing."

Harold leaned back, trying to find that one spot where the throne didn't feel like a torture device. "Great. So, I've got a bunch of disgruntled Normans on one side and a Duchess with a grudge on the other. What else?"

Gyrth hesitated again, then added, "There's more. Someone within your own court has been feeding information to Matilda."

Harold sat up, his eyes narrowing. "A traitor? In my own court?"

Gyrth nodded, looking genuinely concerned for the first time. "I'm afraid so. But we don't know who it is yet. Whoever it is, they've been careful, covering their tracks. But we think they're planning something big—something that could undermine your rule completely."

Harold felt a cold knot forming in his stomach. "So, Matilda's plotting to take back the throne, and she's got an inside man—or woman—helping her. Wonderful. Any good news?"

Gyrth considered this for a moment. "Well, the pies in the kitchen are better than ever."

Harold groaned again. "Brilliant. I'll make sure to enjoy one after I'm assassinated."

As if on cue, a messenger burst into the hall, looking as though he'd just run the length of the kingdom. "Sire! Urgent news from Normandy!"

"Of course," Harold muttered. "What now?"

The messenger caught his breath before speaking. "Matilda is on the move. She's gathered an army and plans to cross the Channel within the week. She's declared that she will reclaim England by force and remove the 'pretender'—that's you, sire—from the throne."

Harold's grip tightened on the armrests of the throne. "The nerve of that woman. I suppose she thinks I'll just step aside and let her waltz in?"

"She's not coming alone," the messenger added nervously. "The nobles who are still loyal to her are rallying their own forces. It's going to be a full-scale invasion."

Harold felt the weight of the crown pressing down harder than ever. "So, it's war again, is it? Fine. Let's prepare. But first, we need to root out this traitor."

The next few days were a whirlwind of preparations. Harold's loyalists scrambled to fortify the coasts, rally troops, and prepare for yet another bloody confrontation. But all the while, the nagging suspicion that someone close to him was betraying him gnawed at Harold's mind.

He called a meeting of his most trusted advisors, each one more paranoid than the last. The atmosphere in the chamber was thick with tension as Harold eyed each of them in turn. "Someone in this room is feeding information to Matilda," he said, his voice deadly calm. "Whoever it is, you've got one chance to come clean."

The silence that followed was so complete that Harold could hear the distant tolling of the city bells. Then, slowly, one of his advisors—Sir Richard, a man who had always seemed just a little too clever for his own good—stepped forward.

"I didn't want it to come to this, Harold," Sir Richard said, not quite meeting the king's eyes. "But Matilda made a compelling argument. You've become too unpredictable, too dangerous. England needs stability, and she can provide it."

Harold shook his head in disbelief. "And you think she's the answer? You've seen what she's capable of."

"Better the devil we know," Sir Richard muttered. "Sorry, Harold. It's nothing personal. Just business."

Before Harold could respond, there was a sudden movement behind him. One of the other advisors, a quiet man named Oswin, who had been with Harold since the beginning, lunged forward, a dagger in his hand. But he wasn't aiming at Harold—he was aiming at Sir Richard.

The blade found its mark with deadly precision, and Sir Richard crumpled to the floor, his betrayal cut short by a swift and silent death.

Oswin wiped the blade clean, then looked up at Harold with a grim expression. "We can't afford any more traitors, sire. We're in this together, or we're finished."

Harold nodded slowly, the shock of the sudden violence giving way to cold resolve. "You're right. No more traitors. And no more second chances."

With the immediate threat dealt with, Harold turned his attention back to the looming invasion. Matilda's forces were advancing quickly, and it was clear that she wasn't coming just to talk. The stage was set for one final showdown—one that would determine the fate of England once and for all.

As Harold rode out to meet his army, the weight of the crown pressing down harder than ever, he couldn't help but think that maybe, just maybe, this throne was cursed after all.

"Matilda wants a fight?" he muttered to himself. "She'll get one. But I'm not going down without taking her with me."

And so, as the dawn broke over England, Harold's forces prepared for what would be the bloodiest and most decisive battle yet.

The Final Backstab (With a Side of Carnage)

The day of reckoning arrived with the kind of ominous fog that even a blind soothsayer could predict meant trouble. Harold Godwinson stood atop a hill overlooking the battlefield, his armor polished to a dull gleam, his sword newly sharpened, and his mood somewhere between grim determination and profound irritation.

"Would it kill the sun to make an appearance today?" Harold muttered, squinting into the gray murk. "I'd like to at least see what I'm dying for."

Gyrth, ever the supportive brother, stood at his side, frowning at the horizon where Matilda's forces were assembling like a particularly aggressive storm cloud. "Maybe it's a blessing in disguise. If we can't see them, they can't see how few of us there are."

Harold grunted. "I'm not sure that's how it works, Gyrth."

As the fog began to lift, revealing the full scope of Matilda's army, Harold's heart sank a little further. Her forces were vast, bristling with armor, swords, and what appeared to be an alarming number of siege weapons.

"Well, she certainly didn't skimp on the preparations," Harold said dryly. "All this just for me? I'm touched."

"Don't be," Gyrth replied. "If she wins, she'll probably bury you with those siege weapons. All of them."

Across the battlefield, Matilda sat astride her warhorse, surveying the English lines with a cold, calculating gaze. She was dressed for war—no more of the diplomatic finery she had once favored. This was a woman who had run out of patience and was ready to claim what she believed was rightfully hers.

"Harold thinks he can keep me from the throne?" Matilda murmured to her second-in-command, a battle-hardened knight named Alain. "He's got another thing coming. And then, after I'm done with him, I'll deal with the rest of these ungrateful nobles."

Alain, a man of few words and even fewer smiles, nodded grimly. "He won't go down without a fight. But we've got the numbers and the element of surprise."

Matilda raised an eyebrow. "Surprise? We've been marching on him for weeks."

"Not that kind of surprise," Alain said, with a glint in his eye. "The other kind. You'll see."

Back on Harold's side of the field, the English army was making its final preparations. Soldiers donned their helmets, sharpened their weapons, and muttered prayers to every deity they could think of. There was an air of tense anticipation, like the calm before a particularly nasty storm.

But as Harold watched his men ready themselves, something didn't sit right. He had learned to trust his gut over the years, and right now, it was telling him that something was off—something more than just the odds stacked against them.

"Gyrth," Harold said, his voice low, "I've got a bad feeling about this. Keep an eye on our ranks. If Matilda's got a trick up her sleeve, I want to know before it hits us."

Gyrth nodded, though his expression was grim. "Let's hope you're wrong."

As the two armies squared off, the tension became almost unbearable. Harold raised his sword, signaling his men to hold the line. Matilda, seeing the movement, gave a slight nod to Alain, who discreetly disappeared into the fog behind her.

And then, with a deafening roar, the battle began.

Matilda's forces charged, crashing into Harold's lines with the force of a tidal wave. The sound of steel on steel filled the air, accompanied by the shouts and cries of men locked in mortal combat. Harold threw himself into the fray, cutting down any enemy that crossed his path, his sword flashing in the dim light.

"For England!" Harold shouted, trying to rally his men as they fought back with all the desperation of those who know they're outmatched.

"For Normandy!" Matilda countered, her voice carrying across the battlefield as she rode through the chaos, directing her troops with ruthless efficiency.

The battle raged on, with neither side gaining a decisive advantage. It was brutal, bloody, and fast becoming a slog of attrition. But just as Harold started to think they might actually hold the line, disaster struck.

From the rear of Harold's forces, a section of his men suddenly broke ranks, turning on their comrades with a viciousness that could only mean one thing: betrayal.

"Traitors!" Gyrth shouted, as he swung his sword at a man who had just moments ago been fighting at his side. "They're turning against us!"

Harold, slashing his way through the melee to get a better look, felt his stomach drop as he saw the full scope of the betrayal. A sizable chunk of his army—men he had trusted, men he had fought alongside—had switched sides, their loyalty bought by Matilda's gold or promises of power.

"So this is the surprise," Harold muttered, his voice thick with anger. "Matilda, you cunning—"

But there was no time to curse his enemy. The battlefield had descended into chaos, with Harold's forces being attacked from both sides. The lines were crumbling, and the battle was quickly spiraling out of control.

Amidst the turmoil, Harold caught sight of Matilda herself, still on horseback, directing the carnage with a cold, merciless precision. She was flanked by a group of her most loyal knights, including Alain, who seemed to be enjoying himself far too much.

"We have to get to her," Harold said through gritted teeth, cutting down another enemy as he tried to carve a path toward Matilda. "If we can take her out, maybe—just maybe—we can turn this around."

But getting to Matilda was easier said than done. The battlefield was a swirling mass of bodies, blood, and chaos. Every step forward was a fight for survival, every enemy slain just another obstacle removed from the path.

And then, just as Harold was beginning to lose hope, he saw an opening.

Matilda's knights had been drawn away by a particularly fierce skirmish, leaving her momentarily unguarded. It was a fleeting opportunity—one that Harold knew he couldn't afford to miss.

With a roar, Harold broke through the enemy line and charged straight for Matilda. She saw him coming and turned to face him, her sword raised, her eyes alight with the fire of battle.

"So, it comes to this," Matilda said, her voice cold and steady. "The pretender against the rightful ruler. Let's see who deserves the crown."

Harold didn't waste time on words. He swung his sword with all the strength he could muster, aiming for Matilda's head. She parried the blow with surprising agility, countering with a strike of her own that nearly took Harold's arm off.

The two fought like demons, neither giving an inch. Each clash of their swords sent sparks flying, each step taken with the intent to kill. The battle around them seemed to fade into the background as they locked in a deadly duel.

"You've got spirit, I'll give you that," Matilda said, grinning fiercely as she blocked another of Harold's strikes. "But spirit won't save you."

"Maybe not," Harold replied, panting with exertion, "but it's all I've got."

And then, in a move that took even Harold by surprise, Matilda lunged forward with a speed that defied the weight of her armor. Her sword slashed through the air, aiming directly for Harold's throat.

Harold barely had time to react. He threw himself to the side, the blade grazing his neck as he stumbled backward. But before Matilda could press the advantage, a shout rang out from behind her.

"Matilda, look out!"

It was Alain, but his warning came too late. A figure emerged from the chaos—a soldier who had somehow made it through the carnage unnoticed. He moved with deadly purpose, raising his sword to strike at Matilda from behind.

Matilda turned just in time to see the blade coming for her, but she was too late to fully dodge it. The sword plunged into her side, the force of the blow knocking her off her horse and onto the blood-soaked ground.

Harold, stunned by the sudden turn of events, stared as Matilda struggled to rise, blood seeping from the wound in her side. Her eyes met his, and for a moment, all the animosity between them seemed to dissolve.

"End it," Matilda gasped, her voice weak but defiant. "End this madness."

Harold hesitated, his sword raised, ready to strike the final blow. But before he could act, Alain was there, pushing him aside with a roar of fury.

"Get away from her!" Alain shouted, his sword flashing as he slashed at Harold.

Harold staggered back, barely managing to deflect the blow. But it was enough to break his concentration, and in that moment of distraction, Matilda made her move.

With the last of her strength, she drove her sword upward, aiming for Harold's unprotected chest. The blade found its mark, piercing through Harold's armor and into his heart.

Harold's eyes widened in shock as the pain hit him like a sledgehammer. He looked down at the sword sticking out of his chest, then back up at Matilda, who was still on the ground, her eyes filled with grim satisfaction.

"For England," she whispered, her voice barely audible.

Harold tried to speak, but the words wouldn't come. His strength was fading fast, his vision growing dark. And then, with a final, shuddering breath, he collapsed beside Matilda, the crown that had caused so much bloodshed slipping from his head and rolling away into the mud.

Alain, who had been too late to save Matilda, knelt beside her, his face a mask of grief and rage. But there was no time for revenge—Matilda's wound was fatal, and she knew it.

"Take the crown," she whispered to Alain, her voice barely more than a breath. "Finish what we started."

But Alain didn't move. He simply stared at her, his expression unreadable.

"You've done enough," he said quietly. "Rest now, my lady."

And with that, Matilda closed her eyes, her hand slipping from the hilt of her sword. Alain stood, his grief turning to cold determination. He looked around at the battlefield, now littered with the bodies of those who had fought and died for a throne that no one truly wanted.

The battle was over, but the cost had been unimaginable. The throne of England, now unclaimed, sat empty—waiting for the next fool to try and take it.

The Crown Nobody Wanted (Except Everyone)

The battlefield outside London was now a grotesque mosaic of mud, blood, and the shattered remnants of England's greatest warriors. Harold and Matilda lay side by side, two would-be rulers who had fought their final battle over a crown that neither of them had lived long enough to enjoy. The sun finally decided to make an appearance, casting an ironic glow over the scene as if mocking the notion that any of this was worth the trouble.

As the bodies were cleared away, and the fog of war lifted, a new struggle began—one that was somehow even more cutthroat than the battle itself: the race to see who would pick up the pieces of the now leaderless kingdom.

In the grand halls of Westminster, a group of English nobles had gathered, each one trying to look more legitimate than the next, while desperately hiding the metaphorical knives they had ready to plunge into each other's backs.

"Gentlemen," began the Earl of Mercia, his voice dripping with false courtesy, "we must act quickly to stabilize the kingdom. Harold is dead, Matilda is dead, and the people are... well, let's just say they're not taking it well."

The Earl of Northumbria, who had all the charm of a damp towel, nodded gravely. "Indeed. It is clear that the crown should pass to the most qualified—"

"Which would be me," interrupted the Duke of Wessex, who had been sharpening his ambition since breakfast.

"Ha! The only thing you're qualified for is running a sheep farm," retorted the Earl of Kent, who was already calculating how many soldiers it would take to claim the throne by force.

The room erupted into a cacophony of accusations, threats, and very creative insults, each noble trying to outmaneuver the others while simultaneously looking like the most obvious choice for king. It was less a council of statesmen and more a pack of wolves deciding who got to devour the carcass first.

As the shouting grew louder, one of the younger, more idealistic nobles—a fresh-faced lad with all the naivety of a newborn lamb—timidly raised his hand. "Perhaps we should consider what's best for England, rather than—"

"Silence!" roared the Earl of Mercia, who had clearly had enough of this whole 'thinking of others' nonsense. "This is about the crown, not about what's 'best.' Now, I propose we settle this the old-fashioned way: with swords."

The room fell silent for a moment, as each noble sized up their rivals. It was clear that diplomacy had been abandoned in favor of something far more immediate and deadly.

Outside the palace, news of the dead rulers and the ensuing chaos spread like wildfire. The common folk, who had seen their fair share of kings come and go (usually violently), began to riot, looting what little there was left to loot. There was a sense of grim resignation among the peasants—another civil war was brewing, and they were the ones who'd have to clean up the mess. Again.

Back inside the palace, the nobles had taken to the courtyard, swords drawn and eyes narrowed. It was a scene straight out of a Shakespearean tragedy—except with less poetry and more outright murder. The Earl of Kent, not one to waste time, lunged at the Duke of Wessex, who parried the blow with a grunt.

"So, this is what it's come to, then?" the Duke said, pushing Kent back. "A bloody free-for-all?"

Kent sneered. "Better than sitting around waiting for you lot to backstab me. At least this way I see it coming."

"Very noble," Wessex shot back, "for a man who'd sell his own mother for a title."

The Earl of Northumbria, not wanting to be left out of the fun, joined the fray, swinging his sword with all the finesse of a drunken ox. "Out of my way! This throne is mine by right!"

Mercia, seeing his opportunity, decided to let the others tire themselves out before making his move. He circled the courtyard, watching for an opening, his eyes gleaming with the cold calculation of a man who had done this before.

As the battle in the courtyard raged, word spread through the city that the nobles were at each other's throats—literally. This news was met with a mix of horror and amusement by the commoners, who had long suspected that their 'betters' were little more than overgrown children with sharper toys.

"Oi, did you hear?" one peasant said to another, watching the palace from a safe distance. "They're killin' each other off for the crown. Can you believe it?"

"Bout time," the other peasant replied, shrugging. "Maybe when they're done, there'll be enough of 'em left to fill a single coffin."

Back at the palace, the fighting had reached a fever pitch. The courtyard was slick with blood, and bodies littered the ground as noble after noble fell to their rivals' blades. The Earl of Mercia, who had waited patiently for his moment, finally saw his chance.

As the Duke of Wessex delivered a fatal blow to the Earl of Kent, Mercia slipped in behind him, driving his sword through Wessex's back with a swift, practiced motion.

Wessex gasped, his eyes widening in shock. "You... treacherous..."

"Survival of the fittest," Mercia said coldly, twisting the blade before pulling it free.

With Wessex out of the way, Mercia turned to face the Earl of Northumbria, who was now the last man standing between him and the throne. Northumbria, bloodied but unbowed, raised his sword in defiance.

"You think you can just take the crown like this?" Northumbria spat, his voice thick with rage. "England won't follow a butcher like you."

Mercia smirked. "We'll see about that."

The two men clashed in a final, brutal duel. The courtyard echoed with the sound of steel meeting steel, each strike more vicious than the last. But in the end, Mercia's patience and cunning paid off. With a swift, brutal stroke, he cut Northumbria down, leaving him to bleed out on the cold stone.

Breathing heavily, Mercia looked around at the carnage. The courtyard was littered with the bodies of his rivals, the blood of England's so-called nobility staining the ground. He had won—but at what cost?

As Mercia sheathed his sword, a slow clap echoed through the courtyard. He turned to see Alain, Matilda's former second-in-command, standing at the entrance, a sardonic smile on his face.

"Well done, Mercia," Alain said, his voice dripping with sarcasm. "You've proven yourself the biggest vulture of the lot. But tell me—what do you plan to do now?"

Mercia narrowed his eyes. "I'll take the crown, of course. Someone has to rule this madhouse."

"Of course," Alain replied, stepping forward. "But before you do, there's one little detail you've overlooked."

Mercia's hand instinctively went to his sword. "And what's that?"

Alain's smile widened. "The people, you fool. While you lot were busy killing each other, they've had enough. There's a mob outside the gates, and they're not exactly keen on letting another noble claim the throne."

Mercia's face paled as the sound of the mob grew louder—angry shouts and the clang of makeshift weapons echoing through the courtyard. He had been so focused on his rivals that he had forgotten the one thing that truly mattered: the people.

"The crown's not worth dying for," Alain said, his tone almost pitying. "But by all means, try to take it. I'll watch."

Mercia hesitated, his mind racing. He had come this far, fought so hard, but now, standing on the brink of victory, he realized that the throne was a poisoned chalice. If he took it, the mob would tear him apart—if not today, then tomorrow.

With a growl of frustration, Mercia turned and fled, leaving the crown lying in the mud where Harold and Matilda had fallen. Alain watched him go, shaking his head in disbelief.

"Smart man," Alain muttered. "Finally."

The mob, having breached the gates, flooded into the courtyard, but by then, Mercia was gone. The crown, bloodied and battered, lay forgotten in the mud—a symbol of the endless violence and ambition that had torn England apart.

In the end, the throne of England remained unclaimed, and the kingdom descended into chaos. The nobles were dead, the people were in revolt, and the once-great realm was left without a ruler.

As the sun set on another day of bloodshed, the crown of England lay in the mud, a reminder that some prizes are best left untouched. And as for the fools who had fought and died for it, their names would be remembered only as a cautionary tale—one that would echo through history as a darkly humorous reminder of the perils of ambition.

The Common Man's Crown (or: How Not to Start a Revolution)

As night fell over the blood-soaked kingdom, England found itself in uncharted territory. The throne was empty, the nobles were either dead or in hiding, and the people—those long-suffering souls who had watched their so-called betters hack each other to pieces—were finally fed up.

In the small village of Mudbury, which had somehow managed to avoid most of the recent unpleasantness, a crowd had gathered in the local tavern. The air was thick with the smell of ale, sweat, and the kind of righteous anger that only a mob with nothing left to lose could muster.

"I'm telling you lot, it's time we took matters into our own hands!" bellowed Big John, the local blacksmith, who had the kind of physique that made people listen whether they wanted to or not. He slammed his tankard down on the table, splashing ale across the rough wooden surface. "No more kings! No more lords! It's time for the common man to rise up and take what's rightfully ours!"

The crowd roared in approval, though whether they understood what "rising up" actually entailed was debatable. Still, it was a compelling idea—especially after several pints of the local brew.

"Yeah!" shouted Old Tom, the village elder who hadn't been this excited since the last good harvest. "Why should those highborn fools get all the power? They couldn't rule a pigsty, let alone a kingdom!"

A chorus of agreements followed, with each villager offering their own colorful critique of the nobility. The butcher, who had never quite forgiven the Earl of Wessex for an unpaid meat order, was particularly enthusiastic about the prospect of beheading someone.

Amidst the growing excitement, a young man named William—known to the villagers as "Willy the Witless" for reasons that were becoming increasingly clear—stood up on a rickety chair. "So, who's going to lead us, then?" he asked, blinking owlishly at the crowd. "We can't all be king."

The room fell silent as the mob collectively realized that they hadn't thought that far ahead. Big John, never one to shy away from a challenge, scratched his chin thoughtfully. "Well, we'll need someone strong, someone who knows how to get things done..."

"And someone who's good with money," added the baker, who had a vested interest in making sure the revolution wouldn't be bad for business.

"And someone who's got all their teeth," muttered Old Tom, who had long since come to the conclusion that dental hygiene was a sure sign of leadership potential.

Just as the debate threatened to devolve into yet another brawl, a voice from the back of the room cut through the noise like a well-aimed arrow.

"What about Wilfred?"

Heads turned to see Mary, the innkeeper's daughter, standing in the doorway, her arms crossed and a knowing smirk on her face. "He's smart, fair, and he's been keeping this place running for years while the rest of you lot were busy grumbling."

Wilfred, the innkeeper who had been quietly polishing a mug behind the bar, froze in place. "Me?" he squeaked, looking around as if hoping someone else named Wilfred might stand up and take the bullet—er, honor.

Mary shrugged. "Why not? You've got more sense than the lot of them put together, and you've never lost a fistfight in your life."

The crowd murmured in agreement, and Wilfred felt a wave of panic wash over him. He was a simple man, with simple ambitions—keeping the inn from burning down, serving good ale, and occasionally winning a game of dice. Leading a revolution was not on his list of life goals.

But before he could protest, the villagers had made up their minds. "Wilfred for king!" they shouted, raising their tankards in a toast to the man who

THE COMMON MAN'S CROWN (OR: HOW NOT TO START A REVOLUTION)

clearly had no idea what he was getting into.

Wilfred, realizing he had been well and truly cornered, gave a weak smile. "Well, if you insist..."

And with that, the Common Man's Revolution was born.

The next morning, armed with whatever weapons they could find—mostly pitchforks, kitchen knives, and the odd rusty sword—the villagers of Mudbury set out for London, determined to take the throne for themselves. Wilfred, who was still trying to figure out how he had ended up leading this motley crew, marched at the front, a rusty old helmet perched awkwardly on his head.

"Are you sure about this?" Wilfred asked Mary, who had appointed herself his unofficial advisor.

"Not even a little," Mary replied cheerfully. "But it's better than letting those nobles muck it up again."

As they approached the city, it became clear that the situation in London was as bad as they had feared. The streets were filled with angry mobs, each one more desperate and dangerous than the last. The palace gates stood open, the crown still lying in the mud where it had fallen, untouched and unwanted.

"Well, here we are," Wilfred said, trying to muster some enthusiasm. "Time to... uh... claim the throne, I suppose."

"Time to show those nobles what's what!" Big John roared, raising his pitchfork like a banner.

But just as they were about to enter the palace, a shout from the rear of the mob made them all turn. Another group of peasants, equally armed and equally disgruntled, was charging toward them from the opposite direction.

"Oi! That's our crown!" shouted their leader, a burly farmer with a face like a pickled walnut. "We're taking it for the people!"

"What do you mean, 'your crown'?" Mary shot back, stepping in front of Wilfred. "We got here first!"

"Finders keepers!" added Old Tom, who was really getting into the spirit of things.

The farmer sneered. "Over my dead body, you will!"

"That can be arranged!" Big John bellowed, brandishing his pitchfork menacingly.

Within moments, the two groups of commoners were at each other's throats, the revolution devolving into yet another free-for-all. Pitchforks clashed, insults were hurled, and Wilfred found himself ducking for cover as the crowd surged around him.

"This is not how I imagined this going," Wilfred muttered, crawling under a nearby cart to avoid a particularly vicious swing from the pickled walnut-faced farmer.

Meanwhile, Mary was fending off attacks with a frying pan she had brought along for just such an occasion. "Wilfred, get out here and do something!" she shouted, knocking a particularly aggressive villager out cold.

"What exactly do you want me to do?" Wilfred called back, his voice muffled by the cart. "Declare myself king? They'd tear me apart before I could finish the sentence!"

The battle raged on, but as more and more commoners joined the fray, it became clear that no one was going to walk away with the crown. The palace courtyard became a chaotic melee, with villagers tripping over each other in their bid to claim the throne that nobody seemed capable of holding onto.

Finally, as the sun began to set, the remaining combatants, exhausted and nursing various bruises and cuts, staggered to a halt. The crown, still lying in the mud, remained unclaimed, a symbol of the futility of the entire endeavor.

Wilfred, covered in dirt and still clinging to his helmet, emerged from under the cart, looking thoroughly dejected. "So... what now?"

Mary, wiping blood and sweat from her brow, shook her head. "Maybe... maybe this whole 'ruling' thing isn't for us after all."

"Maybe it's cursed," Old Tom muttered, eyeing the crown warily. "All it brings is death and madness."

The crowd murmured in agreement, the reality of their situation finally sinking in. The throne, it seemed, was more trouble than it was worth. And with that realization came a sense of grim relief.

Wilfred, sensing that his brief and disastrous foray into leadership was over, took off his helmet and tossed it aside. "Well, I don't know about you lot, but I'm going back to Mudbury. There's ale to be drunk and stories to be told."

The villagers, battered but not broken, slowly began to disperse, each one quietly relieved to be leaving the crown behind. The revolution had failed, but at least they would live to see another day.

As the last of the mob trickled away, leaving the palace courtyard empty once more, the crown of England lay abandoned in the mud—a reminder that sometimes, the best choice is to walk away.

And so, the Common Man's Revolution ended not with a bang, but with a collective shrug. The people of England, having learned the hard way that ruling was far more difficult than it looked, returned to their homes, content to let someone else deal with the mess.

But the crown, still gleaming faintly in the fading light, remained. A symbol of power, ambition, and folly—waiting for the next fool to come along and try their luck.

Edgar's (Final?) Comeback and the Curse of the Crown

As the sun dipped below the horizon, casting long shadows across the empty palace courtyard, the crown of England lay forgotten in the mud—abandoned by peasants, nobles, and would-be rulers alike. It seemed that, at last, the bloody struggle for power had come to a weary end.

But just as the night settled in and the kingdom dared to breathe a sigh of relief, the sound of hooves echoed through the empty streets of London. A lone rider, hunched over and swaddled in a tattered cloak, made his way toward the palace with the determined pace of a man who had nothing left to lose—and absolutely nothing left to prove.

The rider was none other than Edgar the Ætheling, the perpetual also-ran of English politics. The man who had tried (and failed) to claim the throne so many times that even the monks had stopped recording his attempts. But now, with everyone else dead, gone, or too drunk to care, Edgar had come to take what he still believed was rightfully his.

As Edgar dismounted and approached the palace gates, he was greeted by an eerie silence. No guards, no servants, not even a stray dog. The place was as empty as his list of political achievements.

"Well," Edgar muttered to himself, looking around, "I suppose this means no one's going to challenge me this time."

As he entered the courtyard, Edgar's eyes fell on the crown, still lying in the mud where it had been abandoned by the last mob of revolutionaries. He approached it cautiously, half-expecting it to leap up and bite him—or, worse, disappear before he could claim it.

"Finally," Edgar whispered, reaching down to pick up the crown. "Finally, it's mine."

But as his fingers closed around the cold metal, a strange chill ran down his spine. The crown felt heavier than it should have—almost as if it were burdened with something more than just gold and jewels.

"Curse or no curse," Edgar muttered, brushing off the unsettling feeling, "I'm not letting this go."

With a deep breath, Edgar placed the crown on his head, straightened his back, and looked around as if expecting an audience to appear out of thin air and cheer his belated ascension to the throne. But the courtyard remained empty, and the only sound was the distant hoot of an owl.

"Well, this is... anticlimactic," Edgar sighed, wiping the mud off his cloak. "But at least I'm finally king. King Edgar the—"

Before he could finish, a sudden gust of wind howled through the courtyard, snuffing out the torches and plunging the area into darkness. Edgar froze, the crown feeling impossibly heavy on his head.

Then came the whispers.

Low, eerie murmurs seemed to rise from the very stones beneath his feet, swirling around him in a chilling chorus that sent shivers down his spine. Edgar spun around, trying to pinpoint the source of the sound, but the courtyard remained empty.

"Who's there?" Edgar called out, his voice wavering. "Show yourself!"

But the whispers only grew louder, more insistent, like the mutterings of restless spirits—or perhaps the collective sighs of all those who had died in pursuit of the very crown now perched on Edgar's head.

"Curse of the crown... the blood of kings... doomed... all doomed..."

Edgar's eyes darted around wildly. "Stop it! I'm the rightful king! This crown is mine! MINE!"

But the whispers didn't stop. In fact, they seemed to be laughing at him now, mocking him for his arrogance, his ambition, and his all-too-frequent tendency to declare himself king without anyone else agreeing.

As the laughter grew more intense, Edgar felt the weight of the crown pressing down on him even harder. It was as if the very spirits of those who had fought and died for the throne were now condemning him, warning him of the fate that awaited anyone foolish enough to claim the cursed crown.

Then, out of the darkness, a voice much clearer and more authoritative than the rest cut through the din. It was a voice Edgar knew well—one that had haunted his dreams and his failures for years.

"You should have stayed away, Edgar."

Edgar whipped around to see a shadowy figure emerging from the darkness. His heart nearly stopped as the figure stepped into the dim light, revealing none other than the ghost of Harold Godwinson himself, looking rather less dead than Edgar would have liked.

"Harold?!" Edgar gasped, stumbling backward. "But you're—"

"Dead? Yes, thank you for noticing," Harold said, his tone dripping with sarcasm. "But death has its perks—like keeping idiots like you from making the same mistakes I did."

Edgar's mouth opened and closed like a fish out of water. "I-I didn't ask for this! The crown... it was just lying there! What was I supposed to do, leave it?"

"Yes," Harold replied flatly. "That would have been the smart thing to do."

"Since when do you care about 'smart things'?" Edgar shot back, feeling a surge of defiance. "You fought for this crown too, remember? You died for it!"

"And I can tell you, it wasn't worth it," Harold said, crossing his arms. "This crown isn't just cursed, Edgar. It's a trap. It's the reason so many of us are dead—and now it's your turn."

Edgar's bravado faltered. "But... I just want to be king. I deserve this!"

"Deserve?" Harold laughed, though there was no warmth in it. "No one deserves this crown, Edgar. It's cursed, remember? You put it on, you die. That's how it works."

"No! I'm different!" Edgar insisted, his voice tinged with desperation. "I'll break the curse! I'll rule wisely! I'll—"

But before he could finish, the crown suddenly began to tighten around his head, as if it had a mind of its own. Edgar's eyes widened in horror as he tried to claw it off, but the metal seemed to fuse with his skin, the jewels glowing with a sinister light.

Harold watched with a mixture of pity and grim satisfaction. "I warned you," he said quietly. "The crown has claimed another fool."

Edgar's screams echoed through the empty courtyard as the curse of the crown took hold. The whispers intensified, their cruel laughter rising to a crescendo as Edgar fell to his knees, the life draining from his body. The crown, now glowing with an eerie, malevolent light, pulsed with the power it had consumed from yet another would-be king.

As Edgar's body crumpled to the ground, the crown rolled off his head, coming to rest once more in the mud, its glow fading as it waited for the next poor soul to pick it up.

Harold's ghost shook his head, a ghostly sigh escaping his lips. "And so it goes. Another one bites the dust."

But as he turned to leave, Harold couldn't help but glance back at the cursed crown, still lying there, glinting faintly in the moonlight. Despite everything, despite all the death and destruction it had caused, the allure of the throne was still there, tempting, beckoning.

Harold shook his head again. "Some people never learn."

And with that, he disappeared into the night, leaving the crown behind for the next fool to find.

II

When the Crown is Cursed

The Prophecy of Doom

England, having collectively decided that chasing after a cursed crown was about as wise as sticking one's hand into a beehive, found itself in a peculiar situation. With no one willing to touch the damned thing—literally and figuratively—the country was suddenly a kingdom without a king, a state without a ruler, and a people without a clue what to do next.

In a hastily convened meeting of the remaining nobles, a council was formed. They gathered in the grand, if somewhat drafty, hall of Westminster Abbey, the very same place where so many coronations had taken place—though none had ended particularly well. The crown itself had been carefully placed in a locked chest and shoved into the deepest, darkest corner of the abbey, where it could sit and brood like an angsty teenager.

At the head of the council was Lord Eadric of Northumbria, a man who had survived more betrayals than a cat had lives. His reputation for being tough and incredibly difficult to kill made him the perfect candidate to lead the new "Council of England." At least, until someone else tried to stab him in the back.

"Right," Eadric began, rapping his knuckles on the table to get everyone's attention. "We all agree: no more kings. They're more trouble than they're worth, and the crown... well, let's just say it's better off locked away."

The other nobles nodded in agreement, each one eyeing the chest as if it might sprout legs and start causing mischief on its own.

"But what about the prophecy?" asked Lady Ælfwynn of Winchester, a sharp-witted and young noblewoman who had managed to climb the ranks through a combination of cunning and an alarming proficiency with poisons.

"There's always a prophecy."

Eadric sighed, rubbing his temples. "Ah, yes, the prophecy. What was it again? Something about the 'true king' who can lift the curse and bring peace to England?"

"'Only the true king can bear the crown without losing his head,'" quoted Sir Beorhthelm, an aging knight who had somehow survived every battle by sheer luck. "Literally, in some cases."

The council members exchanged glances, each one silently hoping the 'true king' would reveal themselves sooner rather than later. But as they all knew, prophecies were like taxes—unavoidable and always worse than expected.

Just as the council was about to devolve into yet another round of heated debates, the doors to the abbey swung open with a loud creak. A tall, gaunt figure strode in, wearing robes that seemed to have been stitched together from shadows and bad omens. The figure's face was hidden beneath a hood, but the air of authority around them was undeniable.

"Who the devil are you?" Eadric demanded, half-rising from his seat and instinctively reaching for the dagger he kept hidden in his boot.

"I am Brother Mortimer," the figure intoned in a voice that sounded like it had been dragged through a graveyard. "I speak for the One Above All. And I bring a message."

"Oh, wonderful," Lady Ælfwynn muttered under her breath. "A messenger from the divine. Just what we needed."

Brother Mortimer ignored her and swept into the center of the hall, his robes billowing dramatically behind him. "The crown is cursed," he declared, as if this were news to anyone. "It is a punishment for the sins of our forefathers, and it shall bring ruin to any who dare to claim it. But..."

Eadric raised an eyebrow. "There's always a 'but' with these things."

"But," Mortimer continued, his voice dropping to a conspiratorial whisper, "the curse can be lifted. The One Above All has decreed that only the true king, the one chosen by the divine, can wear the crown without being destroyed."

The council members exchanged wary glances. They had heard this kind of talk before, and it rarely ended well.

"And who, pray tell, is this 'true king'?" Sir Beorhthelm asked, his tone skeptical. "Let me guess—it's you?"

Mortimer shook his head slowly. "Nay. The true king is among us, hidden in plain sight. The One Above All has left clues, riddles, signs. The chosen one must seek them out, prove themselves worthy, and only then can they take the crown."

"So, we're supposed to go on some sort of divine scavenger hunt?" Lady Ælfwynn said, her voice dripping with sarcasm. "And here I thought we were done with childish games."

"Perhaps," Mortimer replied, his eyes glinting beneath the hood. "But if the true king does not emerge, the curse will grow stronger. It will consume the land, and England will be plunged into darkness."

"That's the last thing we need," Eadric grumbled, though he couldn't help but feel a chill run down his spine. "But what about the Council? We're supposed to rule together, not chase after fairy tales."

"Ah, but ruling without the crown," Mortimer said, with a slow, ominous nod, "that's where the real danger lies. The curse has already started to take hold. Haven't you noticed the signs? The crops failing, the wolves growing bolder, the rivers turning red..."

"Wait, rivers turning red?" Sir Beorhthelm interrupted, looking genuinely alarmed. "I hadn't heard about that."

Mortimer smiled thinly. "There's more at stake than just the crown. The longer the curse lingers, the more chaos it will bring. The land will suffer, the people will revolt, and everything you've fought for will be for naught."

The council members shifted uncomfortably. They had hoped that locking away the crown would solve their problems, but it seemed that the curse had other ideas.

"Fine," Eadric said, throwing up his hands in exasperation. "If there's a true king out there, let's get on with it. But how do we find them? We're not exactly drowning in worthy candidates."

Brother Mortimer stepped forward, producing a small, weathered scroll from the folds of his robes. "The One Above All has provided a map, of sorts. It will lead the chosen one to the first of the trials—a test of strength, wisdom, and courage."

Lady Ælfwynn leaned over to Eadric, whispering, "You realize this is probably a death trap, right?"

"Oh, undoubtedly," Eadric whispered back. "But what choice do we have? Either we find the true king, or we're stuck ruling a cursed kingdom with no end in sight."

As Mortimer unfurled the scroll, revealing a cryptic set of directions and symbols, the council members realized that their journey was far from over. The prophecy had set them on a path that could lead to salvation—or doom.

The search for the true king was on, but with England's fate hanging in the balance, the council knew that failure was not an option. And so, they reluctantly agreed to send out their most trusted knights, scholars, and even the odd charlatan, hoping that somewhere, somehow, the true king would reveal themselves.

Meanwhile, the cursed crown sat in its chest, waiting for the next fool to try their luck. And if the council's track record was anything to go by, it wouldn't have to wait long.

The Curse That Just Won't Quit

The search for the true king of England began with all the enthusiasm of a drunken knight at a tournament—plenty of bravado, little sense, and absolutely no plan. The Council of England, having grudgingly accepted Brother Mortimer's ominous prophecy, dispatched its finest knights, scholars, and the occasional village idiot on a quest to locate the one person who could lift the curse that was slowly turning their kingdom into the world's most dysfunctional nightmare.

Of course, nothing went according to plan.

The first step on the journey was to find and pass the mysterious "trials" Mortimer had mentioned. These were supposedly ancient tests designed to reveal the true king—though given the current state of England, they were more likely to reveal who was dumb enough to volunteer for this death trap.

Sir Beorhthelm, despite being well past his prime and well aware that his luck had to run out eventually, was one of the first to volunteer. "Can't let these young pups show me up," he muttered, strapping on his rusted armor. "Besides, how hard can it be?"

The first trial took place in a haunted forest where the trees were rumored to whisper secrets—or maybe just insults, depending on who you asked. The task was to retrieve a golden apple from the tallest, creepiest tree in the woods, a feat that sounded much easier than it actually was.

As Sir Beorhthelm approached the tree, the forest seemed to close in around him, the air growing colder with every step. "Well, this is cozy," he muttered, shivering. "Just like my ex-wife's embrace."

He reached for the apple, only for the tree to suddenly spring to life, its branches twisting into claw-like hands. "Not so fast, knight," the tree hissed, its bark cracking with every word. "Only the true king may take the apple."

"Typical," Beorhthelm sighed. "I've fought dragons, bandits, and once a particularly angry goose, but a talking tree? That's a new low."

Undeterred, Beorhthelm swung his sword at the tree, only to have it bounce off the bark with a dull *thud*. The tree retaliated by swatting him aside like a particularly annoying fly. The last thing Beorhthelm heard before losing consciousness was the tree's smug laughter and something about "not being worthy."

Back at the council, Eadric received the news with a groan. "Great. So, that's one knight down. Who's next?"

The trials continued in a similarly disastrous fashion. Another knight was sent to retrieve a cursed sword from a lake only to be dragged underwater by a very uncooperative mermaid. A third was tasked with solving an ancient riddle, but the answer turned out to be something so obscure that even the riddle's creator had probably forgotten it.

As knight after knight failed the trials—usually in embarrassing, if not fatal, ways—the council began to grow desperate. The curse was getting worse by the day: crops were failing, livestock were running off cliffs, and the rivers, true to Mortimer's word, had started turning a worrying shade of red. All signs pointed to doom unless they found the true king.

With the trials proving impossible, a new wave of opportunists saw their chance. Self-proclaimed "kings" began popping up all over the kingdom, each one more ridiculous than the last. Every village seemed to have its own pretender to the throne, all claiming divine favor or ancient lineage—and none of them having the slightest clue about how to actually rule.

The most notorious of these charlatans was "King Oswald the Obvious," a traveling minstrel who had decided that being a bard was too much work and that ruling a kingdom would be easier. He wandered from village to village, dressed in a patchwork cloak he claimed was woven from the hair of a hundred virgins (it wasn't), and carrying a sword that was definitely made of wood.

"Behold, your king has arrived!" Oswald would announce with a dramatic flourish, usually accompanied by a truly awful lute solo. "I am the one true ruler, destined to lift the curse and bring peace to this land!"

The villagers, who were by now desperate for any kind of leadership—even if it came with a terrible soundtrack—would sometimes fall for his act. But as soon as Oswald tried to sit on any throne, cursed or otherwise, the curse would react violently. Livestock would stampede, crops would wither, and on one occasion, the entire village was suddenly overrun by a plague of frogs.

"Maybe I'm not the true king after all," Oswald would say sheepishly, usually while running for his life. "Sorry about the frogs!"

It didn't take long for the council to hear of these pretenders. As each new "king" was exposed as a fraud (often by their inability to withstand even a minor curse), the council's frustration grew.

"I can't take this anymore," Lady Ælfwynn snapped during yet another fruitless meeting. "If I see one more idiot claiming to be king, I swear I'll—"

"—curse them myself?" Eadric finished for her, leaning back in his chair. "Join the club."

With the trials failing and charlatans making a mess of things, the curse began to take on a life of its own. Strange and deadly events started happening all across the kingdom, each one more bizarre than the last.

In the town of Thistledown, the local well suddenly began spewing wine instead of water. At first, this was celebrated as a miracle—until the townsfolk realized the wine was cursed, causing anyone who drank it to dance uncontrollably until they collapsed from exhaustion.

In the coastal village of Driftwood, the sea turned as black as ink, and anyone who dared to fish found their nets full of bones instead of fish. The villagers, normally a hardy bunch, quickly abandoned the coast, convinced that the sea itself was angry at them.

And in the capital, London, things were even worse. The Thames had turned into a frothing river of blood (which, inconveniently, stained everything red), and the once-majestic Tower of London was now infested with rats the size of small dogs. The rats, much to everyone's horror, seemed to be developing a taste for human food—and not in the way anyone liked.

"I'm beginning to think locking the crown away was a mistake," Eadric admitted, staring at the latest reports with a look of pure exasperation.

"Beginning to?" Lady Ælfwynn retorted. "We're sitting on a powder keg, Eadric. If we don't find this so-called true king soon, there won't be a kingdom left to save."

"Maybe the curse is the true king," Sir Beorhthelm suggested, not entirely joking. "It certainly seems to be doing a better job of taking over than we are."

But before Eadric could respond, the abbey doors burst open once more, and Brother Mortimer strode in, looking more ominous than ever.

"I bring news," Mortimer declared, his voice filled with the kind of doom that made everyone wish they were somewhere else. "The One Above All has sent another sign. The trials have not been in vain."

Eadric raised an eyebrow. "Oh? You mean we've finally found our king?"

Mortimer smiled, though it was the kind of smile that suggested bad news was imminent. "Indeed. The true king will reveal themselves at the last trial, in a place where no light shines and no sound is heard."

"And where exactly is that?" Lady Ælfwynn asked, her patience clearly wearing thin.

"The crypts beneath the abbey," Mortimer intoned, his voice sending a chill through the room. "The final trial awaits below, where the true king will face the curse head-on."

The council members exchanged uneasy glances. The crypts were notorious for being the final resting place of kings, queens, and assorted nobility who had died under less-than-pleasant circumstances. It was the kind of place where even the bravest knight would hesitate to tread.

"Well," Eadric said with forced cheer, "nothing like a bit of crypt diving to brighten up the day. Shall we?"

And so, with no other options left, the council prepared to descend into the crypts, hoping that the true king would finally reveal themselves—and that the curse, which had turned their kingdom into a waking nightmare, would at last be lifted.

But as they ventured into the darkness, the cursed crown still hidden away in its chest, they couldn't shake the feeling that their troubles were far from over. If anything, the worst was yet to come.

Crypts and the King Who Wasn't

The crypts beneath Westminster Abbey were exactly as one might expect: dark, dank, and filled with the kind of eerie silence that made even the bravest knights question their life choices. The Council of England, led by the ever-grumpy Lord Eadric of Northumbria, descended into this underground labyrinth with all the enthusiasm of a cat being led to a bath.

"Lovely place," Eadric muttered, his voice echoing off the stone walls. "Perfect for a final trial. Or, you know, a final resting place."

Lady Ælfwynn, who had brought a torch and a healthy dose of skepticism, nodded grimly. "If we find any skeletons down here, I'm not sticking around to ask them who they belonged to."

"Unless they tell us who the true king is," added Sir Beorhthelm, who was trying—and failing—to keep his armor from clanking with every step. "In which case, a chat might be in order."

As the group moved deeper into the crypts, the air grew colder, and the stone walls seemed to close in around them. The flickering torchlight cast long, twisted shadows, making the tombs and statues look like they were watching the intruders with a mix of disdain and morbid curiosity.

Brother Mortimer, who was leading the way with all the solemnity of a man who knew exactly where this was heading (and secretly enjoyed it), suddenly stopped. "We are here," he announced, his voice as ominous as ever.

The council members found themselves in a large chamber, the walls lined with the tombs of long-dead kings and queens. In the center of the room stood a massive stone altar, on which lay a dusty, ancient book bound in cracked leather and ominous runes.

"Well, this is cheerful," Eadric said, eyeing the altar. "What now? Do we chant, light some candles, and hope the curse doesn't eat us?"

"The final trial," Mortimer intoned, ignoring Eadric's sarcasm, "requires the true king to take the book, read the ancient incantation, and face the curse head-on. Only the chosen one will survive."

"Chosen to do what, exactly?" Lady Ælfwynn asked, her eyes narrowing. "Die dramatically?"

"Survive, hopefully," Mortimer replied with a shrug. "But death is always an option."

As the council members exchanged uneasy glances, the ground beneath their feet suddenly began to rumble. The tombs along the walls creaked and groaned, as if the very dead were waking from their eternal slumber.

"Tell me that's just the crypt settling," Sir Beorhthelm said, clutching his sword.

But before anyone could answer, the lids of the tombs started to shift, inching open with a sound that could only be described as the earth's most displeased groan. A moment later, skeletal hands began to emerge, followed by the rest of the long-dead occupants.

"Ah, fantastic," Eadric muttered. "Now we're outnumbered by corpses. Just what I needed."

The council backed away as the skeletons, their bones rattling with every movement, slowly climbed out of their tombs. Some were still wearing the tattered remnants of royal robes, while others held rusted swords and shields, their empty eye sockets glowing with a faint, eerie light.

"I suppose they're here for the trial too?" Lady Ælfwynn asked, raising an eyebrow as one particularly decrepit skeleton pointed a bony finger at her.

"Or maybe they just really don't like visitors," Eadric replied, stepping back as another skeleton staggered toward him.

But before the council could decide whether to fight or flee, a new figure emerged from the shadows at the far end of the chamber. Unlike the skeletons, this figure was fully fleshed, though barely—his skin stretched tight over sharp bones, his eyes sunken and filled with a malevolent gleam.

"I see you've disturbed my rest," the figure said, his voice a dry rasp.

"How... unfortunate for you."

"And you are?" Eadric asked, though he had a sinking feeling he already knew the answer.

The figure stepped into the light, revealing himself to be an emaciated, ghostly figure draped in ancient, tattered robes. A tarnished crown sat crookedly atop his head, and his lips curled into a sneer. "I am the rightful king of England," he declared, "returned from the grave to claim what is mine."

"Oh, lovely," Lady Ælfwynn sighed. "A ghost king. Because regular kings weren't enough trouble."

Brother Mortimer, who seemed unfazed by the sudden appearance of the undead monarch, nodded solemnly. "This is the final trial. The true king must defeat this... pretender, and only then will the curse be lifted."

"Pretender?" the ghost king snarled, his bony fingers flexing. "I am no pretender! I was the last true king before they buried me alive for daring to challenge the usurpers!"

"Sounds like a rough day," Eadric said, inching closer to the altar and the book. "But we're kind of on a schedule, so if you could just—"

"Silence!" the ghost king roared, his voice reverberating through the crypt. The skeletons, sensing his command, began to advance on the council, their rusted weapons raised.

"Well, I guess we're doing this," Sir Beorhthelm said, drawing his sword and preparing for what was surely going to be a very unpleasant fight.

As the skeletons attacked, the council members found themselves in the middle of a brawl that was equal parts terrifying and absurd. Lady Ælfwynn dispatched a particularly aggressive skeleton with a well-aimed torch to the skull, while Sir Beorhthelm hacked away at another, its bones clattering to the ground in a pile.

Eadric, meanwhile, had made it to the altar and was staring down at the ancient book, its runes glowing faintly in the torchlight. "Well, here goes nothing," he muttered, opening the book to the first page.

But as he began to read the incantation, the ghost king let out a chilling laugh. "You think you can defeat me with a few words from a dusty old book?

I am the curse! I am the rightful ruler, and no one will take this crown from me!"

The room began to shake violently, and the crypt walls seemed to close in even further. The ghost king advanced on Eadric, his eyes burning with unholy fire. "You will bow before me, or you will die where you stand!"

Eadric, feeling the weight of the curse pressing down on him like a vice, continued to read the incantation, his voice growing louder as the ancient words flowed from his lips. The ghost king recoiled, as if the very sound of the incantation caused him pain.

"No! Stop!" the ghost king shrieked, his form flickering like a dying flame. "You cannot defeat me!"

But Eadric didn't stop. The incantation reached its climax, the runes on the book blazing with light, and with a final, defiant shout, the ghost king exploded into a cloud of ash, his crown clattering to the ground.

The skeletons, now leaderless, collapsed into heaps of bones, the eerie light fading from their eye sockets. The chamber fell silent once more, save for the heavy breathing of the council members as they tried to process what had just happened.

"Well, that was... something," Lady Ælfwynn said, brushing ash off her cloak. "Is it over?"

Brother Mortimer, who had been watching the whole scene with an unreadable expression, nodded slowly. "The false king has been defeated. The curse should now be lifted."

"'Should'?" Eadric echoed, raising an eyebrow. "I don't like 'should.' I prefer 'definitely.'"

As if on cue, the crypt began to rumble once more, but this time, the shaking was followed by a low, ominous creaking sound. The council looked around in alarm as the tombs began to shift, the stone lids sliding back into place as if the dead were finally returning to their rest.

But before anyone could breathe a sigh of relief, the altar in the center of the chamber split open with a deafening crack, revealing a hidden compartment within. Inside the compartment lay a gleaming, unblemished crown, untouched by time or curse.

Eadric, still holding the ancient book, stared down at the crown. "Oh, you've got to be kidding me."

"The true king's crown," Mortimer whispered, his eyes widening. "It was here all along."

"So, what happens if we put that one on?" Sir Beorhthelm asked, though he didn't seem eager to volunteer.

Mortimer turned to Eadric, his voice filled with reverence. "You have passed the final trial. You are the true king."

Eadric blinked. "Me? The true king? That's... not what I signed up for."

"Nor is it what you want," Lady Ælfwynn added, crossing her arms. "But it seems the crown has chosen."

Eadric stared at the crown, feeling its weight even before he touched it. After everything they had been through—the trials, the charlatans, the curse—it all came down to this. He reached out, hesitated, then finally picked up the crown.

"Fine," he said, placing it on his head with a resigned sigh. "If this thing kills me, at least I won't have to deal with the council anymore."

But as the crown settled on his brow, the chamber grew still, the crypt's oppressive atmosphere lifting as if a great weight had been removed. The curse, it seemed, was finally broken.

Eadric waited for something terrible to happen—a sudden curse, a ghostly apparition, anything—but nothing came. Instead, he felt a strange sense of calm, as if the crown had accepted him as its rightful bearer.

"Well, I'll be damned," Sir Beorhthelm said, breaking the silence. "You really are the true king."

"Great," Eadric replied, though his voice was tinged with sarcasm. "Now I just have to clean up this mess of a kingdom."

As the council members made their way back to the surface, Eadric couldn't help but feel a mix of relief and dread. The curse was lifted, but now he was king—a job he had never wanted, but one he was stuck with all the same.

"Well, Your Majesty," Lady Ælfwynn said with a smirk as they emerged into the light of day, "ready to rule?"

Eadric sighed. "Let's just try not to get cursed again, shall we?"

The Crown and the Council Conundrum

Eadric of Northumbria, the newly minted King of England—though he still hadn't quite gotten used to the title—sat slumped on the now-cursed-no-more throne, surveying the chaos that was his kingdom. The crypts had been left behind, the curse supposedly lifted, and the crown was firmly on his head. Yet, as he looked out at the kingdom he was supposed to rule, he couldn't help but feel that the worst was yet to come.

"Rebuilding a kingdom, they said. It'll be fun, they said," Eadric muttered under his breath, drumming his fingers on the armrest. "It's like trying to fix a sinking ship with a spoon."

Lady Ælfwynn, who had taken up the unenviable position of his chief advisor, leaned against a pillar, arms crossed. "Well, at least the curse is gone. You're not dead, the crown hasn't exploded, and the people aren't rioting... yet."

"Yet," Eadric repeated, his tone dripping with sarcasm. "Always a 'yet.' It's like waiting for the other shoe to drop—except the shoe is made of iron and is likely to land on my head."

Sir Beorhthelm, who had miraculously survived the whole crypt fiasco, strolled into the throne room with the air of a man who was either blissfully unaware of the dangers around him or simply too old to care. "Cheer up, Your Majesty! At least we've got a crown on your head and a kingdom to rule. That's more than we had this morning."

"Yes, but for how long?" Eadric replied, his mood as gray as the clouds gathering outside the palace. "The curse may be gone, but I've still got a kingdom full of angry peasants, scheming nobles, and—let's not forget—the ever-present threat of another curse rearing its ugly head."

And as if on cue, a page burst into the throne room, pale as a ghost and out of breath. "Your Majesty! There's... there's been an incident!"

Eadric sighed deeply, already regretting not just staying in bed. "Of course there has. What now? Plague? Famine? A plague of famines?"

"It's the crops, sire!" the page stammered. "They've... they've started rotting in the fields. And the livestock—well, they're... they're eating each other!"

The room fell silent as everyone processed this latest bit of bad news. Lady Ælfwynn pinched the bridge of her nose. "We lift one curse, and another one pops up like a bad penny. It's almost impressive."

"Impressively infuriating," Eadric corrected, rising from the throne with a weary groan. "It seems the curse wasn't completely lifted after all. Which means we're right back where we started."

Sir Beorhthelm frowned, scratching his head. "But we defeated the ghost king! The crypt trials, the skeletons... that was supposed to be the end of it!"

"Supposed to be," Eadric echoed, striding toward the door. "But curses have a way of lingering, don't they? Like a bad smell."

Lady Ælfwynn fell into step beside him. "So what's the plan, Your Majesty? Besides trying not to get eaten by cursed cows?"

"First, we need to figure out what's causing this new curse," Eadric said, his mind racing. "And if that means we have to go back into those damned crypts, so be it. But we can't do it alone."

"Who else are you planning to drag into this nightmare?" Lady Ælfwynn asked, raising an eyebrow.

"The rest of the council, of course," Eadric replied, his tone laced with irony. "They've been remarkably quiet since I took the throne. Too quiet. I'm beginning to suspect they're up to something."

Sir Beorhthelm nodded sagely. "Nobles are like rats. When you can't see them, it's because they're up to no good."

And so, with the kingdom teetering on the edge of another crisis, Eadric summoned what remained of the council to the throne room. The surviving members—those who hadn't been killed by curses, betrayals, or unfortunate accidents involving falling masonry—arrived with expressions ranging from nervous to downright shifty.

"Your Majesty," began the Earl of Kent, bowing so low that Eadric half-expected him to topple over. "How may we serve you in these troubling times?"

Eadric eyed the gathered nobles with a mixture of suspicion and annoyance. "You can start by telling me what you're plotting. I know you lot didn't survive this long by being loyal and selfless."

The Earl of Kent blinked, looking genuinely surprised. "Plotting? Us? Why, we wouldn't dream of it!"

"Right," Eadric said dryly. "And I'm the Queen of Sheba."

Lady Ælfwynn stepped forward, her gaze sharp. "We know the curse isn't fully lifted. The crops are rotting, the livestock are eating each other, and it's only a matter of time before the people start blaming you—sorry, us—for it. So, I'll ask again: what are you up to?"

The Earl of Kent glanced nervously at his fellow nobles, who were all doing their best to avoid eye contact. Finally, he sighed and straightened up. "Alright, fine. There may have been some... discussions."

"Discussions?" Eadric repeated, his tone dangerously calm. "About what, exactly?"

"About... removing you from the throne," the Earl admitted, his voice barely above a whisper. "Not because we want to, of course! But because we thought... well, we thought you might be cursed."

Eadric stared at the Earl, then burst out laughing—a harsh, humorless sound that echoed through the throne room. "Oh, that's rich! You think I'm cursed, so your brilliant solution is to overthrow me and start this mess all over again? You people really don't learn, do you?"

The Earl of Kent winced. "It's not like that, sire! We were only trying to protect the kingdom."

"By staging a coup?" Lady Ælfwynn asked, her voice dripping with disdain. "That's a novel way to 'protect' something."

Eadric shook his head, still chuckling. "You know what? Fine. You want to play the power game? Let's play. But here's the thing—I'm not cursed. At least, not any more than this whole kingdom is."

The nobles exchanged confused glances. "Then... what do we do?" the Earl of Kent asked hesitantly.

"You help me find out what's causing this new curse," Eadric said, his expression hardening. "Because if you don't, I'll make sure that whatever happens next is a lot worse than rotting crops and cannibal cows. And trust me, I've got ideas."

Lady Ælfwynn smirked. "Good ones, too."

The council members, thoroughly cowed, nodded in unison. "We're at your service, Your Majesty," the Earl said, trying to muster some dignity. "What are your orders?"

"For starters," Eadric said, "I want a full investigation into what's going on with the crops and livestock. Leave no stone unturned, no spell uncast. And if there's any sign of a curse—or, God forbid, another would-be king—deal with it before it becomes a problem."

"Yes, Your Majesty," the council members chorused, eager to be useful.

"Oh, and one more thing," Eadric added, as they began to disperse. "If any of you are thinking about another coup, remember this: I survived the last curse, and I'm more than ready to deal with the next one. So tread carefully."

The nobles, thoroughly chastened, hurried out of the throne room to begin their new tasks. As the last of them departed, Sir Beorhthelm let out a low whistle. "You've got them jumping, Your Majesty."

"For now," Eadric replied, sinking back onto the throne. "But we still have to deal with this curse. And something tells me it's not going to be as simple as hunting down a ghost king."

Lady Ælfwynn nodded in agreement. "If there's one thing I've learned, it's that curses are like weeds. You pull one up, and ten more sprout in its place."

"Then we'll need to dig deeper," Eadric said, rubbing his temples. "And we'd better start soon, before this kingdom turns into a graveyard."

As the council scattered to their new duties, Eadric and his closest advisors prepared for the next stage of their battle against the curse. The road ahead was fraught with danger, betrayal, and—most likely—more than a few close encounters with the undead.

But one thing was certain: Eadric wasn't about to give up his crown without a fight. Even if it killed him.

Again.

Crusaders and the Pope's Problem

Lord Eadric of Northumbria, now reluctantly wearing the crown of England, had thought that his biggest problem would be keeping his head firmly attached to his shoulders. But as he paced the cold, drafty corridors of Westminster Palace, it became increasingly clear that his problems were about to multiply like rabbits on a fertility potion.

"Your Majesty," Lady Ælfwynn began, catching up to Eadric with a stack of scrolls in her arms, "we've just received word from the Vatican. The Pope is... concerned."

Eadric stopped in his tracks, narrowing his eyes. "Concerned? When a pope is 'concerned,' it usually means someone's about to get excommunicated, burned, or both."

Ælfwynn nodded grimly. "Apparently, the Holy See has heard about the curse and our, shall we say, *unorthodox* methods of dealing with it. They're sending an envoy to 'assist' in resolving the matter."

Eadric groaned, rubbing his temples. "Wonderful. As if I didn't have enough problems with crops rotting and cows turning into cannibals. Now I have to deal with a papal envoy breathing down my neck, judging every decision I make."

Sir Beorhthelm, who had been listening nearby, offered his usual brand of unhelpful optimism. "Look on the bright side, Your Majesty. Maybe they'll offer to lift the curse for us?"

Eadric shot him a withering look. "Yes, I'm sure they'll solve everything with a few prayers and a sprinkling of holy water. And then they'll politely ask for the crown and my head on a silver platter."

"Think of it as an opportunity," Lady Ælfwynn suggested, though she didn't sound particularly convinced herself. "If we can show the Pope that the curse is under control, we might avoid a full-blown excommunication. Or worse—a Crusade."

Eadric's eyes widened. "A Crusade? Against England? We've barely finished one crusade, and now they're considering another? What's next, declaring war on us for having bad weather?"

"Apparently, Rome is concerned that England's cursed crown could spread its influence beyond our borders," Ælfwynn explained. "They see it as a threat to Christendom."

"Great," Eadric muttered. "First, I get cursed, and now I'm accused of threatening Christendom. What's next? Am I going to be blamed for the Black Death too?"

Before anyone could respond, a guard hurried into the room, looking as pale as if he'd seen the curse itself. "Your Majesty, there's a group of knights at the gates! They're demanding an audience!"

"Knights?" Eadric repeated, already feeling the headache forming. "Which faction this time? Norman? Viking? Or maybe a band of disgruntled hedge knights looking to add a new chapter to their tragic life stories?"

The guard shook his head. "Crusaders, sire. They've returned from the Holy Land, and they claim they've brought something... divine."

Eadric exchanged a glance with Ælfwynn. "Divine? Oh, this should be good."

"Or deadly," Ælfwynn added, her voice laced with caution. "Best be prepared for either."

The group made their way to the throne room, where the Crusader knights were already waiting. They were a formidable sight—scarred, weathered, and covered in the dust of a thousand battles. At their head was Sir Baldwin, a knight with a permanent scowl etched into his sunburned face, as if he'd spent the entire Crusade brooding in the desert.

"Your Majesty," Baldwin said, bowing stiffly. "We bring you a gift from the Holy Land—a relic of unimaginable power, blessed by the saints themselves."

Eadric, already skeptical, sat back in his throne. "Let me guess. It's a piece of the True Cross? Or perhaps a vial of holy water that turns into wine? Because honestly, I could use a drink right about now."

Baldwin's scowl deepened. "This is no ordinary relic, sire. It is the Spear of Longinus—the very spear that pierced the side of Christ. It has the power to defeat any curse, cleanse any land, and restore any kingdom to glory."

Eadric's sarcasm faded, replaced by a cautious interest. "And you're just... giving this to me? No strings attached?"

Sir Baldwin hesitated, his eyes flicking toward his fellow knights. "We offer it in exchange for a small favor, Your Majesty. We seek to establish a new order here in England—one that will protect the realm from all threats, both mortal and... otherwise."

Lady Ælfwynn raised an eyebrow. "You mean to establish a theocracy? A kingdom ruled by the Church and its knights?"

Baldwin smiled, though it was a smile with all the warmth of a snake in winter. "You misunderstand, my lady. We wish only to serve the crown and the faith. But with the power of the Spear, we can ensure that England remains free from curses, heretics, and... troublesome influences."

"Troublesome influences?" Eadric repeated, his tone dry. "Like the Pope, perhaps?"

Baldwin's expression didn't change. "If necessary."

Eadric stared at the knight, weighing his options. On the one hand, the idea of a relic that could lift the curse was tempting—especially if it meant he could keep the papal envoy from turning England into a battlefield. On the other hand, handing over power to a group of zealots who might decide that Eadric himself was a "troublesome influence" wasn't exactly appealing.

"Thank you for the offer," Eadric said finally, "but I think we'll handle the curse on our own terms."

Baldwin's eyes narrowed. "You would refuse the will of God?"

Eadric smiled thinly. "Let's just say I've learned to be cautious when dealing with relics. You never know when one might come with a curse of its own."

The tension in the room was palpable as the Crusader knights exchanged glances. Baldwin looked ready to argue, but before he could, the doors to the throne room swung open once more, revealing a tall, regal figure clad in the finest ecclesiastical robes.

"The papal envoy," Ælfwynn whispered, her tone flat. "This day just keeps getting better."

The envoy, a severe-looking man with a thin face and eyes that could bore through stone, strode into the room as if he owned it. "King Eadric," he intoned, his voice dripping with authority. "I bring greetings from His Holiness the Pope. And a warning."

Eadric's smile didn't quite reach his eyes. "A warning? How refreshing. Let me guess—you're here to remind me of my mortal sins and threaten me with eternal damnation?"

The envoy's lips curled into something resembling a smile. "Nothing so dramatic, Your Majesty. I am here to ensure that England remains under the protection and guidance of the Church. The curse that plagues this land is a sign—a sign that God's favor has been withdrawn. It is our duty to restore that favor."

"And how do you propose we do that?" Eadric asked, leaning forward slightly. "By handing over the crown to you and your knights?"

"Of course not," the envoy said, his voice smooth. "But by submitting to the will of the Church, allowing us to cleanse the land, and placing the kingdom's governance under the guidance of the Holy See, we can ensure that the curse is lifted, and England is restored to its rightful place."

Eadric raised an eyebrow. "So, in other words, you want to run the kingdom while I sit here and do as I'm told?"

"Precisely," Baldwin added, stepping forward. "With the power of the Spear and the guidance of the Church, England will be invincible."

Eadric looked between the envoy and Baldwin, his mind racing. The curse, the relic, the Pope's influence—it was all a tangled web of politics, power, and religion, and he was the fly caught in the middle. But if there was one thing Eadric knew, it was that he didn't survive this long by letting other people make his decisions for him.

"Here's the problem with your plan," Eadric said, rising to his feet. "I've seen what happens when people put too much faith in relics and holy men. It usually ends with someone getting stabbed in the back—or burned at the stake."

The envoy's expression hardened. "You would defy the will of the Pope?"

"I would defy anyone who thinks they can waltz in here and take my crown," Eadric shot back. "This kingdom may be cursed, but it's still mine. And I'm not about to hand it over to a bunch of zealots with a fancy spear and a penchant for power."

Baldwin's hand moved to the hilt of his sword, but Eadric held up a hand. "You can keep your spear, and you can tell the Pope that England is perfectly capable of handling its own problems. But if you try to take this kingdom by force, you'll find out just how stubborn we English can be."

The room was silent for a moment, the tension thick enough to cut with a knife. Then, the envoy nodded slowly, his eyes narrowing. "Very well, Your Majesty. But know this—if you fail to lift the curse, the Church will intervene. And when we do, there will be no mercy."

With that, the envoy turned on his heel and strode out of the throne room, followed by his retinue of clerics. Baldwin and his knights lingered for a moment longer, their expressions hard and unreadable.

"We will see if your resolve holds, King Eadric," Baldwin said quietly. "But know that we will be watching."

And with that, the Crusaders turned and left, leaving Eadric and his advisors alone in the throne room.

"Well," Eadric said after a moment, rubbing his forehead. "That could have gone better."

"It could have gone a lot worse," Ælfwynn replied, though she didn't sound entirely convinced. "But they're not going to give up, Eadric. The Church, the Crusaders—they're going to keep pushing until they get what they want."

Eadric sighed, sinking back into his throne. "I know. Which means we need to figure out this curse before they come back with an army."

"And the Spear?" Beorhthelm asked. "Do you think it could really lift the curse?"

Eadric thought about it for a moment, then shook his head. "Maybe. But if it does, it'll come at a cost. And I'm not about to trade one curse for another."

"So what's the plan?" Ælfwynn asked.

Eadric looked out at the darkening sky through the high windows of the throne room. "The plan is to survive. To figure out what's really behind this curse, and to keep the Pope and his knights from tearing this kingdom apart."

"And if we can't?" Beorhthelm asked, his voice low.

Eadric smiled, though it was a smile filled with grim determination. "Then we make sure they regret ever underestimating us."

As the storm clouds gathered outside, Eadric knew that the battle for England was far from over. The curse, the Pope, the Crusaders—they were all part of a larger game, and the stakes were higher than ever. But if there was one thing Eadric had learned, it was that he wasn't about to let anyone—alive or dead—take his crown without a fight.

It's Always the King

King Eadric was starting to wonder if someone had cursed him personally, aside from the whole cursed crown debacle. The moment he put the crown on his head, it seemed like every possible disaster had lined up outside Westminster, waiting its turn to knock on his door and demand attention.

But today, the knocking was less polite. It was more like battering-ram-to-the-gates urgent.

"Your Majesty!" Lady Ælfwynn burst into the throne room, breathless, her usually composed demeanor showing the faintest signs of cracking. "We have a problem."

Eadric didn't bother looking up from the map spread out on the table in front of him. "Just one? I'd call that an improvement."

"This one's big," Ælfwynn said, her voice tense. "The Crusaders are making their move. Sir Baldwin and his knights have gathered forces outside the city. They're planning to storm Westminster."

Eadric sighed, rubbing his temples. "And here I thought they'd just leave quietly and never cause trouble again. Silly me."

Sir Beorhthelm, who had become an expert at showing up just in time for bad news, marched into the room with an expression that suggested he'd seen a ghost—or possibly something worse. "Your Majesty, it's not just the Crusaders. We've got another problem."

Eadric looked up sharply. "Another? What is it now? Has the Thames turned into wine? Are the cows rioting again?"

Beorhthelm shook his head, grimacing. "The Pope's sent an Inquisition. They've just landed on the coast, and they're making their way to London.

And from what I've heard, they're not here to discuss theology over tea and biscuits."

Eadric felt the beginnings of a headache. "Of course they are. Why wouldn't they be?"

Ælfwynn looked at Eadric, her eyes narrowing in concern. "This is serious. The Crusaders want the throne, and the Inquisition wants control of the kingdom. If they both attack—"

"—we'll be stuck between a rock and a bunch of religious zealots with torches," Eadric finished, standing up from the table. "Well, we've handled worse... right?"

Ælfwynn raised an eyebrow. "Remind me when we've handled worse?"

"I'm sure it's happened at least once," Eadric replied, though he didn't sound particularly confident. "Anyway, we can't just sit here and wait for them to burn down the palace. We need to figure out what's really behind this curse, and fast. If we can do that, maybe we can throw it in their faces and send them running."

"And if we can't?" Beorhthelm asked, his tone grim.

"Then I'll need to find a better hiding spot," Eadric muttered. "But first things first—let's deal with these Crusaders before they turn Westminster into a cathedral."

As if on cue, the sound of trumpets echoed through the palace, signaling the arrival of the Crusader forces. Eadric and his advisors exchanged quick, determined glances before marching out of the throne room and onto the battlements to assess the situation.

Below, the streets were filled with Baldwin's knights, their armor gleaming in the pale morning light. The Crusaders had surrounded Westminster, their siege engines ready, their banners fluttering in the wind like the wings of vultures circling a soon-to-be corpse.

"Ah, there they are," Eadric said, leaning over the battlements with a grimace. "Our friendly neighborhood zealots."

Sir Baldwin, seated on a massive warhorse that looked like it could have flattened a small village, raised his hand in a gesture that was half-salute, half-challenge. "King Eadric!" he called up to the battlements, his voice

IT'S ALWAYS THE KING

booming. "It's time to end this charade! Surrender the crown and submit to the will of God!"

Eadric cupped his hands around his mouth and shouted back. "Is that a demand, or are you just asking nicely?"

"It's a demand!" Baldwin snapped. "The Pope has declared you unfit to rule! The curse on this land is proof of your failure! Relinquish the throne and allow the Church to restore order!"

Eadric turned to Ælfwynn. "You know, I can't help but notice that whenever something goes wrong, people always blame the king. Never the weather, or bad luck, or that one guy who didn't pray hard enough. It's always the king."

Ælfwynn smirked. "Comes with the crown, Your Majesty."

Eadric sighed, turning back to Baldwin. "And if I refuse?"

Baldwin's eyes narrowed. "Then we'll take the crown by force. And when we do, you'll answer for your sins before the Pope himself."

Beorhthelm leaned in, whispering to Eadric. "Might I suggest something witty and defiant? It's customary before a siege."

Eadric considered this for a moment, then shouted down to Baldwin. "You want the crown? Come and get it! But don't blame me if the curse comes after you next!"

Baldwin scowled, clearly unimpressed with Eadric's bravado. He turned to his knights, raising his sword high. "Prepare for the assault!"

But just as the Crusaders were about to charge, the ground beneath them began to tremble. The air grew thick and heavy, and a low, ominous hum filled the air. Eadric and his advisors exchanged worried glances, knowing all too well what this meant.

"The curse," Ælfwynn whispered, her eyes widening. "It's reacting."

As the tremors grew stronger, the Crusaders hesitated, their horses rearing and neighing in panic. From the cracks in the earth, a thick, black mist began to seep out, curling around the legs of the knights like the fingers of some malevolent spirit.

"Not again," Eadric muttered, gripping the battlements as the mist began to rise higher, enveloping the Crusaders in its suffocating embrace.

Baldwin's horse bucked wildly, throwing him from the saddle as the mist climbed up his armor, seeping into the joints and cracks like a living thing. The other knights, caught in the same deadly cloud, began to thrash and scream as the curse took hold.

"This wasn't part of the plan!" Baldwin shouted, his voice tinged with desperation. "Fight it! Fight the curse!"

But the mist was relentless. It swirled around the Crusaders, choking the life out of them as their armor rusted and their weapons crumbled to dust. Within moments, the mighty force that had surrounded Westminster was reduced to a pile of bones and rusted metal, their banners lying tattered and torn in the street.

Eadric watched in stunned silence as the mist receded, leaving nothing but desolation in its wake. "Well, that was... effective," he said finally, though he didn't sound particularly pleased.

Ælfwynn shook her head, her expression grim. "The curse is getting stronger. If it can do this to an army, what will it do to the rest of the kingdom?"

"And how do we stop it?" Beorhthelm asked, his voice tinged with fear.

Eadric stared down at the remains of the Crusaders, his mind racing. "We need to find the source. Something in this land is feeding the curse, making it more powerful. If we can destroy it, maybe we can save what's left of England."

"But where do we start?" Ælfwynn asked, her brow furrowed. "We've searched the crypts, we've defeated the ghost king... what else could there be?"

As if in answer, the distant sound of marching feet echoed through the city, growing louder with each passing moment. The Inquisition had arrived.

Eadric clenched his fists, his resolve hardening. "We start by surviving. The Pope's Inquisition is here, and they're not going to stop until they've taken control—or until we're all dead."

"And after that?" Beorhthelm asked, though he already knew the answer.

"After that," Eadric said, his eyes narrowing, "we find the source of this curse, we destroy it, and we make sure that no one ever tries to take this throne by force again."

As the Inquisition's forces closed in on Westminster, Eadric knew that the battle for England was far from over. The curse was growing stronger, and the enemies at his gates were more dangerous than ever. But if there was one thing Eadric had learned, it was that he wasn't about to let anyone—Pope, Crusader, or curse—take his crown without a fight.

The Cursed Relic Below

Eadric had faced many challenges since taking the cursed crown of England, but none quite as daunting as the one now bearing down on Westminster. The Pope's Inquisition had arrived in force, bringing with them the cold certainty of divine judgment and the not-so-divine intention of seizing control of the kingdom. And as if that weren't enough, the curse itself seemed to be gaining power, transforming from a troublesome inconvenience into a full-blown, kingdom-wrecking disaster.

"Your Majesty," Lady Ælfwynn said as she strode into the throne room, her tone urgent, "the Inquisition has breached the outer walls. They're moving fast, and they're armed to the teeth."

Eadric looked up from the ancient scroll he'd been studying, his expression a mixture of irritation and resignation. "Of course they are. Because why wouldn't they want to kick a man while he's down?"

Sir Beorhthelm, who had taken to pacing the room like a caged lion, stopped in his tracks. "Your Majesty, we need to prepare for a siege. If the Inquisition gets their hands on Westminster, they'll turn this place into a bonfire—starting with you."

"Thank you for the vote of confidence, Beorhthelm," Eadric replied dryly, rubbing his temples. "But I'm not about to let a bunch of zealots and their torches ruin my day. Or my reign, for that matter."

Ælfwynn stepped closer, lowering her voice. "There's something else, Your Majesty. While you were busy with the Crusaders, we uncovered an ancient map hidden in the crypts. It leads to a hidden chamber deep beneath Westminster—a place that predates the abbey itself."

Eadric arched an eyebrow. "A hidden chamber? Please tell me it's not filled with more skeletons."

"Worse," Ælfwynn said, her expression grim. "According to the map, this chamber holds the relic that's feeding the curse. If we don't destroy it, the curse will keep growing stronger until it consumes the entire kingdom—and probably us along with it."

"So let me get this straight," Eadric said, leaning back in his throne. "We've got the Inquisition trying to turn us into kindling, and at the same time, we need to go on a little treasure hunt in the crypts to find and destroy a cursed relic. All before lunchtime."

"Pretty much," Ælfwynn replied, shrugging. "It's a tight schedule."

Beorhthelm nodded, his hand resting on the hilt of his sword. "I say we split up. I'll lead the defense of Westminster, buy you time to find this relic and destroy it. It's not like I haven't faced impossible odds before."

"Impossible odds are your specialty," Eadric quipped, though there was a hint of genuine appreciation in his voice. "Alright then. Beorhthelm, take whoever you can muster and hold the Inquisition at bay. Ælfwynn and I will go relic-hunting."

As Beorhthelm left to rally the remaining forces, Eadric and Ælfwynn descended into the crypts, torches in hand and the weight of the kingdom's fate pressing down on them like a particularly unwelcome guest. The air grew colder and more oppressive with each step, the shadows flickering eerily along the stone walls as if mocking their every move.

"You know," Eadric said as they wound their way through the labyrinthine passages, "I never thought I'd miss the days when my biggest problem was dealing with unruly nobles and the occasional Viking raid. Those were simpler times."

Ælfwynn smirked. "Now it's just unruly curses and homicidal inquisitors. Progress, I suppose."

"Progress," Eadric muttered, shaking his head. "It's a wonder anyone ever wants this job."

They continued deeper into the crypts, following the map's directions as the air grew thick with a strange, almost electric tension. Finally, they reached a dead end, the stone wall in front of them engraved with ancient symbols that seemed to pulse with a faint, malevolent light.

"This must be it," Ælfwynn said, holding the torch closer to the wall. "The entrance to the hidden chamber."

Eadric studied the symbols for a moment before reaching out to touch the wall. The stone was unnaturally cold, and as his fingers brushed against the engravings, the wall began to tremble. With a low rumble, the stone slid aside, revealing a dark, narrow passageway that seemed to lead straight down into the earth.

"Well, that's inviting," Eadric said with a grimace. "Let's get this over with."

They descended into the passage, the walls closing in around them as they went deeper into the heart of Westminster. The air grew colder still, the oppressive silence broken only by the distant sounds of battle from above—the Inquisition's forces clashing with Beorhthelm's defenders in a desperate struggle to keep the palace from falling.

Finally, they emerged into a vast, circular chamber, the walls lined with rows of ancient, crumbling statues. At the center of the chamber stood a massive stone altar, and atop it rested a black, twisted relic that seemed to pulse with a dark energy.

"There it is," Ælfwynn whispered, her voice tinged with awe and dread. "The source of the curse."

Eadric approached the altar cautiously, his eyes narrowing as he studied the relic. "It looks like something that belongs in the deepest pit of hell, not in the heart of England. How do we destroy it?"

Ælfwynn handed Eadric a small, ornate dagger. "This should do the trick. The dagger's blade is made from the same material as the relic. If we pierce the heart of the relic with it, it should shatter the curse. Or at least, that's what the ancient texts say."

"'Should' again," Eadric muttered, taking the dagger. "I'm starting to hate that word."

As he approached the altar, the chamber began to tremble, the statues lining the walls creaking as if they were coming to life. The relic pulsed more violently, the dark energy radiating from it growing stronger, more oppressive, as if it knew its time was running out.

Eadric steeled himself, raising the dagger. "Here goes nothing."

But just as he was about to strike, a voice echoed through the chamber, cold and mocking. "You cannot destroy what has been forged in darkness, king. The curse is eternal. It will consume you, as it has consumed all before you."

Eadric froze, looking around the chamber for the source of the voice. But there was no one there—only the relic, pulsing ominously on the altar.

"Great," Eadric muttered. "Now it's talking. Just what I needed."

Ælfwynn stepped closer, her voice steady despite the growing tension. "Don't listen to it, Eadric. Destroy the relic. End this."

But the voice laughed, a cruel, bone-chilling sound that echoed through the chamber. "Foolish mortals. You think you can defy the will of the darkness? You will fail, as all others have failed."

Eadric clenched his jaw, tightening his grip on the dagger. "We'll see about that."

With a swift motion, he plunged the dagger into the heart of the relic. The chamber erupted in a blinding flash of light, the force of the explosion sending Eadric and Ælfwynn tumbling to the ground. The relic shattered into a thousand pieces, each fragment dissolving into nothingness as the curse's dark energy was released in a final, deafening roar.

For a moment, everything was silent. Then, slowly, the chamber began to settle, the oppressive darkness lifting as the last remnants of the curse faded away.

Eadric groaned, pushing himself to his feet. "Well, that was... unpleasant."

Ælfwynn stood, dusting herself off. "But effective. The curse is broken."

Eadric looked around the now-empty chamber, the tension in the air finally gone. "Let's hope so. Because if it isn't, I'm going to have some very unpleasant words with whoever made that relic."

As they made their way back up the passage, the sounds of battle above them began to fade, replaced by an eerie silence. When they emerged from the crypts into the throne room, they found Beorhthelm waiting for them, a bloodied sword in his hand and a weary but satisfied expression on his face.

"You did it," Beorhthelm said, a grin breaking through his tired features. "The Inquisition's forces just... collapsed. Like the life was sucked out of them. They're retreating."

Eadric exhaled, relief washing over him. "And the palace?"

"Mostly intact," Beorhthelm replied, though his tone suggested there had been some close calls. "But we held them off, just like you asked."

Ælfwynn nodded, a small smile on her lips. "The curse is broken, Your Majesty. England is safe. For now."

"For now," Eadric echoed, though there was a hint of a smile in his voice. "And maybe, just maybe, we'll get a little peace and quiet."

Beorhthelm chuckled. "That'll be the day."

As the three of them stood in the throne room, battered but victorious, Eadric couldn't help but feel a sense of cautious optimism. The curse was gone, the Inquisition had been repelled, and for the first time in what felt like forever, the kingdom seemed to be on the path to recovery.

Of course, knowing his luck, it wouldn't last long. But for now, Eadric was content to take things one day at a time—and to enjoy the small victories where he could find them.

"Come on," Eadric said, gesturing toward the doors. "Let's get out of here before something else decides to go wrong."

As they left the throne room, the first rays of sunlight broke through the storm clouds outside, casting a warm, golden light over the palace. And for a moment, just a moment, Eadric allowed himself to believe that the worst was truly behind them.

Normans, Scots, and the Pope's New Pet

King Eadric of England was starting to think that wearing a crown was less about ruling a kingdom and more about dealing with constant headaches. Today's headache was particularly nasty and came in the form of two very determined foreign powers: the Normans and the Scots.

It had been only a week since the curse that plagued England was supposedly shattered, but Eadric had barely had time to celebrate. The Inquisition had been repelled, the relic destroyed, and for a brief, shining moment, it seemed like peace might actually be possible. Naturally, that moment was shorter than a Saxon's patience at a Norman banquet.

Eadric's advisors—Ælfwynn and Beorhthelm—stood with him in the war room, staring at a map that looked more like a battlefield than a piece of parchment.

"Your Majesty," Ælfwynn began, her tone as sharp as the dagger she always kept tucked in her belt, "the news isn't good. Henry of Normandy, the son of William the Bastard, has raised an army and is marching toward England. He's got the Pope's blessing and a very persuasive argument for why he should be king."

Eadric raised an eyebrow. "Let me guess—his argument involves a lot of swords and very few polite requests?"

Ælfwynn nodded. "Pretty much. And he's married Matilda of Scotland, daughter of King Malcolm III. Which means the Scots are in on this too. It's a double invasion."

Beorhthelm, who had been frowning at the map as if it had personally insulted him, finally spoke up. "So, we've got the Normans coming from the south, the Scots from the north, and the Pope smiling down from Rome like a particularly smug cat. What's the plan, Your Majesty? Or should I start sharpening my sword now?"

Eadric sighed, leaning over the map. "Oh, sharpen away, Beorhthelm. We'll need every edge we can get. But first, we need to figure out how to deal with this mess. The Pope's backing Henry, which means he's going to try and paint this as a holy war—a crusade against the 'heretical' Saxons."

"And how do we counter that?" Ælfwynn asked, her eyes narrowing. "We're outnumbered, outmaneuvered, and let's be honest, probably out-prayed."

Eadric smirked. "By being cleverer than they are. Henry may have the Pope's blessing, but blessings don't win battles—strategy does. And if we can play our cards right, we can turn these two foreign threats against each other."

Beorhthelm looked intrigued. "How do we do that?"

"First, we spread a little misinformation," Eadric said, a mischievous glint in his eye. "We send word to the Scots that the Normans are planning to take the whole kingdom for themselves, leaving Scotland out in the cold. Meanwhile, we tell Henry that the Scots are only using him to weaken England, planning to swoop in and claim the throne for themselves once he's done all the hard work."

Ælfwynn grinned. "Turn them against each other before they even reach us. Clever."

"But risky," Beorhthelm cautioned. "If they see through it, we'll have both armies on our doorstep, and the Pope will declare us all heretics faster than you can say 'excommunication.'"

"True," Eadric admitted. "But it's a risk we'll have to take. If we just sit here and wait, we'll be crushed between them. We need to sow doubt, cause confusion, and make them second-guess their alliances."

Beorhthelm nodded slowly, considering the plan. "It's not bad, Your Majesty. And while they're busy fighting among themselves, we can gather our forces, fortify our defenses, and be ready for whatever's left of them when they finally get here."

"Exactly," Eadric said, his confidence growing. "And if it all goes wrong, well... we've faced worse."

Ælfwynn snorted. "Like cursed cows?"

"Exactly like cursed cows," Eadric replied with a smirk. "We're practically experts by now."

With the plan set in motion, Ælfwynn and Beorhthelm set out to spread the necessary rumors and misinformation, using every spy, messenger, and tavern drunk they could find. Meanwhile, Eadric focused on preparing for the inevitable conflict, gathering what remained of England's forces and shoring up alliances with any Saxon lord still loyal to the crown.

Days passed, and the tension grew thicker than the fog that often blanketed the English countryside. Reports from the north and south trickled in, each one more unsettling than the last. The Normans were marching with the determination of a man convinced he's doing God's work, while the Scots were moving with the ruthless efficiency of a people who'd been waiting centuries to settle a few old scores.

Finally, the day came when both armies arrived at the outskirts of London, each one eyeing the other with a mix of suspicion and barely concealed hostility. The rumors had done their work—both Henry and Malcolm's forces were uneasy, their alliance fraying at the edges.

Eadric stood on the battlements of Westminster, surveying the scene with a keen eye. "Here they are, just as we planned," he said to Ælfwynn and Beorhthelm, who stood beside him. "Now let's see if they're smart enough to realize they've been played."

"Or if they're stupid enough to start fighting each other over it," Ælfwynn added with a wry smile.

It didn't take long for tensions to boil over. As Henry's forces approached the city from the south, a detachment of Scottish warriors broke ranks, advancing toward the Norman lines with weapons drawn. Shouts rang out, and before anyone could stop it, the two armies clashed in a brutal, chaotic melee.

"Well," Beorhthelm said, watching the carnage unfold below, "that escalated quickly."

Eadric smirked. "I told you—strategy wins battles."

But the victory was far from certain. Even as the Normans and Scots tore into each other, the Pope's influence loomed large. Messengers arrived from Rome, bearing demands for Eadric's immediate surrender and a promise of absolution if he handed over the crown to Henry.

Eadric read the Pope's letter with a mixture of amusement and disdain. "Absolution, is it? How generous of him. And if I refuse?"

"Then you'll be branded a heretic and excommunicated," Ælfwynn replied, her voice dry. "Which, considering the current state of things, is almost an improvement."

Eadric tossed the letter aside. "Then we refuse. Let the Pope send another Inquisition if he likes—there's nothing left for them to burn."

As the battle raged outside the walls, Eadric's forces prepared to make their stand. But just as they braced for the worst, a strange turn of events began to unfold. The Normans and Scots, locked in bitter combat, suddenly found themselves surrounded by a new threat—the remnants of the curse that Eadric had thought destroyed.

The cursed mist, still lingering in the dark corners of the land, had sensed the bloodshed and risen once more. It crept through the battlefield like a silent predator, wrapping itself around the combatants and sowing panic in their ranks.

"What in God's name...?" Beorhthelm muttered, his eyes widening as he watched the mist consume the battlefield.

"It's the curse," Ælfwynn said, her voice tense. "It's not done with us yet."

Eadric watched in stunned silence as the mist began to wreak havoc on the invading forces. Norman knights were torn from their horses by unseen hands, while Scottish warriors found themselves stumbling blindly through the fog, cut down by enemies they couldn't see.

"This isn't what I expected," Eadric admitted, a touch of awe in his voice. "But I'm not going to complain."

The mist, seemingly indiscriminate in its wrath, soon turned the battlefield into a scene of utter chaos. Henry's forces, caught between the cursed fog and the furious Scots, began to fall back in disarray. The Scots, realizing they were just as vulnerable, retreated in turn, leaving the battlefield littered with the dead and dying.

Eadric, Ælfwynn, and Beorhthelm exchanged glances as the mist finally began to dissipate, leaving behind only silence and destruction.

"Well," Eadric said, breaking the tense quiet, "that was... unexpected."

Ælfwynn nodded, still processing what they'd just witnessed. "The curse isn't gone. It's just... changed. And now it's taken out half our enemies for us."

Beorhthelm chuckled darkly. "I suppose that's one way to win a battle. Let the curse do the dirty work."

"But it's not over," Eadric warned, his tone serious. "The Pope won't give up that easily. He'll send more forces, more Inquisitors, and next time, they might not be so easily distracted."

Ælfwynn nodded. "Then we need to figure out what's really driving this curse—once and for all. Because if we don't, it'll destroy everything we've fought to protect."

"And maybe us along with it," Beorhthelm added grimly.

Eadric sighed, his mind racing with the possibilities. "Then we go back to the source. Whatever we missed, whatever piece of the puzzle we didn't find, we need to uncover it—and fast."

As the three of them stood on the battlements, looking out at the ruined battlefield below, Eadric knew that the fight was far from over. The curse was still out there, lurking in the shadows, waiting for its moment to strike again. And with the Pope's forces still determined to take England, the kingdom's future was anything but secure.

But Eadric wasn't about to give up. He'd survived this long by being clever, by outmaneuvering his enemies, and by never backing down from a challenge. And now, with the fate of England hanging in the balance, he was ready to face whatever came next—whether it was the Pope, the curse, or something even worse.

"Come on," Eadric said, turning away from the battlefield. "We've got work to do."

And with that, the three of them descended from the battlements, ready to face the next chapter in their ongoing struggle for the kingdom.

Prophecies and the Perils of Ancient Enemies

King Eadric of England had a sinking feeling that no amount of ale would be enough to get him through the next few weeks. The Normans had been beaten back, the Scots had retreated, and the cursed mist had done more damage to his enemies than any sword ever could. But the victory felt hollow, like winning a game of chess only to realize your opponent has set the board on fire.

Now, standing in the war room with Ælfwynn and Beorhthelm, Eadric couldn't shake the sense that the real trouble was just beginning.

"Well, that went better than expected," Beorhthelm said, rubbing his hands together with grim satisfaction. "I'd say we dodged an arrow, Your Majesty."

Eadric gave him a sidelong glance. "More like we dodged a whole quiver, and they're all stuck in someone else's back. But let's not break out the mead just yet."

Ælfwynn, ever the voice of reason, nodded in agreement. "The curse is still out there, Your Majesty. We might have bought ourselves some time, but whatever's behind it isn't done with us. And let's not forget the Pope. He's not going to take this defeat lightly."

Eadric sighed, running a hand through his hair. "The Pope. Of course. Because what's a cursed kingdom without a vengeful pontiff breathing down our necks?"

As if on cue, a messenger burst into the room, looking like he'd run all the way from Rome. "Your Majesty! Urgent news from the coast! The Pope's fleet has been spotted. He's coming to England—personally!"

Eadric blinked. "Personally? Since when does a Pope do his own dirty work?"

"Since he's really, really mad," Ælfwynn replied dryly. "He's coming to make sure you either bend the knee or lose your head."

Eadric shook his head in disbelief. "Well, isn't this just the cherry on top? We've got an ancient curse trying to turn England into a ghost story, and now we have the Pope himself storming over here to finish the job. What's next? Dragons?"

"Let's hope not," Beorhthelm muttered. "Though at this rate, I wouldn't be surprised."

Eadric leaned over the table, his gaze fixed on the map spread out before him. "We need answers. Real ones. Something we can use to end this curse and send the Pope back to Rome with his tail between his legs."

Ælfwynn reached into her cloak and pulled out an old, weathered scroll, the edges frayed and the ink faded. "I might have just the thing, Your Majesty. I found this in the crypts, hidden in the same chamber where we destroyed the relic. It's a prophecy—an ancient one."

Eadric arched an eyebrow. "A prophecy? Of course there's a prophecy. What does it say? Something vague and ominous, I assume?"

Ælfwynn unrolled the scroll and began to read aloud. "'When the land is torn by strife and shadow, and the cursed crown sits upon the head of the unwary, the ancient enemy shall rise from the depths. Only the blood of the first king, mixed with the tears of the fallen, can break the chains of darkness and restore the light.'"

Beorhthelm frowned. "Well, that's as clear as mud."

Eadric snorted. "That's the thing about prophecies—always more poetry than practicality. But this 'ancient enemy'… that sounds like something we should be worried about."

"Indeed," Ælfwynn said, her expression serious. "If this prophecy is to be believed, the curse isn't just a random plague. It's the work of something far older and far more dangerous than we thought. And if it rises, we could be facing a threat that makes the Pope look like a grumpy monk."

Eadric grimaced. "Wonderful. So we're fighting a war on two fronts—one against a man who thinks he's God's right-hand enforcer, and one against... what? A demon? A dark spirit? A really angry ghost?"

"Possibly all three," Beorhthelm said, only half-joking.

The room fell into a heavy silence as the weight of the situation sank in. Eadric knew they were running out of time. The Pope was on his way, the curse was still lurking in the shadows, and now there was this 'ancient enemy' to deal with. It was starting to feel like the universe had a personal vendetta against him.

"Well," Eadric said at last, straightening up with a resigned sigh, "if this prophecy is right, then we need to find out who—or what—this ancient enemy is, and fast. We also need to figure out who the 'first king' was and what exactly we're supposed to do with his blood."

"And don't forget the tears of the fallen," Ælfwynn added with a hint of sarcasm. "Because nothing says 'let's end a curse' like mixing bodily fluids."

Eadric chuckled despite himself. "Right. Tears of the fallen. I'm sure that'll be easy to come by. Now, where do we start?"

Ælfwynn thought for a moment, then pointed to a spot on the map. "The prophecy speaks of the first king. That likely refers to Æthelstan, the first true king of all England. His tomb is in Malmesbury Abbey. If there are answers to be found, they might be there."

Eadric nodded. "Then we head to Malmesbury. Beorhthelm, you stay here and keep an eye on things. If the Pope's fleet lands, do whatever you can to stall them."

Beorhthelm grinned, his hand resting on the hilt of his sword. "Stalling's my specialty, Your Majesty. And if it comes to it, I'll give them a fight they won't soon forget."

With the plan set, Eadric and Ælfwynn made preparations for their journey to Malmesbury. As they rode out from Westminster, Eadric couldn't shake the feeling that they were heading straight into the heart of a storm—one that might swallow them whole if they weren't careful.

The ride to Malmesbury was long and tense, the countryside eerily quiet as if the land itself was holding its breath. When they finally arrived at the abbey, the sun was setting, casting long shadows across the ancient stone walls. The monks greeted them with a mixture of awe and trepidation, their eyes lingering on the cursed crown that still rested on Eadric's head.

"We seek the tomb of King Æthelstan," Eadric said to the abbot, his voice firm. "There's something we need to find."

The abbot, a wiry old man with a beard like a bird's nest, nodded solemnly. "The tomb lies within, Your Majesty. But beware—many have sought the secrets of Æthelstan's tomb, and few have returned."

"Sounds like a party," Eadric muttered under his breath. "Lead the way."

The abbot led them through the dimly lit corridors of the abbey, the flickering torchlight casting strange, twisted shadows on the walls. As they descended into the crypts, the air grew colder, and the sense of foreboding grew stronger with each step.

Finally, they reached a massive stone door, engraved with the image of a king holding a sword in one hand and a cross in the other. The abbot stepped back, his expression grave. "The tomb of Æthelstan. May God watch over you."

Eadric took a deep breath, pushing open the heavy door. Inside, the tomb was a grand, imposing chamber, the walls lined with ancient carvings depicting the life and deeds of King Æthelstan. At the center of the room lay the king's sarcophagus, a massive stone structure covered in intricate runes and symbols.

"Let's hope this isn't another trap," Eadric said as he approached the sarcophagus. "I've had enough of those to last a lifetime."

Ælfwynn followed closely, her eyes scanning the carvings for any sign of the prophecy. "We need to find out how this 'blood of the first king' ties into the curse. If there's something we're missing, it has to be here."

As they examined the sarcophagus, a strange, low hum began to fill the chamber, growing louder with each passing moment. The air crackled with energy, and the runes on the sarcophagus began to glow with an eerie, otherworldly light.

Eadric stepped back, his hand instinctively moving to the hilt of his sword. "That can't be good."

Suddenly, the sarcophagus began to shift, the lid sliding open with a deafening grind of stone against stone. From within, a dark, swirling mist began to rise, coalescing into a towering, shadowy figure that seemed to suck the light from the room.

"The ancient enemy," Ælfwynn whispered, her voice barely audible over the rising hum. "It's been here all along."

The shadowy figure loomed over them, its eyes glowing with a malevolent red light. When it spoke, its voice was a low, rumbling growl that seemed to vibrate through the very stones of the crypt. "You dare disturb the rest of the first king? You dare challenge the darkness?"

Eadric gritted his teeth, drawing his sword. "I'm starting to regret it, but yes, we dare. Now, who—or what—are you?"

The figure's laughter echoed through the chamber, a sound devoid of any warmth. "I am the darkness that was sealed within the first king's blood. I am the curse that was forged from the sins of your ancestors. And now, I am free to claim what is mine."

As the shadowy figure advanced, Eadric realized they were facing something far more dangerous than he'd anticipated. The ancient enemy wasn't just a spirit or a demon—it was the embodiment of the curse itself, a force of pure darkness that had been waiting centuries for its chance to rise again.

"Ælfwynn," Eadric said, keeping his voice steady despite the rising panic, "find whatever's left of Æthelstan's blood. If the prophecy is right, we need it to stop this thing."

Ælfwynn nodded, her eyes scanning the chamber for any sign of the ancient king's remains. "On it, Your Majesty. Just try not to get killed while I'm busy."

As she searched, the shadowy figure raised a hand, and the room was suddenly filled with a howling wind that tore at their clothes and threatened to rip the very stones from the walls. The darkness pressed in from all sides, and Eadric found himself struggling to keep his footing.

"Enough of this!" Eadric shouted, raising his sword and charging at the figure. But as his blade connected, it passed straight through the shadowy form, striking nothing but air.

PROPHECIES AND THE PERILS OF ANCIENT ENEMIES

The figure laughed again, a cold, mocking sound that sent shivers down Eadric's spine. "You cannot harm me, mortal. I am the curse. I am the darkness that your kind has feared since the dawn of time."

Eadric staggered back, his mind racing. "Then how do we stop you?"

The figure's eyes glowed brighter, and its voice was filled with dark amusement. "You cannot. The curse is eternal, as is my power. Your kingdom will fall, your people will suffer, and I will rule over the ruins."

Just as all hope seemed lost, Ælfwynn let out a triumphant cry. "Here! I found it!"

Eadric turned to see her holding up a small, ancient vial, the contents glowing faintly in the dim light. "The blood of Æthelstan," she said, her voice filled with determination. "This is our last chance, Eadric. We have to mix it with the tears of the fallen."

Eadric frowned. "And where do we get those?"

As if in answer, the shadowy figure let out a roar of fury, the wind howling even louder as the darkness closed in around them. Eadric realized with a sinking feeling that the only tears they were going to get were their own—if they survived long enough to shed them.

"Fine," Eadric muttered, feeling the sting of the wind in his eyes as it whipped up dust and debris. "Guess I'll just have to get emotional."

With a swift motion, Ælfwynn handed him the vial, and Eadric uncorked it, mixing a single tear with the ancient blood. As the two mingled, the mixture began to glow with a fierce, blinding light, the very air crackling with energy.

The shadowy figure recoiled, its form wavering as the light grew brighter. "No! You cannot do this! The curse cannot be broken!"

"Watch me," Eadric growled, raising the vial high. "For England!"

With that, he hurled the vial at the shadowy figure, the glowing liquid splashing across its dark form. The figure let out a deafening scream as the light consumed it, the darkness unraveling like smoke in the wind.

For a moment, the chamber was filled with a blinding light, the air humming with the release of ancient power. Then, as quickly as it had begun, it was over. The light faded, the wind died down, and the shadowy figure was gone—reduced to nothing more than a whisper on the air.

Eadric and Ælfwynn stood in the silent chamber, the weight of what they'd just done slowly sinking in.

"Is it over?" Ælfwynn asked, her voice barely above a whisper.

Eadric nodded, still catching his breath. "I think so. The curse... the darkness... it's gone."

As they made their way back up to the surface, Eadric couldn't help but feel a strange mix of relief and exhaustion. They'd faced down an ancient curse, battled against impossible odds, and somehow, miraculously, they'd come out on top.

But as they emerged into the daylight, there was no time to celebrate. The Pope's fleet was still approaching, and the battle for England wasn't over yet.

"Come on," Eadric said, squaring his shoulders as he prepared for the next challenge. "We've got a kingdom to save. Again."

And with that, they rode out to meet whatever fate had in store for them, ready to face whatever darkness—or pontiff—dared to stand in their way.

The Pope and the King Who Fell

King Eadric of England had faced curses, curses with swords, and curses with creepy Latin incantations, but none of that had prepared him for facing off against the Pope himself. Now, as the Pope's fleet loomed off the coast, Eadric knew this would be the final battle. Win, and England would be free. Lose, and... well, losing wasn't an option. Not after everything he'd been through.

He stood on the battlements of Westminster, staring out at the horizon, where the papal ships were anchored like a swarm of angry bees. Ælfwynn and Beorhthelm stood at his side, their faces grim but resolute.

"Your Majesty," Beorhthelm began, "the Pope's forces are landing as we speak. They've brought enough men to make the last invasion look like a tavern brawl."

Eadric sighed, rubbing his temples. "Of course they have. Because what's a final showdown without overwhelming odds?"

Ælfwynn nodded, her eyes narrowed as she surveyed the scene. "But we're not alone. We've received word from a surprising source—King Sigurd of Denmark. He's sent ships and warriors to aid us."

Eadric blinked, caught off guard by the unexpected news. "Sigurd? The same Sigurd who swore he'd never get involved in English affairs after that... incident with the herring?"

"The very same," Ælfwynn confirmed with a smirk. "Apparently, he's decided that a world where the Pope controls England isn't one he wants to live in. Plus, he still owes you for saving his son from that dragon."

Eadric chuckled, though the sound was tinged with weariness. "Ah, yes. That dragon. The one that turned out to be a particularly aggressive sheep."

"Details," Beorhthelm muttered, clearly trying to keep the mood light. "But we've got a fighting chance now, Your Majesty. With the Danes at our side, we might just pull this off."

Eadric nodded, feeling a flicker of hope. "Then let's give them a fight they'll never forget. We'll meet the Pope's forces head-on, and when we're done, he'll wish he'd stayed in Rome."

With the plan set, Eadric and his forces prepared for the battle of their lives. The Saxons and their Danish allies rallied together, forming a united front against the approaching papal army. As the sun began to rise over the battlefield, Eadric took his place at the head of his troops, his sword gleaming in the morning light.

"Men of England!" Eadric called out, his voice carrying across the ranks. "Today, we fight not just for our land, but for our freedom! The Pope thinks he can take our kingdom, our lives, and our very souls—but we're not going to let him!"

A roar of approval rose from the ranks, the Saxons and Danes ready to defend their homeland with every ounce of strength they had.

"Let's give them hell," Ælfwynn added with a grin, drawing her own sword.

Eadric shot her a sideways glance. "I thought you didn't believe in hell."

"I don't," she replied. "But I'm happy to make an exception today."

As the papal forces advanced, the battlefield erupted into chaos. The clang of steel on steel, the shouts of battle, and the cries of the wounded filled the air, mingling with the distant crash of the sea against the shore. Eadric fought at the front, his sword cutting through the enemy ranks with a determination born of desperation and pride.

But the Pope's forces were relentless. Wave after wave of soldiers crashed against the Saxon and Danish lines, each one more determined than the last. Eadric knew they couldn't hold out forever, but he also knew they couldn't afford to lose.

Amid the chaos, Eadric spotted a figure clad in gleaming white armor, standing at the center of the papal forces like a beacon of arrogance. The Pope himself, flanked by his personal guard, watching the battle unfold as if it were a mere chess game.

"Ælfwynn! Beorhthelm!" Eadric shouted over the din of battle. "We need to take the fight to him. The Pope's the key. If we can bring him down, the rest will crumble."

Beorhthelm grinned, his sword already slick with blood. "You're speaking my language, Your Majesty."

The three of them fought their way through the throng of enemies, cutting a path toward the Pope. Eadric's blade flashed in the sunlight as he parried blows and struck down enemies, each step bringing them closer to the heart of the papal army.

Finally, they reached the Pope, who stood atop a makeshift dais, his eyes cold and calculating as he surveyed the battlefield. He raised a hand, and his guards closed in around him, their swords drawn and ready.

"So," the Pope said, his voice dripping with disdain, "the cursed king of England thinks he can defy the will of God."

Eadric smirked, his grip tightening on his sword. "I'm not defying God. I'm defying you. And let's be honest—you're not exactly on speaking terms with the Almighty right now."

The Pope's eyes narrowed, and he gestured to his guards. "Kill them."

The battle that followed was fierce and brutal. Eadric, Ælfwynn, and Beorhthelm fought with everything they had, their swords clashing against the steel of the Pope's elite guards. The air was thick with the sounds of battle, the clash of swords and the cries of the dying.

But even as they fought, Eadric could feel his strength waning. The curse might have been broken, but the toll it had taken on him was undeniable. His movements grew slower, his breath more labored, and he knew, deep down, that this fight would be his last.

Ælfwynn, ever perceptive, glanced at him with concern. "Eadric, you're slowing down."

"Noticed that, did you?" Eadric replied with a grim smile. "Just keep fighting. We're almost there."

With a final, desperate push, Eadric broke through the Pope's guards, his sword slashing through the air toward the pontiff himself. But before the blade could connect, a sharp pain tore through Eadric's side, and he staggered, dropping to one knee.

"Eadric!" Ælfwynn shouted, cutting down the guard who had struck the blow and rushing to his side.

Eadric looked up at the Pope, who stood over him, a cold smile on his lips. "You may have broken the curse, but you cannot break the will of the Church."

Eadric coughed, blood staining his lips, but he managed a defiant grin. "Funny. I was about to say the same thing."

With a last burst of strength, Eadric thrust his sword upward, driving it through the Pope's armor and into his chest. The Pope's eyes widened in shock as he staggered back, blood pouring from the wound.

As the Pope fell to the ground, his guards hesitated, their confidence shattered along with their leader. The Saxons and Danes, seeing their chance, surged forward, cutting down the remaining papal forces with a renewed ferocity.

The battle was won, but the cost was high. Eadric collapsed to the ground, his strength finally giving out as the pain in his side spread through his body like fire.

Ælfwynn knelt beside him, her face pale with fear and sorrow. "Eadric, stay with me."

Eadric smiled weakly, his vision beginning to blur. "Looks like I'm the 'fallen' the prophecy was talking about, huh? Could've done without that part."

Ælfwynn shook her head, tears welling up in her eyes. "Don't say that. You're not done yet."

But Eadric knew better. The prophecy had been clear, even if he hadn't wanted to admit it. "Ælfwynn... you've always been the clever one. The strong one. England needs a ruler who can keep it safe, who can lead with both strength and wisdom. That's you."

Ælfwynn's breath hitched. "Eadric..."

"I'm naming you Queen of England," Eadric said, his voice barely above a whisper. "You'll do better than I ever did. And don't let anyone tell you otherwise."

Before Ælfwynn could protest, Beorhthelm approached, his expression grim. "Your Majesty," he said, addressing Ælfwynn, "the Pope's forces are retreating. We've won."

Eadric smiled faintly. "Good. Then it's done."

With his last breath, Eadric looked up at Ælfwynn, his eyes filled with a mixture of pride and sorrow. "Rule well, Ælfwynn. England's in your hands now."

And with that, Eadric, King of England, closed his eyes for the last time.

The battlefield grew silent as the Saxons and Danes, victorious but weary, gathered around their fallen king. Ælfwynn, now Queen of England, stood tall, her grief held in check by the knowledge of the responsibility that had just been placed upon her shoulders.

Beorhthelm placed a hand on her shoulder, his voice gentle. "He chose well, Your Majesty. You'll make him proud."

Ælfwynn nodded, swallowing back her tears. "Let's make sure this victory wasn't in vain. We've got a kingdom to rebuild, and I won't let Eadric's sacrifice be forgotten."

As the sun set over the battlefield, casting a warm, golden light over the scene, the people of England gathered around their new queen, ready to follow her into whatever future awaited them.

The curse was broken, the Pope defeated, and England was free. But the memory of Eadric, the fallen king, would live on in the hearts of those who fought for their land and their freedom.

And as Ælfwynn took up the mantle of queen, she knew that, like Eadric, she would face every challenge with courage, wit, and a good dose of sarcasm—just as he had taught her.

The Queen of England

Queen Ælfwynn of England, once merely the sharp-tongued advisor to King Eadric, now found herself on the throne—an unexpected turn of events that seemed to surprise everyone, including herself. It hadn't taken long for the whispers to start, though: *Could a woman really rule England? Was she strong enough? Smart enough?* And, most importantly, could she wield sarcasm as effectively as her predecessor?

Ælfwynn was determined to answer all those questions with a resounding yes—especially the last one.

She stood on the balcony of Westminster, surveying the city below. Despite the victory over the Pope's forces, England was still in shambles. The scars of battle marked the land, the people, and even the buildings. Rebuilding wasn't just a necessity; it was a chance to reshape England into something stronger, something that could withstand whatever the future might throw at it.

"Your Majesty," Beorhthelm said, approaching with a stack of reports that looked heavier than his sword. "The lords have gathered in the great hall. They're... eager to hear your plans."

Ælfwynn turned to him, arching an eyebrow. "Eager? That's one way to put it. I'm sure they're chomping at the bit to tell me how I should be ruling."

Beorhthelm grinned. "Aye, but they've yet to face someone who can outwit them in both strategy and insults. Shall we?"

Ælfwynn nodded and strode into the great hall, where the Saxon lords were assembled, their expressions a mixture of curiosity and skepticism. The room fell silent as she took her place at the head of the table, her presence commanding despite the murmurs that followed her every move.

"Lords of England," Ælfwynn began, her voice steady and clear, "we've faced down curses, invasions, and a rather unpleasant Pope. But our work is far from done. This kingdom needs rebuilding—physically, culturally, and militarily. We're not just going to patch up the cracks; we're going to forge something stronger from the ashes."

One of the older lords, Lord Eadwine, leaned forward, his eyes narrowing. "And how do you propose we do that, Your Majesty? With all due respect, England has never been ruled by a woman before. We need strong leadership."

Ælfwynn's smile was as sharp as the sword at her side. "Then it's a good thing you've got me, isn't it?"

The lords exchanged uneasy glances, but Ælfwynn pressed on. "We'll start by restoring Saxon traditions and strengthening our military. We've been too reliant on foreign alliances and mercenaries. It's time we reminded the world what England can do on its own."

Beorhthelm stepped forward, unrolling a large map of England and the surrounding regions. "We'll begin with rebuilding the fortifications along the coast. The Vikings may have backed off for now, but they'll be back, and we need to be ready."

"And while we're at it," Ælfwynn added, her tone casual but firm, "we'll be reinforcing our laws—Saxon laws. No more bending to foreign influences or papal decrees. This is England, and we'll rule it as we see fit."

The lords murmured their approval, though some were still clearly wary. Ælfwynn wasn't just proposing a restoration—she was leading a revival, one that would assert England's independence from both Rome and any other would-be conquerors. But as the meeting drew to a close, Ælfwynn knew she couldn't let her guard down. There were still too many enemies lurking in the shadows.

As the lords departed, Beorhthelm leaned in, his voice low. "Word's come from the north, Your Majesty. Matilda, now Queen of Scotland, has been making moves. With all of her brothers and husband dead, she's got nothing left to lose—and she's gathering support from the Welsh and any Norman sympathizers she can find."

Ælfwynn sighed, rubbing her temples. "Of course she is. Because what's a day without another vengeful relative trying to seize the throne?"

Beorhthelm shrugged. "Revenge seems to run in the family. She's claiming that the throne should rightfully belong to her, through her late husband, and she's not exactly sending you a friendly invitation to discuss it over tea."

Ælfwynn snorted. "Tea with Matilda? I'd rather drink poison. And I'm sure that's exactly what she'd serve."

But Ælfwynn knew better than to underestimate Matilda. The Scottish queen had a reputation for being as ruthless as she was cunning, and with her husband Henry dead and all of her brothers out of the picture, Matilda was free to act on her darkest impulses. And apparently, those impulses involved claiming the English throne.

"We can't afford to let her gather more support," Ælfwynn said, her mind already racing with strategies. "We need to cut her off before she gets any closer to uniting the Welsh and Normans under her banner."

Beorhthelm nodded. "Agreed. But it won't be easy. She's already made inroads with some of the more discontented Saxon lords—those who aren't thrilled about being ruled by a woman."

Ælfwynn's eyes narrowed. "Then we'll need to remind them why they chose me. And if that doesn't work, we'll remind them what happens to traitors."

As Ælfwynn prepared for the coming conflict, she couldn't help but feel a strange mixture of anticipation and dread. The revival of Saxon power and tradition was crucial, but it wouldn't matter if she couldn't stop Matilda's march on England. It was a game of chess, and Matilda had just made her move.

That night, as Ælfwynn sat in her chambers, poring over maps and reports, she couldn't shake the feeling that the final battle for England was looming on the horizon. She had faced curses, Popes, and invading armies, but this—this was personal.

She smiled grimly as she thought of Matilda, plotting her revenge up in Scotland. "If she thinks she can take England from me, she's in for a rude awakening."

The next morning, Ælfwynn summoned her most trusted allies, including Beorhthelm and the leaders of the newly reformed Saxon army. They would need to move quickly, striking at the heart of Matilda's forces before she could unite her allies and bring them to bear against England.

"We'll start by securing the border," Ælfwynn said, her voice firm. "We'll cut off any support from Wales and isolate her forces. Then, we'll force her to meet us on the battlefield—on our terms."

Beorhthelm grinned, clearly relishing the idea of another fight. "Sounds like a plan, Your Majesty. And if we're lucky, we'll send her running back to Scotland with her tail between her legs."

"Or better yet," Ælfwynn added, her eyes flashing with determination, "we'll send her back in a box."

As the plans were set in motion, Ælfwynn couldn't help but feel a surge of confidence. Matilda might be cunning, but she had never faced an opponent like Ælfwynn—a queen who had learned from the best and who wasn't about to let anyone, especially a vengeful widow, take away what she had fought so hard to build.

The days that followed were a whirlwind of preparations, as Ælfwynn's forces fortified their positions and cut off Matilda's supply lines. The Saxon revival was in full swing, with Ælfwynn leading the charge, her resolve unshakable.

When the time finally came, Ælfwynn led her army to the borderlands, where Matilda's forces had gathered. The two queens met on the battlefield, their armies arrayed behind them, the tension so thick it could be cut with a knife.

"Matilda," Ælfwynn called out, her voice carrying across the field. "It's not too late to turn back. You don't have to die for a cause that was never yours to begin with."

Matilda, dressed in armor that gleamed like cold steel, sneered. "This throne is mine by right! You're nothing but a usurper, a pretender who thinks she can hold a kingdom together with wit and sarcasm. But this is war, Ælfwynn, and you're out of your depth."

Ælfwynn smiled, though there was no warmth in it. "If you think I'm just a pretender, you haven't been paying attention. But don't worry—I'll make sure you understand before this is over."

With that, the battle began, the two armies clashing in a storm of steel and blood. Ælfwynn fought at the front, her sword flashing as she cut through the enemy ranks. Beorhthelm was at her side, his laughter ringing out as he dispatched any Norman or Scot foolish enough to come within reach.

The battle was fierce, but Ælfwynn's forces had the upper hand. The Saxon revival had brought with it a renewed sense of purpose and pride, and her soldiers fought with a determination that couldn't be matched.

As the sun began to set, casting a bloody light over the battlefield, Ælfwynn finally confronted Matilda in the midst of the chaos. The two queens faced each other, swords drawn, the fate of England hanging in the balance.

"This is your last chance, Matilda," Ælfwynn said, her voice low and dangerous. "Surrender, and you might live to see another day."

Matilda's eyes blazed with fury. "Never! I'll take what's mine, even if I have to kill you to do it!"

With a scream of rage, Matilda charged at Ælfwynn, her sword aimed for the queen's heart. But Ælfwynn was faster, her blade flashing as she parried the blow and countered with a swift strike that sent Matilda's sword flying from her hand.

Matilda staggered back, her eyes wide with shock and fear. "You... you can't..."

Ælfwynn stepped forward, her sword at Matilda's throat. "I can. And I will."

With a swift motion, Ælfwynn ended the battle, her sword cutting through the air in a deadly arc. Matilda fell to the ground, her eyes staring up at the sky as the life drained from her body.

The battlefield fell silent, the fighting coming to an abrupt halt as both sides realized that the battle was over. The Saxons had won. Ælfwynn had won.

As she stood over Matilda's lifeless body, Ælfwynn couldn't help but feel a pang of sorrow. The two women had been drawn into a conflict not of their own making, each driven by duty, pride, and the weight of history. But in the end, there could only be one ruler of England.

Beorhthelm approached, wiping blood from his sword as he surveyed the scene. "It's over, Your Majesty. The day is ours."

Ælfwynn nodded, though the victory felt bittersweet. "Yes. But there's still so much to do. Rebuilding, restoring, and making sure that England stands strong—stronger than ever."

Beorhthelm grinned, though his eyes were serious. "If anyone can do it, it's you, Ælfwynn. Eadric chose well."

Ælfwynn smiled, the weight of the crown feeling both lighter and heavier at the same time. "Then let's get to work, Beorhthelm. We've got a kingdom to rebuild—and a legacy to secure."

And so, with the battle won and the future of England in her hands, Queen Ælfwynn began the next chapter of her reign. The Saxon revival was just beginning, and under her leadership, England would rise from the ashes, stronger and more united than ever before.

But even as she looked to the future, Ælfwynn knew that there would always be new challenges, new enemies, and new battles to fight. And she would face them all with the same courage, wit, and unyielding determination that had brought her this far.

After all, she was the Queen of England—and she wasn't about to let anyone forget it.

III

When It's England vs the World

Suitors and the Pope's Latest Ploy

Queen Ælfwynn of England had fought off curses, crusades, and more conniving nobles than she could count, but now she was faced with a challenge that made even those seem almost manageable: marriage. It wasn't as if she was opposed to the idea in principle, but when half of Europe's royalty lined up at her door like a parade of overdressed peacocks, each with their own agenda, it became clear that this was about more than just matrimony—it was about power.

The council chamber in Westminster buzzed with activity as Ælfwynn's advisors presented her with the latest batch of proposals. Beorhthelm, ever the loyal and battle-hardened soldier, stood to one side, looking thoroughly unimpressed with the proceedings.

"So, let me get this straight," Ælfwynn began, eyeing the stack of letters on the table with a mixture of amusement and irritation. "I'm expected to choose a husband from this lot, secure an alliance, and prevent half the kingdom from tearing itself apart in the process?"

"That about sums it up, Your Majesty," Beorhthelm replied, his tone dry. "And might I add, you're expected to do all of that while fending off a fresh Crusade from the Pope, who seems to think you're the Antichrist in chainmail."

Ælfwynn sighed, rubbing her temples. "Of course. Because why wouldn't the Pope call for another Crusade? It's not as if we've already been through this dance before."

Ælfwynn had just finished dispatching Matilda of Scotland, restoring some semblance of order to the kingdom, when the latest Papal Bull had arrived.

The new Pope, clearly still holding a grudge after his predecessor's defeat, had declared England a land of heretics and lawlessness, calling on all good Christians to take up arms and reclaim it. The fact that this was less about religion and more about grabbing some prime English real estate wasn't lost on anyone.

"Your Majesty," Ælfwynn's chief diplomat, Lord Eadwine, said cautiously, "we must take these suitors seriously. A marriage alliance could provide us with the military support we need to fend off this new Crusade."

"Couldn't we just tell the Pope to go find a new hobby?" Ælfwynn quipped, though her eyes were serious as she scanned the letters. "I'm sure there's some heretics in Rome he's overlooked."

Beorhthelm chuckled, but Eadwine remained grave. "I'm afraid the Pope is quite serious, Your Majesty. He's already rallied several European powers to his cause, including the French."

Ælfwynn looked up sharply. "The French? I thought we were negotiating with them."

"We were," Eadwine said, shifting uncomfortably. "Until, well... the unfortunate incident with their emissary."

"Ah, yes," Ælfwynn said, her voice heavy with sarcasm. "The unfortunate incident where he was found face-down in a wine barrel. Some would call that a tragedy. Others might call it an improvement in his personality."

"Either way," Beorhthelm added, "it didn't go over well. The French were looking for any excuse to turn on us, and now they've got one."

Ælfwynn sighed. "So, to recap: I'm supposed to marry one of these royal peacocks, secure an alliance with someone who won't immediately stab me in the back, and somehow convince France not to join the Crusade against us—all while ensuring I don't end up poisoned, assassinated, or worse."

Eadwine nodded solemnly. "That's the general idea, Your Majesty."

"Well," Ælfwynn said, her tone lightening as she picked up one of the letters, "let's see what our options are."

The first letter was from a certain Prince Louis of France, a cousin of the French king. It extolled his virtues as a brave knight, a devout Christian, and a man who knew how to handle a sword—both in battle and, as the letter

SUITORS AND THE POPE'S LATEST PLOY

hinted not so subtly, in more personal matters.

"Louis of France," Ælfwynn said, raising an eyebrow. "So, he wants to marry me, then join the Crusade against my own kingdom? Ambitious, if nothing else."

Beorhthelm snorted. "He's a Frenchman, Your Majesty. Ambition is about all they've got going for them."

Ælfwynn set the letter aside, moving on to the next one. This one was from King Alfonso of Castile, who was apparently looking to expand his influence beyond the Iberian Peninsula. His letter was filled with flowery language about uniting their kingdoms under God's watchful eye, but Ælfwynn couldn't help but notice the subtext: he wanted to use England as a stepping stone to greater power in Europe.

"Alfonso of Castile," Ælfwynn mused. "He's got the Pope's ear, but I'd wager he's more interested in my land than in me."

"Most likely," Eadwine agreed. "And if you marry him, he'll expect you to play the dutiful wife while he runs the kingdom."

"That'll be the day," Ælfwynn muttered, setting the letter aside.

The third letter was from a Scandinavian prince—Sven of Norway, a man known for his skill in battle and his, let's say, *vigorous* approach to life. His proposal was blunt, almost comically so: marry him, and he'd bring his armies to crush anyone who dared challenge their rule.

"Sven of Norway," Ælfwynn said with a smirk. "He's direct, I'll give him that. But I don't fancy spending my nights listening to tales of Viking conquests while he sharpens his axe."

"Could be worse," Beorhthelm said with a grin. "He might teach you to drink like a Norseman."

"And then I'd be dead within a week," Ælfwynn replied, shaking her head. "Pass."

After going through the rest of the letters—each one more unimpressive than the last—Ælfwynn finally tossed the stack aside, leaning back in her chair with a sigh.

"So, where does that leave us?" she asked, though she already knew the answer.

"With a lot of enemies and no allies," Eadwine said grimly. "And a Crusade headed our way."

Beorhthelm, always the pragmatist, leaned forward. "There is another option, Your Majesty. You don't have to marry any of them. We could use the threat of marriage to buy time—string them along while we build our defenses and rally support from those who don't want to see England fall."

Ælfwynn considered this, her mind racing. It was a risky strategy, but then again, everything about her reign had been risky. And if there was one thing she had learned from Eadric, it was that sometimes, the best way to win was to play the long game.

"You know," Ælfwynn said with a sly smile, "that just might work. We'll keep the suitors guessing, keep the negotiations with France open just enough to keep them interested, and in the meantime, we'll prepare for the worst."

"And when the Crusade arrives?" Eadwine asked, though he already knew the answer.

Ælfwynn's smile turned cold. "We'll give them a fight they won't soon forget. England may be outnumbered, but we're not outmatched. We'll remind them why the last Crusade ended in disaster."

Beorhthelm grinned. "Now that's a plan I can get behind."

As the preparations began in earnest, Ælfwynn sent out letters to the various suitors, each one carefully worded to keep them interested without making any promises. She met with her generals, overseeing the strengthening of fortifications and the training of her troops. And all the while, she kept a wary eye on France, knowing that their allegiance could swing either way depending on how the wind blew.

The days turned into weeks, and the tension grew thicker with each passing moment. The Pope's forces were gathering strength, and reports of their progress were grim. But Ælfwynn refused to be intimidated. She had faced down curses, kings, and would-be conquerors—she wasn't about to let a few thousand Crusaders and a handful of suitors dictate her fate.

Finally, the day came when the Pope's fleet was spotted off the coast, their banners flying high and their ships bristling with soldiers. The time for negotiations was over—the battle for England was about to begin.

Ælfwynn stood on the walls of Dover Castle, her eyes fixed on the horizon as the enemy fleet approached. Beorhthelm stood beside her, his sword at the ready.

"Any last-minute marriage proposals?" he asked, half-joking.

Ælfwynn chuckled. "Not unless the Pope himself wants to try his luck. And something tells me he's more interested in my crown than my hand."

Beorhthelm nodded, his expression serious. "Then let's give them a welcome they'll never forget."

As the Pope's forces began to disembark, Ælfwynn turned to her troops, her voice ringing out across the battlements.

"Men of England! Today we face a foe that thinks it can take our land, our lives, and our freedom. But they've forgotten one thing: this is *our* land, and we will defend it with everything we have!"

A cheer went up from the troops, the sound echoing across the cliffs as they prepared to face the invaders.

As the first wave of Crusaders charged up the beach, Ælfwynn drew her sword, the steel glinting in the sunlight. "Let's show them what happens when they try to take what's ours."

The battle that followed was brutal and relentless. The Pope's forces, confident in their numbers and their divine mandate, threw themselves at the English defenses with a ferocity that would have broken lesser armies. But Ælfwynn's troops held firm, their determination bolstered by the knowledge that they were fighting not just for their queen, but for their very way of life.

Beorhthelm fought like a man possessed, cutting down Crusaders left and right with a mixture of skill and brute force. Ælfwynn, too, was in the thick of the fighting, her sword flashing as she led her men in the defense of their homeland.

As the day wore on, it became clear that the Pope's forces had underestimated their opponent. The English, though outnumbered, fought with a ferocity that the Crusaders hadn't anticipated. And with every wave that crashed against the English defenses, the invaders lost more ground, their morale crumbling under the relentless assault.

Finally, as the sun began to set, the Pope's forces broke. The remaining

Crusaders fled back to their ships, leaving the beach littered with the dead and dying. The day was won, but the cost had been high.

As the last of the Crusaders retreated, Ælfwynn stood on the blood-soaked beach, her sword still in hand. Beorhthelm approached, his armor dented and bloodied but his grin as wide as ever.

"We did it, Your Majesty," he said, his voice filled with pride.

Ælfwynn nodded, though her expression was somber. "Yes. But this is only the beginning. The Pope won't give up that easily, and neither will the rest of Europe. We've won the battle, but the war is far from over."

Beorhthelm nodded, his grin fading as the reality of the situation sank in. "What now?"

Ælfwynn sheathed her sword, her eyes fixed on the horizon. "Now, we rebuild. We prepare for whatever comes next. And we remind the world that England is not a prize to be won—it's a kingdom that will fight to the last breath."

As the sun dipped below the horizon, casting a golden glow over the battlefield, Ælfwynn turned back to her troops, her voice ringing out clear and strong.

"Today, we have shown the world what it means to be English. We are not just a kingdom—we are a force to be reckoned with. And let anyone who dares challenge us remember this day, and remember what we are capable of."

The troops cheered, their voices echoing across the cliffs as they celebrated their hard-won victory. But even as the cheers rang out, Ælfwynn knew that the road ahead would be long and treacherous. The Pope, the suitors, and the ever-looming threat of invasion—they were all pieces in a game that was far from over.

But as she looked out over her kingdom, Ælfwynn felt a surge of determination. She had fought too hard and come too far to let anyone take what was hers. And if that meant facing down the Pope, a dozen suitors, and half of Europe—well, she'd done worse.

After all, she was the Queen of England, and she wasn't about to let anyone forget it.

Knights, Lords, and the Papal Sword

Queen Ælfwynn sat at the head of the long, polished table in the council chamber of Westminster Palace, her fingers drumming lightly on the wood as she surveyed the faces of her advisors. It was another one of those days—one where the weight of the crown seemed just a bit heavier, and the choices before her a bit more treacherous.

"Well, gentlemen," she began, her voice laced with dry amusement, "it seems we've got more suitors than a barrel of ale at a Saxon feast. Each one is convinced he's the answer to all our problems, and each one comes with enough baggage to sink a ship."

Beorhthelm, her ever-faithful warrior and chief advisor, grinned from his seat at her right. "Aye, Your Majesty, and some of them are heavy enough to sink a fleet. We've got French dukes, Saxon lords, and now the Pope's trying to pawn off one of his favorites on you. I'd say it's flattering, if it weren't so damned irritating."

Ælfwynn smiled thinly. "Flattering, indeed. It's not every day that a queen gets a marriage proposal from the Pope—well, technically from the Duke of Aquitaine, but we all know who's pulling the strings."

Lord Eadwine, the oldest and most conservative of her advisors, cleared his throat. "Your Majesty, the offer from the Duke of Aquitaine is not without merit. An alliance with France could secure our southern borders and, more importantly, put an end to this damned Crusade. The Pope is offering a peace treaty in exchange for your hand."

Ælfwynn raised an eyebrow. "And what does the Pope expect in return? Besides my undying loyalty, of course."

Eadwine hesitated, clearly uncomfortable with the answer. "He would expect England to follow the directives of the Church more closely. To align with Rome in matters of governance and faith."

Beorhthelm snorted. "In other words, he wants you to play the obedient wife, bow to the Vatican, and let the Pope run England from his throne in Rome."

"Charming," Ælfwynn said, her tone dripping with sarcasm. "And I'm sure the Duke of Aquitaine is just thrilled at the idea of being the Pope's errand boy. Not to mention the fact that half of my nobles would revolt at the thought of a Frenchman on the throne."

"True," Beorhthelm added. "But it gets better. While you're busy trying to avoid getting tangled up with the French, there's a Saxon lord who's got his own idea of how you should be ruling."

"Lord Wulfric of Mercia," Eadwine said, nodding. "He's proposed a marriage between you and his son, Osric. The idea is to unify the Saxon factions under your rule, solidifying your position as the true Saxon queen."

"Osric of Mercia?" Ælfwynn mused, her brow furrowing. "He's a bit... young, isn't he? Last I heard, he was still playing with wooden swords."

"Barely a man," Beorhthelm agreed, a hint of a smirk on his lips. "But his father's the real power behind the throne, and he's been pushing this idea hard. Thinks he can run the kingdom through his son, with you as the figurehead."

"And if I refuse?" Ælfwynn asked, though she already knew the answer.

Eadwine sighed. "Then Wulfric might take matters into his own hands. He's got the support of several other Saxon lords who aren't thrilled with the idea of a woman ruling alone. There's talk of rebellion, Your Majesty. They'll use any excuse to undermine your authority."

"So, to recap," Ælfwynn said, leaning back in her chair, "I've got the Pope trying to sell me off to a French duke, a Saxon lord trying to marry me to his barely-bearded son, and a looming rebellion if I don't comply. Did I miss anything?"

Beorhthelm grinned. "Only that you're supposed to do all this without losing your head—literally or figuratively."

Ælfwynn chuckled, though there was a sharp edge to it. "Wonderful. Well, it seems we have a choice to make. We could accept the Pope's offer and try to buy peace with Rome, but at the cost of our independence. Or we could marry into the Mercian line and risk being overshadowed by Wulfric's ambitions. Or..."

"Or?" Eadwine prompted.

"Or," Ælfwynn continued, "we could do what I do best: play them all against each other and come out on top. We keep the negotiations with Aquitaine open, just enough to keep the Pope interested. Meanwhile, we placate Wulfric with promises of a possible union—until we can find a way to neutralize his threat."

"Dangerous game, Your Majesty," Beorhthelm said, though there was a note of admiration in his voice. "But if anyone can pull it off, it's you."

Ælfwynn smiled, her eyes gleaming with determination. "And while they're all busy vying for my hand, we'll be preparing for the worst. The Pope's Crusade is still a threat, and we need to be ready. I won't let England fall to a bunch of sanctimonious knights and a power-hungry pontiff."

The council nodded in agreement, and the meeting soon adjourned, with each advisor heading off to put their queen's plans into motion. But as Ælfwynn retired to her chambers, she couldn't help but feel the weight of the decisions she was making. One wrong move, one miscalculation, and everything she'd fought for could come crashing down.

That night, as she sat by the fire, Ælfwynn found herself contemplating the future. The Pope, the French, the Saxons—each was a threat in their own way, and each needed to be handled with care. But she couldn't let herself be overwhelmed. She was the Queen of England, after all, and she had a kingdom to protect.

As the fire crackled in the hearth, a knock at the door interrupted her thoughts. It was Beorhthelm, his expression unusually serious.

"Your Majesty," he said, stepping into the room, "there's something you need to see."

Ælfwynn frowned. "What is it?"

Beorhthelm handed her a letter, the seal already broken. "A message from the Pope. It's... unsettling."

Ælfwynn took the letter, her eyes scanning the parchment. As she read, her expression darkened. The Pope's tone was no longer one of negotiation—it was a veiled threat. He implied that if she refused his offer, the Crusade would be relentless, and England would be brought to its knees.

"And here I thought we were done with curses," Ælfwynn muttered, tossing the letter into the fire. "It seems the Pope isn't willing to play nice."

"What's the plan, Your Majesty?" Beorhthelm asked, his hand resting on the hilt of his sword.

Ælfwynn stared into the flames, her mind racing. "We stick to the plan. Keep them guessing, keep them off balance. But we need to be ready for anything. The Pope's not going to back down, and neither will I. If it comes to war, we'll be ready."

"And Wulfric?" Beorhthelm pressed.

Ælfwynn's eyes narrowed. "Wulfric will get what's coming to him. But not yet. Let him think he's got the upper hand. When the time is right, we'll deal with him—and anyone else who stands in our way."

Beorhthelm nodded, satisfied. "Very well, Your Majesty. I'll see to it."

As he left, Ælfwynn stood by the fire, her resolve hardening. The road ahead was treacherous, but she had no intention of backing down. England was her kingdom, and she would do whatever it took to protect it—even if that meant facing down the Pope, the Saxons, and the entire continent of Europe.

Unholy Alliances and Unruly Lords

Queen Ælfwynn of England was not in the habit of visiting the dungeons, especially not before breakfast. But this particular morning had presented her with a rather compelling reason to make an exception.

The torchlight flickered off the damp stone walls as she descended the winding stairs, the sound of her boots echoing through the narrow passageway. Beorhthelm, ever her shadow, walked beside her, his hand resting on the hilt of his sword.

"You know," Ælfwynn said, her voice cutting through the gloom, "when I imagined myself as queen, I didn't exactly picture starting my days with interrogations in a dungeon. I'm more of a breakfast-in-bed type, really."

Beorhthelm grinned, though there was a hard edge to it. "Look on the bright side, Your Majesty. At least this one can't run away."

At the bottom of the stairs, two guards stood at attention, their faces blank but their eyes betraying curiosity. Ælfwynn nodded to them, and they stepped aside, revealing the heavy iron door behind them. One of the guards pulled a large key from his belt and unlocked the door, the hinges creaking ominously as it swung open.

Inside the small, dimly lit cell sat Wulfric of Mercia, stripped of his armor and his dignity, his hands shackled to the wall. His normally proud and defiant expression was marred by a fresh bruise on his cheek, courtesy of the rather rough arrest that had taken place the night before.

"Wulfric," Ælfwynn greeted him, her tone almost friendly. "I hope the accommodations are to your liking. We don't usually have noble guests down here."

Wulfric glared at her, his eyes flashing with hatred. "You won't get away with this, Ælfwynn. The Saxon lords won't stand for it."

Ælfwynn sighed, almost pitying him. Almost. "You see, that's where you're mistaken. The Saxon lords won't stand for *you*. They're loyal to England, not to some overambitious noble who thought he could seize the throne by force."

Wulfric spat on the floor. "Loyal to you? They'll never accept a woman on the throne! You're nothing but a usurper, hiding behind that crown!"

Ælfwynn's smile was sharp enough to cut through steel. "I'm not hiding behind anything, Wulfric. I'm wearing the crown because I earned it—something you wouldn't understand. But since you're so concerned about the Saxon lords, let me ease your mind. They've already made their choice. And it wasn't you."

Wulfric's defiance wavered for a moment, but he quickly recovered. "You think you've won, but the Pope—"

"Ah, yes, the Pope," Ælfwynn interrupted, waving a hand dismissively. "He's sent me a lovely letter, threatening excommunication and a Crusade if I don't fall in line. Typical papal overreach, really. But what I'm more interested in is how you managed to get involved with him."

Wulfric's mouth twisted into a bitter smile. "The Pope knows a weak ruler when he sees one. He offered me his blessing—and a very powerful ally—in exchange for your crown."

"Let me guess," Ælfwynn said, her voice dripping with sarcasm, "he suggested a cozy little marriage to his favorite European prince, who would then help you overthrow me? How original."

Wulfric didn't reply, but the look on his face said it all.

Beorhthelm leaned in, his tone almost conversational. "You see, Wulfric, that's where you really miscalculated. You thought you could play the Pope's game and come out on top, but all you've done is paint a big target on your back. And now, you're sitting here in this cell, while your so-called allies are busy planning how to take what's left of your lands."

Ælfwynn stepped closer, her gaze fixed on Wulfric's. "But I'll give you this, Wulfric—you were right about one thing. The Pope doesn't like me. Which is why I'm going to have to do something about that."

Wulfric's eyes narrowed. "What are you planning?"

Ælfwynn smiled, but it was a smile that held no warmth. "Something you wouldn't have the patience or the subtlety for. But don't worry—you'll find out soon enough."

With that, she turned on her heel and left the cell, Beorhthelm following close behind. As they ascended the stairs, she could feel the weight of the decisions she had to make pressing down on her, but she pushed it aside. There was no time for doubt—not when the fate of England was at stake.

Once back above ground, Ælfwynn headed straight to her private chambers, where a letter awaited her on the desk. The seal had already been broken—Beorhthelm, ever vigilant, had read it before she arrived.

"What do you make of it?" Ælfwynn asked, picking up the letter and scanning its contents.

Beorhthelm frowned. "The Pope's making his move, all right. He's offering you a deal—marriage to one of his favored princes in exchange for an end to the Crusade and papal recognition of your rule. But it's a trap, Your Majesty. If you accept, you'll be under the Church's thumb, and England will be little more than a puppet state."

Ælfwynn nodded, her eyes narrowing as she read the flowery language and veiled threats. "The Pope's gotten bold, hasn't he? But I'm not about to let Rome dictate how I rule. There's only one way out of this, and it involves finding a way to break free of the Pope's influence entirely."

"That brings us to the Danes," Beorhthelm said, his tone cautious. "We've had word from Prince Harald of Denmark. He's offering an alliance—through marriage, of course. He'll provide troops to counter the Crusade and support your claim to the throne. But..."

"But he's a Viking," Ælfwynn finished, setting the letter down. "And the last time England got involved with Vikings, we ended up with half the country on fire."

"True," Beorhthelm agreed. "But Harald's different. He's more interested in securing his own power than raiding our coasts. And frankly, we could use his warriors if the Pope decides to press the attack."

Ælfwynn considered this, weighing her options. "Harald's ambitious, no doubt about that. But if we can keep him in check, he might be the ally we need. And if it comes down to it, I'd rather deal with a Viking than a Pope."

Beorhthelm grinned. "I never thought I'd hear a Saxon queen say that."

Ælfwynn smirked. "Desperate times, Beorhthelm. Desperate times."

But as she spoke, her mind was already working through the implications. The Pope was a dangerous enemy, and Wulfric's conspiracy had shown just how fragile her hold on the throne could be. An alliance with Denmark could tip the scales in her favor—but it could also bring new dangers, ones she might not be able to foresee.

As the day wore on, Ælfwynn sent word to Harald, agreeing to meet him on neutral ground to discuss the terms of an alliance. She also summoned her most trusted advisors, instructing them to begin preparations for the worst-case scenario: a full-scale Crusade, backed by the Pope's mightiest allies.

But deep down, she knew that no matter what alliances she forged or what battles she won, the real struggle was for the soul of England itself. The Pope wanted her subservient, Wulfric wanted her overthrown, and the Danish prince saw an opportunity to expand his power. And somewhere in the middle of it all, Ælfwynn was determined to keep her kingdom intact—and her head firmly on her shoulders.

As the sun set over Westminster, casting long shadows across the stone walls, Ælfwynn stood at the window of her chambers, looking out over her city. The future was uncertain, and the path ahead was fraught with danger. But she had faced worse before, and she would face it again.

With a final glance at the letter from the Pope, she crumpled it in her hand and tossed it into the fire.

"Let him come," she murmured, watching the flames consume the parchment. "I'll be ready."

Vikings, Vows, and Vatican Vipers

The smell of salt hung heavy in the air as Queen Ælfwynn stood at the edge of the docks, watching the Danish longship glide through the mist like a ghostly serpent. The oars cut through the water in perfect rhythm, and the dragon-headed prow seemed to glare at her as if daring her to look away. But Ælfwynn held her ground, her gaze steady and unflinching. If she was going to meet a Viking prince, she was damn well going to do it on her own terms.

Beside her, Beorhthelm adjusted his sword belt, his expression a mix of wariness and amusement. "Quite the entrance, wouldn't you say, Your Majesty? Nothing like a boatload of armed Vikings to start your day off right."

Ælfwynn smirked. "I'll give them this—they know how to make an impression. Let's just hope they're better at diplomacy than they are at raiding."

As the ship docked, a figure leaped from the deck to the shore in one fluid motion—a tall man with broad shoulders, clad in a fur-trimmed cloak and polished armor that gleamed even in the muted light. Prince Harald of Denmark was every inch the warrior, his presence commanding as he strode toward Ælfwynn with a confident grin.

"Queen Ælfwynn," Harald greeted her, his voice deep and rich with a hint of a challenge. "I see England's as welcoming as ever."

Ælfwynn raised an eyebrow. "And I see the Danes are as subtle as a battle-axe. Welcome to England, Prince Harald."

He chuckled, clearly amused by her sharp tongue. "I appreciate a queen who doesn't mince words. We have much to discuss."

"Indeed we do," Ælfwynn replied, motioning for him to follow her. "But first, a word of advice: when negotiating with me, it's best to keep your sword sheathed and your wits sharp."

Harald's grin widened. "I wouldn't have it any other way."

They made their way to a nearby tavern that Ælfwynn had chosen for its discretion and strong ale, the kind of place where secrets could be shared without fear of loose tongues. The tavern was dimly lit, with a few rough-looking patrons nursing drinks and keeping to themselves. The perfect setting for a meeting that could decide the fate of a kingdom.

As they sat down at a corner table, Harald wasted no time. "You've got a problem, Ælfwynn. The Pope's got his eye on England, and he's not going to let a defiant queen stand in his way. You need my help, and I need an ally with a throne."

Ælfwynn leaned back, studying him carefully. "And what exactly do you want in return, Harald? I doubt you're here out of the goodness of your heart."

"Let's not pretend we're here to talk about hearts," Harald said with a sly smile. "I want land. A foothold in England, where I can secure my own power and keep the Vikings from raiding your coasts every other week. Marry me, and you'll have the might of Denmark at your back. Together, we can send the Pope's forces packing."

It was a tempting offer—one that could solve several of Ælfwynn's problems in one fell swoop. But there was something about Harald's eagerness that set off alarm bells in her mind. She wasn't about to hand over a chunk of England to a Viking prince without knowing exactly what he was planning.

"I'll admit, Harald," she began, her tone measured, "the idea of an alliance is appealing. But I've learned the hard way that nothing comes without strings attached. What's your real game here? You want a foothold in England—but for what? To protect it, or to carve out your own kingdom?"

Harald's expression hardened, his blue eyes narrowing slightly. "You're smart, Ælfwynn. I like that. So I'll be honest: I want both. Protecting England serves my interests, but I'm also looking out for my own. We're not so different, you and I. We both know power is what keeps the wolves at bay."

Before Ælfwynn could respond, Beorhthelm, who had been quietly observing, cleared his throat. "Your Majesty, we have company."

Ælfwynn followed his gaze and saw a cloaked figure slipping into the tavern, moving with the kind of careful grace that suggested they didn't want to be seen. The figure glanced around before heading toward a shadowy corner, where another man was already seated, his face hidden by a hood.

"Friends of yours?" Harald asked, his tone light but his hand drifting toward the hilt of his axe.

Ælfwynn shook her head. "Not mine. But I'm curious to know who they are."

She gave a quick nod to Beorhthelm, who immediately rose and moved toward the two men, his hand resting on his sword. Ælfwynn and Harald watched as Beorhthelm leaned over their table, saying something too low to hear. The two men stiffened, but before they could react, Beorhthelm's sword was at one man's throat, the other hand gripping the cloak of the second figure.

"Gentlemen," Beorhthelm said in a voice that carried just enough threat to freeze blood, "Her Majesty would like a word."

The two men were quickly brought to Ælfwynn's table, their faces now visible—and one of them, to Ælfwynn's surprise, was a familiar face. It was Brother Aldred, one of the monks from a local abbey who had always seemed too pious for his own good. The other man was a stranger, but the insignia on his cloak—an embroidered cross—told her everything she needed to know.

"Aldred," Ælfwynn said calmly, though her eyes were sharp. "I didn't realize you'd taken up drinking in taverns. And with such... interesting company."

Aldred's face flushed with a mix of fear and guilt. "Your Majesty, I—this is a misunderstanding. I was only—"

"Only what?" Ælfwynn interrupted, her voice cold. "Only meeting with a Vatican spy? Only plotting against your queen?"

The man beside Aldred scowled. "I am no spy. I am an envoy of the Church, here on official business."

"Official business?" Harald scoffed. "That's a new one. Usually, they just send assassins."

Ælfwynn's gaze didn't waver. "What were you discussing, Aldred? And don't lie to me, because I'm not in the mood."

Aldred swallowed hard. "Your Majesty, please—I didn't mean to betray you. I only—"

"Betrayal was the intention, then," Beorhthelm cut in, his voice a low growl.

"The Pope has offered a pardon," the Vatican envoy said, clearly realizing the jig was up. "For any who oppose the queen and support the rightful rule of the Church. Brother Aldred was merely hearing us out."

"Pardon in exchange for treason," Ælfwynn said, her voice like ice. "How very generous of him."

The envoy glared at her, his fear replaced by righteous indignation. "Your defiance of the Holy Father will bring ruin upon this land, Queen Ælfwynn. You can't stand against the will of God."

Ælfwynn leaned forward, her eyes locking onto his. "You're in England now, and in England, we stand against anyone who threatens our freedom. Take that message back to your Pope."

The envoy's mouth twisted into a sneer. "You'll regret this, Your Majesty."

"No," Ælfwynn said, her voice calm and deadly, "you will."

With a nod to Beorhthelm, the two men were dragged out of the tavern, leaving Ælfwynn and Harald alone once more. Harald was grinning, clearly impressed by how Ælfwynn had handled the situation.

"You've got fire, Ælfwynn," he said, raising his mug in a mock toast. "But you've also got enemies on all sides. You can't fight them all on your own."

Ælfwynn smiled faintly, though her mind was still racing. "No, I can't. Which is why I need to choose my allies carefully."

Harald's gaze softened, his tone becoming more serious. "I meant what I said earlier. We're stronger together. The Pope won't stop until he's crushed you—or until you crush him."

Ælfwynn met his gaze, seeing the truth in his words. But there was still the matter of trust—trust that Harald's ambitions wouldn't endanger England in the long run. Still, the immediate threat from the Pope's forces was very real, and the idea of facing them without Danish support was less appealing by the minute.

She took a deep breath, weighing her options one last time. "Very well, Harald. We'll form an alliance—but it's on my terms. We'll face the Pope together, but England remains mine. I won't trade one enemy for another."

Harald grinned, raising his mug again. "To an alliance of steel and blood, then. May our enemies tremble."

As they sealed the deal, Ælfwynn couldn't shake the feeling that this was just the beginning of a much larger game—one where the stakes were higher than ever, and the players far more dangerous.

Rebellion and Retaliation

The smell of roasting venison wafted through the banquet hall, mingling with the laughter and clinking of goblets. It was a rare evening of respite at Westminster, and Queen Ælfwynn had decided to let her court indulge in a feast before the storm inevitably rolled in. After all, if they were going to face off against the Pope and a potential Saxon rebellion, they might as well do it with full stomachs.

Ælfwynn herself sat at the head of the long table, watching the revelry with a mixture of amusement and caution. Across the hall, Beorhthelm was regaling a group of soldiers with exaggerated tales of battle, his booming laughter echoing off the stone walls. Prince Harald of Denmark, their newest ally, was deep in conversation with a group of nobles, clearly enjoying the English ale a bit too much.

"Do you think it's wise to let the Danes drink so freely, Your Majesty?" Lord Eadwine whispered as he leaned in from her left.

Ælfwynn smirked, taking a sip from her own goblet. "Let them. They'll be more manageable with hangovers tomorrow."

Eadwine's lips twitched in a reluctant smile. "You always did know how to play the long game."

"Speaking of games," Ælfwynn said, lowering her voice, "how are our guests in the dungeon?"

"Wulfric is still nursing his bruises, and Brother Aldred has been muttering prayers to every saint he can think of," Eadwine replied. "But it's the Saxon lords who concern me. There's been talk of rallying behind Wulfric. They see him as a martyr now, and they're using his imprisonment as a rallying cry."

Ælfwynn sighed, setting down her goblet. "Of course they are. Because nothing says 'good leadership' like backing a man who got himself thrown in the dungeon for conspiring with the Pope."

Before Eadwine could respond, the doors to the banquet hall flew open with a crash, and a guard stumbled in, blood streaming from a wound on his forehead.

"Your Majesty!" the guard gasped, his voice hoarse. "The Saxon lords—they're marching on London! They've raised their banners in revolt!"

The hall fell silent, the revelry snuffed out like a candle in a storm. Ælfwynn shot to her feet, her eyes narrowing. "How many?"

"Hundreds, maybe more," the guard replied, wincing as he clutched his side. "They're claiming Wulfric's their rightful leader, that he's been unjustly imprisoned. They're demanding his release—or they'll take it by force."

Harald, who had been leaning back in his chair with a contented grin, suddenly looked much more sober. "Sounds like your lords have a death wish, Ælfwynn."

"More like a suicide pact," Beorhthelm muttered, already rising to grab his sword.

Ælfwynn clenched her fists, her mind racing. The rebellion was moving faster than she'd anticipated, and with the Pope's forces still looming on the horizon, they couldn't afford to be divided. But releasing Wulfric would only embolden the rebels—and undermine her authority.

"There's no time to waste," she said, her voice steady despite the urgency in the air. "We need to crush this rebellion before it gains any more momentum. Harald, I need your men."

Harald nodded, his expression grim. "You'll have them. But this won't be easy—those lords have been waiting for an excuse to revolt. They're not going to back down without a fight."

"Then we'll give them one," Ælfwynn replied, her eyes hard as steel. "And if they want Wulfric, they'll have to come and get him—over our dead bodies."

The feast was over in an instant, the revelers turning to warriors as they rushed to prepare for battle. Ælfwynn gave orders with the precision of a general, rallying her forces and sending out messengers to loyal lords who might still be able to help. Beorhthelm, ever her right hand, was already strategizing the defense of London, while Harald prepared his Danish warriors for the coming clash.

As Ælfwynn made her way through the corridors of Westminster, she couldn't shake the feeling that the rebellion was just the beginning. The Pope's threat still loomed, and she knew that the Saxon lords weren't the only enemies she had to worry about.

Her thoughts were interrupted when a shadowy figure emerged from a side corridor, slipping in front of her with the grace of a cat. Ælfwynn instinctively reached for her sword, but the figure held up a hand in a gesture of peace.

"Your Majesty," the figure said in a low, urgent voice. "I bring news from the Vatican."

Ælfwynn's eyes narrowed. "And who might you be?"

The figure pulled back the hood, revealing a gaunt, sharp-featured man with a scar running down one side of his face. His eyes were dark and intense, but there was something in them that hinted at desperation.

"My name is Pietro," he said, glancing around to ensure they weren't being overheard. "I was once a servant of the Pope—but no longer. I've come to warn you."

Ælfwynn kept her hand on her sword, not yet ready to trust him. "Warn me about what?"

"The Pope's plans," Pietro replied, his voice tight. "He's not content with a simple Crusade. He's sending assassins to England, to eliminate anyone who stands in his way—including you. But the assassins aren't just any mercenaries—they're trained by the Vatican's most secretive order. They'll stop at nothing to see you dead."

Ælfwynn felt a cold knot form in her stomach, but she didn't let it show. "And why should I believe you?"

"Because I've seen what they're capable of," Pietro said, his eyes haunted. "And because I know where they're coming from. I can help you stop them—if you let me."

Before Ælfwynn could respond, another guard rushed down the corridor, his face pale. "Your Majesty, the rebels have reached the outskirts of the city!

They're burning everything in their path!"

Ælfwynn cursed under her breath. The rebellion was moving faster than she'd expected, and now she had to deal with both the Saxon lords and the threat of assassins from the Vatican.

"Fine," she said, turning to Pietro. "You'll come with me. But if this is a trap, I'll make sure you regret it."

Pietro nodded, clearly relieved. "I'll do whatever it takes to help you, Your Majesty."

Together, they hurried to the war room, where Beorhthelm and Harald were already waiting, maps and weapons spread out before them.

"The rebels are closing in," Beorhthelm said grimly. "They've already torched several villages on the way here. We need to move fast."

"And we will," Ælfwynn replied, her mind racing as she formulated a plan. "But there's more. Pietro here claims the Vatican is sending assassins—trained killers, and they're already on their way."

Harald let out a low whistle. "As if things weren't complicated enough."

Beorhthelm's eyes narrowed as he sized up Pietro. "And we're supposed to trust this man? He could be leading them right to you, Your Majesty."

"Then we'll keep a close eye on him," Ælfwynn said, her voice firm. "But right now, we need every advantage we can get. Pietro, do you know where the assassins will strike?"

"They'll try to hit you when you're vulnerable," Pietro replied, his voice steady. "Possibly during the battle, when you're focused on the rebels. But I know where they're hiding—and I can lead you to them."

"Good," Ælfwynn said, her gaze hardening. "Beorhthelm, you'll take a small force and deal with the assassins. Harald and I will lead the main army against the rebels."

"Understood, Your Majesty," Beorhthelm replied, already preparing to move out.

Harald grinned, his hand on his sword. "Let's remind these lords who the real ruler of England is."

As the war room buzzed with activity, Ælfwynn felt the weight of the coming battle settle on her shoulders. The rebellion, the assassins, the looming threat of the Pope—it all seemed impossible to overcome. But she wasn't about to back down. Not now, not ever.

"Let's end this," she said, her voice filled with determination.

The battle for London was fierce and bloody, with the rebel lords throwing everything they had at Ælfwynn's forces. But Ælfwynn, flanked by Harald and his Danish warriors, fought with the ferocity of a queen defending her throne. As the sun set over the city, the tide began to turn in their favor, the rebels' lines breaking under the relentless assault.

Meanwhile, Beorhthelm and Pietro led a small team through the narrow streets of London, hunting down the Vatican assassins before they could strike. The fight was brutal, the assassins skilled and deadly, but in the end, Beorhthelm's men prevailed, leaving a trail of bloodied bodies in their wake.

By the time the battle ended, the rebel forces were shattered, and Wulfric's hopes of seizing the throne were crushed. The Saxon lords who had rallied to his cause were either dead or captured, and London remained firmly in Ælfwynn's control.

As Ælfwynn stood on the battlements, overlooking the battlefield strewn with the fallen, she couldn't help but feel a surge of triumph. The rebellion had been quelled, the assassins thwarted, and the Pope's forces were still on the horizon, waiting for their chance.

Feast and False Foes

The first rays of dawn crept over the horizon, casting a pale light over the misty fields outside London. It was the kind of morning that seemed impossibly quiet, as if the world itself was holding its breath. In a secluded grove, a dozen of Ælfwynn's most trusted warriors stood in a loose circle, their swords drawn, their eyes fixed on the center of the clearing.

There, Queen Ælfwynn and Prince Harald of Denmark faced each other, each holding a sword in one hand and a goblet of wine in the other.

"You know," Ælfwynn said, breaking the silence, "most people just exchange rings."

Harald grinned, his teeth flashing in the early light. "Most people aren't Vikings, Your Majesty. We prefer to seal our alliances with something a bit more... exciting."

"By 'exciting,' I assume you mean 'dangerous,'" Ælfwynn replied, her tone dry as she took a sip of the wine.

The ceremony they were about to perform was an ancient Viking custom—a blood oath, where each participant would make a small cut on their hand and let the blood drip into their goblets before drinking. It was symbolic of a bond forged in blood, unbreakable and sacred.

Or at least that's what Harald had told her. Ælfwynn suspected it was more about proving that she wasn't afraid to get her hands dirty—literally and figuratively.

She raised her sword, and Harald did the same. With a quick, precise motion, they both made a shallow cut across their palms, letting the blood drip into their goblets. Ælfwynn watched as her blood mingled with the wine, the deep red swirling in the cup.

"To our alliance," Harald said, raising his goblet.

"To our alliance," Ælfwynn echoed, and they both drank.

The wine burned as it went down, but Ælfwynn didn't flinch. She could feel the eyes of her warriors on her, and she knew that any sign of weakness would be seized upon—by her own people as well as the Danes. But as she lowered the goblet, she allowed herself a small smile.

"Was that exciting enough for you?" she asked Harald, arching an eyebrow.

Harald chuckled, wiping the blood from his hand. "You're a brave woman, Ælfwynn. No wonder your people follow you."

"They don't follow me out of bravery," Ælfwynn replied, her voice steady. "They follow me because I give them no other choice."

Harald's smile widened. "And that's why I'm marrying you."

With the blood oath complete, the two of them made their way back to the palace, where preparations for the wedding feast were already underway. It was to be a grand affair, with lords and warriors from both England and Denmark in attendance, all there to witness the union that would, they hoped, bring peace and strength to both kingdoms.

But as Ælfwynn entered the bustling hall, she couldn't shake the feeling that peace was still a long way off.

The great hall of Westminster was alive with the sounds of celebration. The smell of roasted meat filled the air, mingling with the laughter of warriors and the clinking of goblets. Ælfwynn sat at the head of the table, resplendent in a gown of deep crimson, a crown of gold resting lightly on her brow. Beside her, Harald looked every bit the Viking prince, his rough edges only slightly smoothed by the trappings of royalty.

The feast was a carefully orchestrated display of unity, with Saxon lords and Danish warriors mingling under the watchful eyes of their respective leaders. But beneath the surface, Ælfwynn knew that tensions were simmering. There were still lords who questioned her decision to marry Harald, seeing it as a betrayal of Saxon traditions. And there were Danes who saw England as ripe for the taking, despite the marriage.

Still, Ælfwynn had a plan—one that involved more than just good food and wine.

As the feast reached its peak, she rose from her seat, raising her goblet high. The hall fell silent, all eyes turning to her.

"Lords, warriors, friends," she began, her voice carrying easily over the gathered throng, "tonight, we celebrate a union that will strengthen both our peoples. England and Denmark, united in purpose, standing together against those who would seek to divide us."

A cheer went up, but Ælfwynn wasn't finished.

"But let us not be complacent," she continued, her tone taking on a more serious edge. "We face threats not just from without, but from within. There are those who would see this alliance fail, who would prefer to see us divided and weak. We must be vigilant, for our enemies are clever—and closer than we might think."

She let the words hang in the air for a moment, watching as they sank in. The Saxon lords exchanged uneasy glances, while the Danish warriors shifted in their seats. Harald looked at her with a mixture of admiration and curiosity, clearly wondering where she was going with this.

"I have received word of a new threat," Ælfwynn said, lowering her voice slightly, forcing everyone to lean in closer. "A rival kingdom—one that seeks to exploit any perceived weakness in our alliance. They are spreading rumors of an invasion, hoping to drive a wedge between us."

The hall buzzed with murmurs, the lords and warriors trying to guess which kingdom she was referring to. The Welsh? The Scots? The Irish? Each had reason to resent England's growing power, and any of them could be behind the rumored threat.

"But we will not be idle," she declared, her eyes flashing with determination. "We will strengthen our bonds. We will unite our forces as never before. Let the world see that England and Denmark are not divided—they are one."

The cheers erupted.

Ælfwynn watched with satisfaction as the Saxon lords began to mingle more freely with the Danes, their earlier suspicions fading in the face of a common cause.

As she sat back down, Harald leaned in close, his voice low. "You're a clever woman, Ælfwynn. Turning a false threat from a common enemy into a rallying cry—your lords will follow you anywhere now."

"That was the idea," Ælfwynn replied with a sly smile. "But don't think I've forgotten the real threats. The Pope, the rebels, the assassins—they're still out there, waiting for us to let our guard down."

Harald nodded, his expression serious. "And when they strike?"

Ælfwynn's smile didn't waver. "We'll be ready."

As the feast wound down and the guests began to retire to their quarters, Ælfwynn and Harald found themselves alone in a private chamber, away from the prying eyes of the court. A fire crackled in the hearth, casting flickering shadows on the stone walls.

"I must admit," Harald said, breaking the comfortable silence, "I wasn't expecting to enjoy myself so much tonight. Your Saxon lords are an interesting bunch—stubborn, but loyal."

"They're loyal because they know what's at stake," Ælfwynn replied, swirling the wine in her goblet. "But I can't help but wonder—how loyal are your men, Harald? Do they see this marriage as an alliance or as an opportunity?"

Harald's expression darkened slightly. "You're asking if they plan to betray me."

"Let's just say I've learned to trust my instincts," Ælfwynn said, her tone careful. "And my instincts tell me that not everyone in your camp is thrilled with this union."

Harald sighed, running a hand through his hair. "You're not wrong. There are those who would rather see me seize power than share it. They think England should be ruled by a Viking king, not a Saxon queen."

"And what do you think?" Ælfwynn asked, her eyes fixed on his.

"I think," Harald said slowly, "that those men are fools. They don't understand that we're stronger together. But if they're plotting something, I need to know."

Ælfwynn nodded. "Agreed. Which is why I suggest we keep a close eye on them. If there's a conspiracy brewing, we'll root it out—together."

Harald's gaze softened, and he reached out to take her hand. "You're a remarkable woman, Ælfwynn. I never thought I'd find a partner like you."

Ælfwynn smiled, though her mind was still racing. "And I never thought I'd find myself married to a Viking. But here we are."

As they sat together, the firelight dancing in their eyes, Ælfwynn knew that the road ahead would be anything but easy. The unity she had forged tonight was a fragile thing, and there were still many who would see it broken. But for now, she had Harald's loyalty—and that was a start.

Daggers in the Dark

The moon hung low over Westminster, casting long shadows across the stone walls as the castle settled into the quiet of night. The feast had ended hours ago, and the hallways were empty, save for the occasional guard making their rounds. In her chambers, Queen Ælfwynn was finally allowing herself a moment of peace, the weight of the day's events pressing heavily on her.

But peace, it seemed, was not in the cards.

A flicker of movement in the corner of the room caught her eye, just as the candlelight wavered. Ælfwynn's hand instinctively went to the dagger she kept under her pillow—a habit she'd developed since the first attempt on her life. The door to her chamber was locked, and there were guards posted outside, but the feeling of unease wouldn't leave her.

And for good reason.

The silence was shattered by the sudden crash of glass—a window breaking. Before she could react, three figures dressed in black, their faces masked, dropped into the room, their movements swift and deadly.

Assassins.

"Really?" Ælfwynn muttered, leaping to her feet, dagger in hand. "And here I thought I'd get a full night's sleep for once."

The first assassin lunged at her, but Ælfwynn was quicker, sidestepping his attack and driving her dagger into his side. He let out a grunt of pain, but before she could finish him off, the second assassin was upon her, swinging a blade that caught the edge of her gown, tearing the fabric but missing flesh.

"Nice try," she said, ducking under his next strike and kicking out at his knee. The man stumbled, and she used the opening to slash at his throat. He dropped to the floor, blood pooling around him.

But the third assassin was more cautious. He circled her, his eyes cold and calculating, clearly the leader of the group. Ælfwynn felt a bead of sweat trickle down her back—this one was going to be trouble.

"Let me guess," she said, her voice laced with sarcasm even as she braced herself for the fight. "You're here on behalf of the Pope? He really doesn't know when to quit, does he?"

The assassin didn't respond, but the flicker of anger in his eyes told her everything she needed to know. He feinted to the left, then lunged to the right, his blade flashing in the moonlight.

But before he could strike, the door to her chamber burst open, and Harald stormed in, sword in hand. "Ælfwynn!"

The assassin spun around just in time to see the Viking prince charging at him. Harald didn't hesitate—his sword cleaved through the air with deadly precision, forcing the assassin to retreat. The two men clashed, their blades ringing out in the confined space of the chamber.

"Couldn't let you have all the fun," Harald grunted, parrying a strike and driving his sword into the assassin's chest. The man gasped, blood spurting from the wound, and crumpled to the floor.

Ælfwynn lowered her dagger, catching her breath as she surveyed the carnage. "I'd say thank you, but I had it under control."

"Of course you did," Harald replied, grinning as he wiped the blood from his sword. "But I couldn't resist."

She rolled her eyes, though there was a hint of a smile on her lips. "Well, that's one way to end a night."

As they caught their breath, the guards finally arrived, drawn by the noise. Ælfwynn gave them a sharp look. "Took your time, didn't you?"

"Apologies, Your Majesty," one of the guards stammered, clearly mortified. "We'll search the grounds immediately. There could be more of them."

"Do that," Ælfwynn said, her voice cold. "And double the guard. I don't want another repeat of tonight."

As the guards rushed off to follow her orders, Harald turned to her, his expression serious. "These assassins—they're getting bolder. The Pope's making his move."

Ælfwynn nodded, her mind already racing ahead. "Yes, but we've dealt with his assassins before. It's time we stopped playing defense and started taking the fight to him."

The next morning, the great hall of Westminster was transformed into a courtroom. The bodies of the assassins had been cleared away, and in their place stood the conspirators who had been captured over the past few weeks. Brother Aldred was among them, his head bowed in what Ælfwynn suspected was a show of piety rather than genuine remorse.

The trial was a spectacle, with the Saxon lords and Danish warriors watching from the galleries, their faces a mix of anger and anticipation. Ælfwynn sat on the throne, flanked by Harald and Beorhthelm, her gaze fixed on the accused.

"Brother Aldred," she began, her voice carrying through the hall, "you stand accused of treason against the crown, conspiring with the Vatican, and aiding assassins in their attempt to murder your queen. How do you plead?"

Aldred raised his head, his eyes filled with a fervor that Ælfwynn found both disturbing and pitiful. "I plead guilty, Your Majesty. Guilty of following the will of God, which is higher than any earthly law."

Ælfwynn sighed inwardly. "And this will of God—did it also command you to murder in His name?"

Aldred didn't flinch. "The Pope is the voice of God on Earth. His commands are divine."

"And yet here you are, in chains," Ælfwynn said, her tone sharp. "It seems your divine commandment didn't extend to protecting you from the consequences of your actions."

There was a murmur of approval from the gathered lords, and Ælfwynn pressed on. "You and your fellow conspirators sought to sow chaos and discord in my kingdom. You wanted to weaken England, to make it ripe for conquest by foreign powers. But you failed. And now, you will answer for your crimes."

She paused, letting the silence hang in the air before delivering the sentence. "You are sentenced to death for treason. Your execution will serve as a reminder to all who would conspire against the crown—England will not bow to the whims of the Vatican, or to anyone who seeks to divide us."

Aldred's face twisted in fury, but he said nothing more. As the guards led him away, Ælfwynn stood, addressing the court.

"Let this be a lesson to all," she declared, her voice firm. "We will not tolerate treachery in our midst. We are stronger together, and we will not be divided."

The trial had served its purpose. The Saxon lords, seeing how Ælfwynn dealt with traitors, were reminded of the strength of her rule. The Danish warriors, too, were impressed by her decisive action, solidifying their loyalty.

But Ælfwynn knew that trials and executions wouldn't be enough. The Pope was still out there, and so were other threats. It was time to expand her alliances beyond England and Denmark.

A week after the trial, Ælfwynn sat in her study, surrounded by maps of the British Isles. The Welsh, the Scots, the Irish—all of them had the potential to be either allies or enemies in the coming conflict. She needed them on her side, or at least neutralized, if she was to stand any chance against the Pope's forces.

Harald entered the room, his brow furrowed as he looked over the maps. "You're planning something big, aren't you?"

"I'm always planning something big," Ælfwynn replied with a wry smile. "But this time, it's a bit more ambitious. I'm going to unite the Celtic kingdoms—or force them to bend the knee."

Harald raised an eyebrow. "And how do you plan to do that? The Celts aren't exactly known for their love of Saxon queens or Viking princes."

Ælfwynn tapped one of the maps, where the borders of Wales, Scotland, and Ireland were marked in ink. "I'm going to play on their fears. The Pope's reach is long, but it's not infinite. If they see England as the strongest power on the Isles, they'll be more inclined to align with us—especially if the alternative is facing us in battle."

"And if they refuse?" Harald asked, a hint of amusement in his voice.

"Then we remind them why it's better to be our friend than our enemy," Ælfwynn said, her eyes gleaming with determination. "I'll send emissaries to each of the kingdoms, offering them favorable terms for an alliance. But

I'll also make it clear that if they refuse, they'll face the full might of England and Denmark."

Harald chuckled. "You've got a way with words, Ælfwynn. I wouldn't want to be on the receiving end of that ultimatum."

"Neither would I," she replied, her tone light but her resolve unshakable. "We'll give them the choice—join us, or face us. Either way, we win."

Celtic Complications

The sun hung low in the sky as the Welsh hills loomed before the small party of emissaries sent by Queen Ælfwynn. Led by Lord Beorhthelm, the group was a mix of Saxon warriors, Danish soldiers, and one unfortunate scribe who looked as though he'd much rather be anywhere else. As they approached the border, the wind whipped through the grass, carrying with it the scent of the sea and a sense of foreboding.

"Remind me again why I volunteered for this," Beorhthelm muttered, adjusting the sword at his hip as he eyed the rocky terrain. "Because I'm starting to think I was drunk at the time."

The scribe, a lanky young man named Oswald, cleared his throat nervously. "Your Majesty—I mean, Lord Beorhthelm—perhaps it's because you wanted to see the world? Expand your horizons?"

Beorhthelm snorted. "I'd rather expand my ale collection. And for the record, if I get skewered by a Welsh spear, I'm blaming you."

As they crested the final hill, the Welsh stronghold of Dinas Emrys came into view—a fortress perched precariously on a rocky outcrop, its walls as old as the legends that surrounded it. The Welsh, it seemed, had a flair for the dramatic.

"Now remember," Beorhthelm said, turning to his men, "we're here to make an alliance, not start a war. So try not to insult anyone's sheep or mention anything about their legendary dragons. We don't need to give them any more reason to dislike us."

"Dislike us?" one of the Danish warriors chuckled. "I thought they hated us."

"Semantics," Beorhthelm replied with a grin. "Just keep your wits about you and your weapons sheathed—unless they don't. Then feel free to unsheathe away."

With that, the group made their way to the gates of the fortress, where they were greeted by a wary-looking group of Welsh soldiers. The leader, a grizzled man with a scar that ran from his eyebrow to his jaw, stepped forward.

"Lord Beorhthelm of England, here on behalf of Queen Ælfwynn," Beorhthelm said, bowing slightly—a gesture that looked a bit odd from a man who could break bones with a single glance. "We seek an audience with your king."

The Welshman grunted, clearly unimpressed. "King Gruffydd isn't one for audiences with Saxons. Or Danes. Or anyone who doesn't have Welsh blood, for that matter."

Beorhthelm smiled disarmingly. "Then we're in luck, because I'm not just any Saxon—I'm the charming kind. And besides, we're here with an offer that even King Gruffydd won't want to refuse."

The Welsh soldier narrowed his eyes but nodded. "Follow me."

As they were led through the winding corridors of the fortress, Beorhthelm couldn't help but notice the wary looks they received from the Welsh soldiers. It was clear that their presence was not exactly welcome, but then again, when was it ever?

Finally, they were brought before King Gruffydd, a man who looked as though he'd been carved from the very rocks his fortress was built on. He sat on a simple wooden throne, his gaze sharp and unyielding as he regarded the emissaries with thinly veiled disdain.

"So," Gruffydd said, his voice a low rumble, "the Saxons have sent a warrior to do a diplomat's job. And they've brought Danes, too. What do you want?"

Beorhthelm stepped forward, all traces of humor gone from his face. "We bring a message from Queen Ælfwynn. She seeks an alliance with the Welsh people, to stand united against a common enemy—the Pope and his forces. England and Denmark have already joined forces, and together with Wales, we can ensure that the British Isles remain free from foreign control."

Gruffydd's eyes narrowed. "And what does your queen offer in return? Wales has stood independent for centuries—we have no need for Saxon help."

"Independence is a fine thing," Beorhthelm said, his tone measured, "but it's hard to maintain when you're facing the might of Europe. The Pope's forces won't stop at England—they'll come for Wales, too. And when they do, you'll either stand with us, or be overrun."

Gruffydd leaned back in his chair, considering this. "And if we refuse?"

Beorhthelm smiled, but it didn't reach his eyes. "Then we'll leave, and you can take your chances with the Pope. But consider this—if you refuse our offer, you'll not only be facing his forces but ours as well. And I don't think I need to remind you that a divided Britain is a weak Britain."

The room was silent as Gruffydd weighed his options. Finally, he nodded, a grudging respect in his eyes. "Very well. We will consider your queen's offer. But know this—if she betrays us, there will be no place on this island where she can hide."

Beorhthelm inclined his head. "She wouldn't dream of it, Your Majesty."

With the Welsh alliance tentatively secured, Beorhthelm and his men made their way back to England, knowing that they had bought themselves a valuable ally—but also a potential enemy, should things go wrong.

Meanwhile, across the sea in Ireland, another of Ælfwynn's emissaries was having a decidedly less formal conversation with the Irish king, Brian of Munster, a man known for his love of war, whiskey, and witticisms—often in that order.

"So," Brian said, leaning back in his chair and taking a swig of whiskey, "the Saxons and Danes think they can waltz in here and tell us what to do, eh? And what's this about an alliance? I've got half a mind to tell you where to stick your alliance."

Oswald, the unfortunate scribe who had been sent to Ireland (and who now found himself wondering what he had done to deserve this), forced a nervous smile. "We offer you a partnership, Your Majesty. Together, we can resist the Pope's forces and ensure that Ireland remains free from foreign rule."

Brian snorted, setting his goblet down with a thud. "Foreign rule? And what do you call Saxon rule? Or Viking rule? You're all foreigners to us, lad.

But I'll admit, I've no love for the Pope. And if it's a fight he wants, well, I've never been one to turn down a good scrap."

Oswald nodded eagerly, trying to keep the conversation on track. "Exactly, Your Majesty. And with England, Denmark, and Wales united, we can—"

"Spare me the details," Brian interrupted with a wave of his hand. "The truth is, I don't trust your queen any more than I trust a snake in a bog. But I trust the Pope even less. So here's my offer—I'll join your alliance, but only if your queen agrees to keep her Saxon and Viking noses out of Irish affairs. Ireland will fight alongside you, but we won't be taking orders from England. Understood?"

Oswald gulped but nodded. "Understood, Your Majesty. I'll relay your terms to Queen Ælfwynn."

Brian grinned, his teeth flashing. "Good lad. Now, how about a drink to seal the deal?"

Oswald hesitated for only a moment before accepting the goblet handed to him. After all, refusing an Irish king's offer of whiskey was a surefire way to end up on the wrong side of his sword.

As Oswald raised the goblet, he silently prayed that Ælfwynn would find a way to manage this alliance without sparking another war.

While her emissaries were busy securing alliances with Wales and Ireland, Queen Ælfwynn herself had traveled north to Scotland, where she was meeting with King David I in the grand hall of Stirling Castle. The atmosphere was tense, to say the least. The Scots had no love for the English, and the feeling was mutual. The wars between the two nations had left scars that were far from healed—scars that ran deep, especially for David.

His sister, Matilda of Scotland, had been a key player in the conflict that had nearly torn England apart. She had fought fiercely, and she had died for it, leaving behind a legacy of bitterness and enmity that David had inherited. Now, he sat on the throne of Scotland, a wary and battle-hardened king who had no reason to trust the Saxon queen who had bested his sister.

"So," David said, his voice as cold as the stone walls around them, "the woman who killed my sister comes to my court, asking for an alliance. You've got nerve, Ælfwynn, I'll give you that."

Ælfwynn met his gaze without flinching. "Matilda was a formidable opponent, David. I respected her, even if we were enemies. But we're not here to dredge up old grudges. We're here because the Pope's forces are coming, and when they do, they won't care about our past conflicts. They'll see us both as obstacles to be crushed."

David's eyes narrowed. "And why should I believe that you won't crush us first? The English have been trying to subdue Scotland for generations. What makes you any different?"

Ælfwynn leaned forward, her voice low and intense. "Because I know that fighting each other is a waste of time and lives. We've both lost too much already. But if we don't stand together now, we'll lose everything. You want to avenge your sister? Fine. But do it by beating the Pope's forces, not by tearing each other apart."

David was silent for a long moment, his expression unreadable. Finally, he spoke, his tone measured. "And what do you offer in return? Scotland has no desire to bow to an English queen, no matter how persuasive she might be."

"I'm not asking you to bow," Ælfwynn replied, her voice firm. "I'm asking you to stand with us as equals. Scotland will remain independent, and so will England. But we'll fight together against our common enemies. And when this is over, we can settle our differences—if there are any left to settle."

David studied her, his gaze piercing. "You're asking a lot, Ælfwynn. Trust doesn't come easily to the Scots, especially not when it comes to the English."

Ælfwynn nodded. "I know. But I'm not asking for trust. I'm asking for a chance to prove that this alliance is in both our interests. Let the Pope and his forces come, and we'll show them that the British Isles are not theirs to conquer."

There was another long pause, the tension in the room thick enough to cut with a sword. Finally, David stood, his expression grim but resolute.

"Very well," he said. "Scotland will stand with you—on one condition. If you break your word, if you so much as think about turning on us, I'll make sure Scotland never forgets it. And you'll find that the wrath of the Scots is not something you want to face."

Ælfwynn rose as well, meeting his gaze with steely determination. "You have my word, David. We'll fight this battle together, and we'll win it together."

With the tentative alliance secured, Ælfwynn left Stirling Castle with a mixture of relief and caution. The Scots were fierce and proud, and they would not tolerate any sign of weakness or betrayal. But for now, they were allies, and that was all she could ask for.

Allies and Ambushes

The flickering light of the hearth cast long shadows across the map-strewn table in Queen Ælfwynn's war chamber. She leaned over the parchment, her eyes scanning the borders of Europe with a sharp intensity that had become second nature. Beside her, Beorhthelm traced a finger along the routes that messengers would take to reach their potential allies.

"It's not enough to have the British Isles on our side," Ælfwynn murmured, her voice as sharp as the steel dagger she kept strapped to her thigh. "We need to reach across the Channel, find those in Europe who've got as much reason to hate the Pope as we do. The more thorns in his side, the better."

Beorhthelm grinned, his scarred face lighting up with the thrill of the plan. "Aye, Your Majesty. And I can think of a few names who might be more than happy to thumb their noses at Rome."

Ælfwynn's lips curled into a sly smile. "Good. Let's start with those who have a bone to pick with His Holiness—and perhaps a few of their own to grind into dust."

She paused, her finger hovering over the map. "Who's first on the list?"

Beorhthelm leaned in closer, tapping a spot on the map. "How about Henry, the Holy Roman Emperor? The Pope tried to pull his strings more than once, and Henry cut those strings with a sword. He's not likely to be singing hymns of praise to the Vatican anytime soon."

Ælfwynn's smile broadened. "Henry. A man after my own heart. Let's see if we can turn his grudge into an alliance. Send an emissary to his court, Beorhthelm—but choose wisely. We need someone who knows how to navigate imperial politics without getting beheaded."

Beorhthelm nodded. "And if the Emperor plays hard to get?"

"Then remind him of the Pope's habit of meddling in affairs that don't concern him," Ælfwynn replied, her tone icy. "And suggest that an alliance with England could ensure that Rome keeps its nose out of Germany's business."

"Clever," Beorhthelm said, clearly impressed. "Who's next?"

Ælfwynn moved her finger to another part of the map, tracing the coastline of Sicily. "Roger of Sicily. The Pope's never been too fond of the Sicilian kingdom, and I doubt Roger's forgotten how Rome tried to meddle in his coronation."

Beorhthelm raised an eyebrow. "You think Roger will join us?"

Ælfwynn's smile turned wicked. "I think Roger's a man who knows the value of keeping his enemies close—and his friends even closer. Besides, an alliance with Sicily would give us a foothold in the Mediterranean, something the Pope would loathe."

Beorhthelm nodded, already picturing the possibilities. "We'll send him an offer he can't refuse—unless he wants to find himself isolated when Rome comes knocking."

"And while we're at it," Ælfwynn added, "we might as well reach out to Alfonso of Aragon. He's been waging his own war with the Moors, and the last thing he needs is the Pope interfering. A little support from England might convince him that his true enemy isn't just across the Mediterranean, but sitting on a throne in Rome."

Beorhthelm smirked. "Three kings with a grudge against the Pope—this is shaping up nicely."

Just as they were about to move on, Beorhthelm's finger hovered over Normandy, and the room seemed to chill.

"And then there's William Clito," he said, his tone dropping a notch. "The grandson of William the Bastard. He's been claiming the English throne ever since he became the Duke of Normandy. He's ambitious, cunning, and more dangerous than any other rival you've faced. Trying to turn him into an ally might be like trying to befriend a viper."

Ælfwynn's smile faded slightly. "Clito's a wild card, no doubt. He's got a legitimate claim to England, and he's never stopped reminding the world of it. But if we don't reach out to him, he could easily become our greatest enemy. Better to keep him close, even if it's with one hand on the hilt of a knife."

Beorhthelm frowned. "And if he refuses to play nice?"

Ælfwynn's eyes darkened. "Then we remind him that England is not his birthright, and never will be. But first, we'll see if he can be swayed. If we can offer him something that appeals to his ambition, we might just avoid a future conflict—or at least delay it."

Beorhthelm nodded slowly. "I'll send a messenger, but I'll make sure he understands the risks. Clito isn't the type to let a perceived slight go unpunished."

"Good," Ælfwynn said. "And make sure the message is clear: England is willing to work with him, but not under him. He can either be an ally or an obstacle—his choice."

With the plans set, Beorhthelm left the chamber to dispatch the messengers. Ælfwynn stared at the map for a moment longer, her mind whirring with possibilities and potential threats. The alliances she was attempting to forge were as fragile as they were necessary, and any misstep could lead to disaster.

As the emissaries were sent out to their respective destinations, Ælfwynn allowed herself a moment of satisfaction. The plan was bold, but if it worked, it could shift the balance of power in her favor. She had already secured alliances with the Welsh, the Irish, and the Scots, but now it was time to cast a wider net.

Yet, as with all things in politics, nothing ever went smoothly.

A few days later, as Ælfwynn was poring over the latest reports from her spies, a commotion broke out in the courtyard. The sound of clashing steel and shouts of alarm reached her ears, and she was on her feet in an instant, sword in hand.

Rushing to the window, she saw a group of figures, dressed in the dark robes of monks, engaged in a fierce battle with her guards. But these were no ordinary monks—their movements were swift, calculated, and deadly.

Assassins. Again.

"Persistent bastards, aren't they?" Ælfwynn muttered, already making her way to the door.

By the time she reached the courtyard, the fight was in full swing. Harald was there, his massive sword cleaving through one of the assassins with a savage roar. Beorhthelm was at his side, directing the guards as they fended off the attackers.

"Nice of you to join the party, Your Majesty!" Harald called out, his voice thick with battle lust.

"I wouldn't miss it for the world," Ælfwynn shot back, driving her sword into the back of an assassin who had gotten too close to one of her guards.

The assassins fought with the desperation of men who knew they had already failed. One by one, they were cut down, until only one remained—an older man, his eyes filled with a fanatical zeal that sent a chill down Ælfwynn's spine.

"You may kill me," the assassin spat, blood trickling from the corner of his mouth, "but the Pope's will is divine. He will not rest until you are dead, heretic!"

Ælfwynn raised her sword, her expression cold. "I've heard that before. But I'm still standing."

With one swift motion, she ended the assassin's life, watching dispassionately as he crumpled to the ground. The courtyard fell silent, save for the heavy breathing of the surviving guards.

"Well," Harald said, wiping his blade clean on the robe of a fallen assassin, "that was invigorating."

Ælfwynn sheathed her sword, her mind already racing. "It's more than that. It's a message from the Pope—he's not going to stop. But neither will we."

"Damn right," Beorhthelm growled, kicking one of the dead assassins for good measure. "But we've got our own message to send, don't we?"

Ælfwynn nodded, her eyes narrowing. "Indeed. Let the Pope and his allies know that England is not a kingdom to be trifled with. We'll see how they fare when the wolves start circling."

With the assassins dealt with, Ælfwynn turned her attention back to her plan. The letters had been sent, the wheels set in motion. Now, it was time to see which of Europe's monarchs would respond to her call.

Deals, Deceits, and Dangerous Waters

The war chamber buzzed with activity as Ælfwynn paced in front of the hearth, her mind racing through the latest developments. The letters had come back—some with promises, others with threats, and one with enough veiled menace to warrant a few extra guards at the door.

Beorhthelm, as usual, stood by with a grin that suggested he was enjoying this far more than anyone should. "Well, Your Majesty, seems we've stirred the pot nicely. Now the question is—what's the next move?"

Ælfwynn stopped pacing long enough to shoot him a look. "The next move, Beorhthelm, is figuring out how to juggle these so-called allies without letting them drop on our heads. The Pope's already sent assassins, and now he's sending mercenaries. If we're not careful, England's going to look like a battlefield before the real fight even begins."

Beorhthelm shrugged, clearly unbothered by the prospect of more bloodshed. "Better England look like a battlefield than the Pope thinking he can waltz in here without a fight."

"True," Ælfwynn conceded, her voice laced with sarcasm, "but I'd rather not be the one cleaning up after the dance."

She turned back to the map, her finger tracing the Mediterranean coastline. "Roger of Sicily is interested in our offer—but he wants us to send troops to secure some fortress that's under threat from a rival claimant. I'm not keen on sending my best soldiers halfway across Europe to fight someone else's war."

Beorhthelm snorted. "Especially when we've got our own battles to worry about. But Roger's no fool—he'll want something solid before he signs on with us."

"Then we'll give him something solid," Ælfwynn said, her eyes narrowing. "Offer him naval support instead of troops—ships, supplies, whatever he needs to secure that fortress. We can keep our forces closer to home, and he still gets his victory."

Beorhthelm nodded, already mentally drafting the letter. "And if he asks for more?"

"Then we remind him that England's help doesn't come cheap," Ælfwynn replied, her tone firm. "He either takes the offer, or he can deal with his rival on his own."

With Sicily dealt with, Ælfwynn turned her attention to the Holy Roman Empire. Henry had shown interest in an alliance, but he'd insisted on meeting her personally to finalize the details—a request that Ælfwynn found less than appealing.

"I'm not about to trek all the way to Germany just to shake hands with an emperor," Ælfwynn muttered, shaking her head. "Not when there's a war brewing on our doorstep."

"Then don't go," Beorhthelm suggested with a shrug. "Send someone else—a trusted envoy who can sweet-talk the emperor without you having to leave the kingdom."

"Or better yet," Ælfwynn said, a spark of cunning in her eyes, "we make him come to us. Offer to meet him on neutral ground—somewhere close, like Flanders. If he really wants this alliance, he'll make the journey."

Beorhthelm grinned. "You'd make a fine chess player, Your Majesty."

"I've always preferred games where the pieces bleed," Ælfwynn quipped, before her expression darkened as she moved to the next issue on her plate.

William Clito.

The Duke of Normandy had responded to her overtures with a letter that dripped with arrogance. He reminded her, in no uncertain terms, of his claim to the English throne and offered a tentative alliance—on the condition that she recognize his claim.

"As if I'd hand over England on a silver platter," Ælfwynn muttered, her grip tightening on the edge of the table. "Clito's a problem we'll need to solve—with swords, not words. But for now, we'll play along. Tell him we're open to discussing terms, but make it clear that any claim to the English throne is off the table."

Beorhthelm's grin faded slightly, replaced by a look of concern. "And when he inevitably gets tired of talking?"

Ælfwynn's smile was cold. "Then we remind him why his grandfather failed to take England in the first place. And why we'll make sure there's no 'Clito the Conqueror' to follow."

The final piece of bad news came in the form of a report from the coast—mercenaries, sent by the Pope, had begun raiding English villages. They weren't a large force, but they were skilled and ruthless, leaving a trail of destruction in their wake.

Beorhthelm slammed his fist on the table, the grin finally gone from his face. "Bloody mercenaries. They're not enough to take a town, but they're more than enough to make a mess of our defenses."

"They're a pain in the ass," Ælfwynn agreed, her eyes narrowing as she studied the map. "But they're also an opportunity. Send word to our forces along the coast—set a trap for them. Let the mercenaries think they've got the upper hand, then crush them. Make it clear that any more incursions will be met with the same fate."

"And what if the Pope sends more?" Beorhthelm asked, his tone grim.

Ælfwynn's smile returned, sharp as a blade. "Then we make sure he regrets every coin he spent on them."

The plan was set in motion swiftly. Ælfwynn dispatched messengers to Sicily, offering Roger naval support instead of troops. To Henry, she suggested a meeting in Flanders—a place close enough to England to be convenient, yet neutral enough to avoid offending the Emperor's pride. As for William Clito, Ælfwynn's response was carefully worded, offering to discuss an alliance while firmly dismissing any talk of his claim to her throne.

Meanwhile, along the coast, Beorhthelm led a force of English and Danish soldiers, setting a trap for the Pope's mercenaries. They let the mercenaries raid a few more villages, luring them into a false sense of security before springing the ambush. The battle was swift and brutal—just the way

Beorhthelm liked it.

As the last of the mercenaries fell, Beorhthelm wiped the blood from his sword and turned to his men. "Let that be a lesson to anyone who thinks they can raid our lands and get away with it. We'll send what's left of them back to the Pope in a sack."

* * *

Months passed. The war chamber was filled with the usual bustle—maps spread out, messengers coming and going, and Beorhthelm standing at the ready, his arms crossed and a gleam of anticipation in his eyes. But the atmosphere was tense, and Queen Ælfwynn's mood was anything but light.

The letters from Roger of Sicily and Alfonso of Aragon lay before her, their demands clear: more ships, more men, more resources. It was the kind of request that would have drained England dry if she entertained it.

"Greedy bastards," Ælfwynn muttered, tossing the letters onto the table. "They think I'm sitting on a mountain of gold, just waiting to be handed out."

Beorhthelm grunted in agreement. "Sicily and Aragon are miles away. Why should we bleed for their wars?"

"We won't," Ælfwynn replied, her tone firm. "We'll stall them. Offer some token support—enough to keep them interested, but not enough to break the bank. We can't afford to spread ourselves too thin, not with Clito making moves."

Beorhthelm nodded, a grim smile forming on his lips. "Speaking of Clito, the latest reports are in. He's trying to get the Pope's blessing to support his claim to the English throne. Apparently, he thinks a papal endorsement will give him the legitimacy he needs."

"Clito's always been delusional," Ælfwynn said, rolling her eyes. "As if a piece of parchment from the Pope would make me hand over England. Still, it's a problem—if the Pope backs him, we could see more nobles rally to his side."

Beorhthelm's grin widened. "Then why wait for him to make the first move? Our fleet's ready, and the Danes, the Welsh, and the Scots are itching for some action—and some of Clito's land."

Ælfwynn's eyes gleamed with a mixture of resolve and dark humor. "Why indeed? If Clito wants to play at kingship, let's remind him that England doesn't take kindly to pretenders. We'll strike Normandy before he even knows what's happening."

She turned to her map, her finger tracing the coastline of Normandy. "We'll hit him hard and fast—take his castle, seize his lands, and send him running with his tail between his legs. And if the Pope wants to back him after that, he can bless the ashes."

Beorhthelm chuckled, already eager for the fight. "I'll prepare the troops. The Danes will be pleased—they've been eyeing Normandy's shores for years."

"And the Scots?" Ælfwynn asked, her voice tinged with sarcasm.

Beorhthelm grinned. "They're in it for the gold. Gruffydd of Wales too. As long as they get their share of the spoils, they'll follow you to the ends of the earth."

"Good," Ælfwynn said, a satisfied smile on her lips. "Then let's give Clito the surprise of his life."

The Queen's Conquest

The English Channel was not known for being kind to those who crossed it, but on this particular day, it seemed to be in a rare, cooperative mood. The fleet Ælfwynn had assembled cut through the water with surprising ease, the sails of the English, Danish, Welsh, and Scottish ships billowing in the wind like the wings of some vast, predatory bird.

On the deck of her flagship, Ælfwynn watched the Normandy coast draw closer, her sharp eyes narrowing as she surveyed the horizon. The air was thick with the scent of salt and opportunity—a heady combination that had always put her in a dangerous sort of mood.

"Beorhthelm," she called, not taking her eyes off the distant shoreline, "remind me again why Clito thought it was a good idea to poke the English lion while he's still nursing his grandfather's wounds?"

Beorhthelm, standing beside her with one hand resting on the hilt of his sword, chuckled. "Because he's got more ambition than brains, Your Majesty. He's a fool who believes that a papal blessing is worth more than a castle full of soldiers."

Ælfwynn smirked. "A papal blessing won't stop an arrow—or a sword to the gut. But let's be kind. We'll let him figure that out for himself."

As they neared the coast, the first signs of Normandy's unpreparedness became clear. The sentries on the cliffs looked more bored than vigilant, their attention more focused on their dice games than the sea. If Clito had been expecting an attack, it was obvious he hadn't expected it today.

"Pathetic," Ælfwynn muttered. "I've seen village festivals better prepared for a surprise."

Beorhthelm grinned. "Maybe we should've sent them a warning—a nicely worded note, something like 'Dear Clito, we're coming to knock on your door with a few thousand of our closest friends. Be home. Yours truly, Ælfwynn.'"

"Too subtle," Ælfwynn said with a smile. "But let's not waste this gift. If Clito wants to sleep through his own downfall, who are we to wake him?"

The fleet landed with swift precision. The soldiers disembarked silently, the only sound the faint clinking of armor and the occasional barked order. The Danes were the first to reach the shore, their battle axes gleaming in the morning light. Behind them, the Welsh and Scots followed, eager for the promise of gold and land.

"Move quickly and quietly," Ælfwynn ordered as she stepped onto the sand. "I want that castle taken before Clito even knows we're here."

The march inland was swift, the landscape rolling by in a blur of green fields and stone walls. As they approached Clito's stronghold, the full scope of Normandy's unpreparedness became even more apparent. The gates were open, the walls undermanned, and the few guards who were awake looked more startled than defiant at the sight of an invading army.

Ælfwynn's forces surrounded the castle before the alarm was even raised. The Welsh archers took up positions on the hills, their bows ready to rain down death on any who dared resist. The Scots, with their fierce determination and lust for plunder, positioned themselves at the gates, eager to be the first to breach the walls.

And the Danes—well, the Danes were already sharpening their axes and making bets on how many heads they'd collect before lunch.

Ælfwynn stood at the front, her sword drawn, a gleam of cold satisfaction in her eyes. "Beorhthelm, remind me again—how long will it take us to conquer Normandy?"

Beorhthelm looked up at the sun, then back at the castle. "At this rate? We'll be home in time for supper."

"Good," Ælfwynn said with a smirk. "Let's not keep the cooks waiting."

The assault began with the Scots at the front, charging the gates with a fury that would've made their ancestors proud. The defenders, caught off guard, barely managed to lower the portcullis before the first wave hit. The clash of steel on steel echoed through the air, mingling with the battle cries of the attackers and the panicked shouts of the defenders.

It was, as Ælfwynn had anticipated, a massacre.

The Welsh archers unleashed volley after volley of arrows, cutting down anyone who dared show their face above the battlements. The Danes, true to their word, hacked their way through the defenders with brutal efficiency, their laughter mingling with the screams of the dying.

Ælfwynn watched it all with the calm detachment of a queen who knew she had already won.

"Clito won't even have time to pack," Beorhthelm commented as he sliced through a particularly stubborn defender.

"Let's hope he at least grabs a change of clothes," Ælfwynn replied, stepping over a fallen guard as she made her way toward the inner courtyard. "It's a long road to nowhere, and it would be a shame if he caught a cold."

The gates fell with a resounding crash, and the allied forces poured into the castle. The defenders, realizing the hopelessness of their situation, began to surrender—or flee, though the latter proved just as futile.

As Ælfwynn entered the courtyard, she was greeted by the sight of Clito's standard being torn down from the keep. The man himself was nowhere to be seen, but that didn't concern her. He was running, and that was enough.

"Search the keep," Ælfwynn ordered, her voice carrying over the din of battle. "Find Clito—and if you can, bring him to me. Alive, if possible."

The search didn't take long. Clito's chambers were empty, his bed still warm. The coward had fled, leaving his men to die in his place.

Beorhthelm returned with a look of mock disappointment. "No sign of him, Your Majesty. The rat's gone to ground."

Ælfwynn sighed, though there was a note of satisfaction in her voice. "He can run all he likes, but he'll find no refuge in Normandy—or anywhere else. We've taken his lands, his power, and his pride. All that's left is a title with no substance."

Beorhthelm grinned. "And if he shows his face again?"

Ælfwynn's smile was cold. "Then we'll finish what we started."

The castle fell silent as the last of the resistance was crushed. The courtyard was littered with the bodies of those foolish enough to stand against Ælfwynn's might. The allied forces began to strip the castle of its valuables, claiming their rewards with the eagerness of men who had earned them.

As Ælfwynn watched, the satisfaction of victory settled over her like a warm cloak. Normandy was in her hands, and Clito, once a thorn in her side, was now little more than a fugitive.

"Send word to the Pope," she said, her voice carrying the weight of authority. "Tell him that William Clito is no longer the Duke of Normandy. And if he wishes to continue supporting pretenders, he'll find England ready and waiting."

Beorhthelm grinned. "I'll make sure the message is delivered with all the subtlety it deserves."

As the sun began to set over the blood-stained courtyard, Ælfwynn allowed herself a rare moment of satisfaction. Clito was broken, Normandy was hers, and the Pope had been sent a clear message: England would not bow, and Ælfwynn would not be trifled with.

But the queen knew better than to let victory go to her head. The war was far from over, and the Pope, furious at the loss of his chosen puppet, would undoubtedly retaliate.

Still, for now, the spoils of war were hers, and Clito was just another footnote in the history of those who had dared to challenge the Queen of England.

IV

When Kingdoms Clash

French Fury and the Imperial Favor

The castle at Rouen, once William Clito's stronghold and now Ælfwynn's latest acquisition, was bustling with activity. Soldiers moved about with purpose, reinforcing walls and preparing defenses. The air was thick with the scent of smoke from the forges and the tension of an impending storm—both metaphorical and very real.

Inside the great hall, Ælfwynn was holding court with her closest advisors. Beorhthelm stood beside her, arms crossed, his usual grin replaced by a more serious expression. Even he knew that things were about to get interesting—and not necessarily in a good way.

"Well, Beorhthelm," Ælfwynn said, a wry smile playing on her lips as she looked over the latest reports, "it seems we've gone and poked a bear. And not just any bear—a very large, very angry French one."

"More like we kicked it where it hurts," Beorhthelm replied, shaking his head. "Louis is fuming. Word is he's rallying every knight and vassal from Paris to Provence. They're all marching this way to take Normandy back."

"Of course they are," Ælfwynn said, sighing with exaggerated exasperation. "Because why not? The French have nothing better to do than reclaim lands they were never competent enough to hold in the first place."

Beorhthelm grunted. "It's worse than that. He's declared it a personal insult. Louis isn't just coming to retake Normandy—he's out for blood. Yours, specifically."

Ælfwynn rolled her eyes. "I'm flattered, really. But if Louis wants to make this personal, I'm more than happy to oblige. What's the latest from Henry?"

"Ah, the good news for once," Beorhthelm said, a grin returning to his face. "The Holy Roman Emperor is downright gleeful that we've snatched Normandy from under the French noses. He's agreed to an alliance, but naturally, he wants something in return."

"Of course he does," Ælfwynn said dryly. "Let me guess: he wants gold, lands, and maybe my firstborn child?"

"Close enough," Beorhthelm chuckled. "He's demanding a significant tribute from Normandy's wealth. And he's not shy about it—if we want his support against France, we'll have to pay up. Or offer him some strategic concessions."

Ælfwynn tapped her fingers on the armrest of her chair, considering. "It's a steep price, but not one we can refuse. If Henry is on our side, it'll keep France on its toes. I'd rather bleed gold than soldiers—especially when we'll need every blade to hold this territory."

Beorhthelm nodded. "Agreed. I'll draft the terms. We'll make sure Henry gets his tribute, but Normandy stays under your control."

"Excellent," Ælfwynn replied, her tone clipped. "But that's not our only problem. Have we heard from the Duke of Brittany?"

Beorhthelm's grin widened. "We have, and it's actually good news—if you like playing with fire. The Duke of Brittany, Conan, sees our conquest of Normandy as his golden ticket to break free from France's influence. He's offering to ally with us against the French in exchange for us recognizing his independence."

Ælfwynn raised an eyebrow. "So, the Duke wants to bite the hand that's been holding his leash. Interesting. What's the catch?"

"Well," Beorhthelm said, scratching his beard, "he's asking for some lands in Normandy as part of the deal. Just a few choice pieces, of course—nothing too extravagant."

"Of course," Ælfwynn said, sarcasm dripping from her voice. "He helps us hold Normandy, and in return, he gets to carve out a little piece for himself. It's tempting—if only because it'll irritate Louis to no end."

"And we do enjoy irritating kings, don't we?" Beorhthelm said, his grin back in full force.

"It's one of life's simple pleasures," Ælfwynn replied, her smile turning wicked. "But let's not get too carried away. We need Brittany's help, but we also need to ensure Conan doesn't get too ambitious. If he's going to be our ally, he needs to remember who's in charge."

Beorhthelm's eyes gleamed with anticipation. "So, we accept his offer?"

"With conditions," Ælfwynn said, her voice firm. "We'll recognize Brittany's independence and give him some land—but nothing too valuable. And we'll make it clear that if he steps out of line, we'll remind him why Normandy is ours and not his."

"Understood," Beorhthelm said, nodding. "I'll make sure the terms are clear."

As the day wore on, Ælfwynn finalized her plans. The alliance with Henry was essential, even if it meant parting with some of Normandy's wealth. And the Duke of Brittany, with his ambitions, could be a useful ally—provided he didn't overstep. But the looming threat of France was the most pressing concern. Louis was furious, and it was only a matter of time before he marched on Normandy with all the forces he could muster.

But Ælfwynn was not one to sit and wait for the storm to come to her. If Louis wanted a fight, he'd get one—but on her terms, not his.

The next few weeks were a whirlwind of preparations. Troops were gathered, fortifications strengthened, and supplies stockpiled. Normandy, once a peaceful duchy under Clito's questionable rule, was now a fortress bristling with the might of England, Denmark, Wales, and Scotland.

And yet, in the midst of all this, Ælfwynn found herself almost enjoying the chaos. There was something invigorating about preparing for war—especially when you knew you had the upper hand.

One afternoon, as she reviewed the latest reports with Beorhthelm, a messenger burst into the hall, his face flushed with excitement.

"Your Majesty!" he cried, bowing deeply. "Word from Brittany—the Duke has mobilized his forces and is marching to join us. He's eager to begin the campaign against the French."

"Eager, is he?" Ælfwynn said, her lips curling into a smirk. "Well, we wouldn't want to disappoint him, would we?"

Beorhthelm chuckled. "Seems like everyone's eager to take a piece out of

France. Can't say I blame them—it's not every day you get to stick it to a king."

"No, it's not," Ælfwynn agreed. "And when Louis does arrive, I want him to find Normandy ready for him. We'll give him a welcome he won't soon forget."

As the preparations continued, Ælfwynn's thoughts turned to the future. Normandy was just the beginning—if she could hold this territory and fend off the French, her position would be stronger than ever. And with allies like Henry and Conan , she might just turn the tables on Louis and take the fight into France itself.

But that was a plan for another day. For now, Ælfwynn focused on the task at hand: defending her newly conquered lands and reminding the world that England, under her rule, was not to be trifled with.

The Emperor's Tribute and the Scottish Demand

In the grand scheme of things, one might think that conquering Normandy would give a queen some breathing room, a moment to bask in the glory of victory. But Ælfwynn had learned long ago that peace was for the dead, and as long as she was alive, there'd be no rest.

The war chamber at Rouen was alive with the hum of activity—advisors, soldiers, and emissaries moved in and out, all vying for a moment of the Queen's attention. At the center of it all, Ælfwynn sat with Beorhthelm, a map of northern France spread out before them, as if Normandy's troubles could be solved by simply pinning them down on parchment.

"Your Majesty," Beorhthelm began, his tone somewhere between amusement and exasperation, "the Scottish King's emissary has arrived. Again."

Ælfwynn sighed, her fingers tracing the borders of Normandy on the map. "Let me guess—David has decided that his 'friendship' with us requires more land. How much is he asking for this time?"

"More than last time, but less than he'll ask for next time," Beorhthelm replied with a wry grin. "He wants a chunk of Northumbria. Says it's only fair, given the success of our alliance."

"Fair?" Ælfwynn scoffed. "And here I thought the Scots were content with haggis and hills. But Northumbria? That's more than ambitious—it's greedy."

Beorhthelm leaned in, lowering his voice. "You could refuse him, of course, but the Scots are not the most patient allies. And with the French breathing down our necks, a rebellion in the north is the last thing we need."

"Patience was never a Scottish virtue," Ælfwynn muttered, tapping her fingers on the table. "But a rebellion in the north could be… inconvenient. We need David on our side, but I'll be damned if I'm handing over Northumbria."

Beorhthelm smiled, clearly enjoying the mental chess match. "Perhaps a compromise? Offer him something less valuable, but make it look like a grand gesture."

Ælfwynn's eyes lit up with a cunning glint. "Give him the borderlands—enough to satisfy his pride but not enough to weaken us. And remind him that any further demands will come with consequences."

"Subtle as ever, Your Majesty," Beorhthelm said, bowing slightly.

Ælfwynn returned his smile with one of her own, though it was more the smile of a wolf than a queen. "Now, let's talk about Henry."

Henry, the Holy Roman Emperor, was a man who knew how to strike a deal, but he was also a man who knew how to extract a price. The message he'd sent had been clear: Normandy's wealth for his support. It was a demand that Ælfwynn had no choice but to consider seriously.

As she and Beorhthelm discussed the terms, Ælfwynn's mind was already working through the possibilities.

"Henry's no fool," Ælfwynn said, leaning back in her chair. "He knows we need his support against Louis, and he's going to milk that for all it's worth. But if we give him everything he's asking for, we'll be weakened before the real fight even begins."

Beorhthelm nodded. "He's demanding a hefty tribute, but he's also offering to meet in Flanders. The problem, of course, is that Flanders is under French control. We can't exactly stroll in and have a friendly chat with the Emperor while the French are in the way."

"That's precisely why Henry suggested Flanders," Ælfwynn replied, her tone sharp with realization. "He's testing us. If we want his help, we'll have to earn it by clearing the way."

Beorhthelm's grin widened. "So, we suggest that Henry takes Flanders from the French. After all, it's in his best interest too—weakening Louis on two fronts."

"And we sweeten the deal," Ælfwynn added, her eyes gleaming with a plan. "We agree to his tribute, but only after he seizes Flanders. That way, he's committed to the fight, and we don't pay a single coin until he delivers."

Beorhthelm chuckled. "Clever. If Henry wants his tribute, he'll have to work for it. And if he takes Flanders, it'll drag Louis deeper into this mess, spreading the French forces thin."

"Exactly," Ælfwynn said, her voice laced with satisfaction. "Henry gets his victory, we get a weakened France, and the Emperor's forced to be our ally whether he likes it or not."

The message was sent, and Henry, never one to shy away from a challenge—or an opportunity to humiliate the French—agreed to the plan. He would march on Flanders, seize the territory, and open the path for the much-anticipated meeting.

The French Fury Unleashed

When word reached Louis that Henry had launched an attack on Flanders, it was said the French king's roar could be heard from Paris to Provence. Already enraged by Ælfwynn's conquest of Normandy, the news that the Holy Roman Emperor was now openly challenging him on another front pushed him to the brink.

"Louis must be fuming," Beorhthelm said with a wicked grin. "First Normandy, now Flanders. He's probably foaming at the mouth."

"Good," Ælfwynn replied with a smile that was equal parts amusement and malice. "Let him rage. The more he spreads his forces, the more vulnerable he becomes. We've turned this into a war of attrition, and Louis doesn't even realize it yet."

Beorhthelm's grin widened. "And when he does?"

"It'll be too late," Ælfwynn said, her voice cold. "Louis can throw as many men as he likes at us—he'll find Normandy ready for him. And while he's busy trying to reclaim what's lost, we'll be tightening the noose."

The days that followed were filled with reports of battles in Flanders as Henry's forces clashed with the French. The fighting was fierce, but the Emperor's armies, bolstered by the promise of English tribute, were relentless. Slowly but surely, Flanders began to fall into Henry's hands, and Louis found himself embroiled in a war that was growing larger by the day.

Back in Normandy, Ælfwynn prepared for the inevitable French response. She knew that once Flanders fell, Louis would turn his full attention to reclaiming Normandy. But she was ready for him. The castles were fortified, the troops drilled, and the supply lines secured. And with Henry now committed to the fight, the scales were tipping in her favor.

Still, there was no denying that the war was entering a new, more dangerous phase. The French king was furious, and furious kings were prone to recklessness. Ælfwynn knew that the next move could make or break her campaign.

But if there was one thing she relished, it was a challenge.

The French Counterstrike

The skies over Normandy had darkened, as if sensing the storm of blood and steel that was about to be unleashed. Queen Ælfwynn stood atop the battlements of a border fortress, her gaze fixed on the horizon where the first signs of the French army were beginning to emerge. The distant rumble of drums and the glint of sunlight on armor signaled what she had been expecting: Louis was bringing the fight to her doorstep, and he wasn't coming alone.

Beorhthelm stood beside her, arms crossed and a wicked grin plastered across his face. "Well, Your Majesty, looks like Louis is bringing half of France with him. Should we send him a thank-you note for making this more interesting?"

Ælfwynn smirked, though her eyes remained locked on the approaching forces. "He's certainly not one to disappoint. But then again, when you've got a face like his, disappointing people comes naturally."

As the French army drew closer, the banners of Louis's allies came into view. There was William Clito, skulking like a wolf in borrowed armor, eager to reclaim the lands he'd lost and settle old scores. Next to him rode Thibaut of Blois, known as 'Thibaut the Fat'—a nickname he wore with surprising pride, given his tendency to consume more wine than wisdom. And then there was Robert of Dreux, Louis's younger brother, whose ambition far outstripped his competence.

"Quite the motley crew," Beorhthelm observed, his tone laced with sarcasm. "I'm almost disappointed we're not facing someone who actually knows what they're doing."

"They've got numbers, and we've got brains," Ælfwynn replied, her voice calm. "And when Henry's forces arrive from Flanders, we'll have both. For now, we hold the line."

The French army was massive, stretching across the fields like a tide of steel and banners. Clito, at the head of his own contingent, was clearly out for blood. He'd been nursing his wounds ever since Ælfwynn had chased him out of Normandy, and now he was back with vengeance in his eyes.

"The prodigal fool returns," Ælfwynn muttered, watching Clito's banner flutter in the wind. "He should've stayed in exile. It's safer there."

Beorhthelm chuckled. "You think he's still sore about losing Normandy?"

"I think he's still sore about losing his dignity," Ælfwynn shot back. "Not that he had much to begin with."

The French forces began to fan out, preparing to encircle the fortresses that stood as the first line of defense. Ælfwynn's troops—Saxons, Danes, Scots, Welsh, and the Bretons under Conan—took up their positions along the walls and in the fields beyond, ready to meet the onslaught.

The air was thick with tension, the kind that made men grip their swords tighter and whisper prayers they didn't believe in. Ælfwynn, however, had little use for prayers. She believed in strategy, steel, and the ability to outthink an enemy too blinded by rage to see straight.

"Louis must be desperate," Beorhthelm commented as he watched the French knights form up for the charge. "Throwing Clito into the mix—he's hoping the promise of an English throne will keep Clito from realizing he's just a pawn."

"Desperate men make desperate decisions," Ælfwynn replied, her tone sharp. "And desperate decisions lead to mistakes. Let's make sure Louis regrets this one."

The French charge came with the force of a tidal wave. Clito led the vanguard, his knights crashing against the walls like a storm. The earth trembled under the weight of thousands of hooves, and the air was filled with the clash of steel and the shouts of men.

But Ælfwynn's forces were ready. The Danes, with their brutal efficiency, held the walls, their axes cleaving through French knights who dared get too close. The Scots, ever eager to prove their mettle, met the French cavalry in the open fields, their pikes bristling like a forest of death. The Welsh archers, perched on the high ground, rained arrows down on the enemy with deadly accuracy, turning the fields into a killing ground.

Beorhthelm, in the thick of the fighting, laughed as he drove his sword through the chest of a particularly unfortunate French knight. "Well, that's one less fool for Louis to throw at us. How many more do you think he's got?"

"Plenty," Ælfwynn replied, her voice cool as she dispatched an enemy who'd gotten too close. "But let's not make it too easy for them."

Clito, determined to breach the fortress walls, led a charge straight at the gate. But Ælfwynn had anticipated this. As his forces surged forward, the gates swung open—not to admit them, but to unleash a wave of spearmen who slammed into Clito's ranks, driving them back with brutal efficiency.

"Surprise, surprise," Ælfwynn said with a smirk. "Did Clito really think we'd just let him waltz in?"

Clito, his face a mask of fury, rallied his men for another charge. But the trap had already been sprung. The Bretons, led by Conan, swept down from the hills, cutting off Clito's retreat and sending his men into disarray. The French knights, now surrounded, fought desperately, but they were outmatched and outmaneuvered.

Louis, seeing the chaos unfolding, ordered his reserves forward. Thibaut the Fat and Robert of Dreux led the reinforcements, but they quickly found themselves entangled in the same trap. The Scots and Welsh, with grim determination, held their ground, turning the battlefield into a scene of carnage.

"Louis really should've thought this through," Beorhthelm called out as he parried a blow from a French knight. "But then, thinking's never been his strong suit."

"Or Clito's," Ælfwynn added, cutting down another enemy. "They're like a pair of blind men trying to find their way out of a forest—no sense of direction and no hope of survival."

As the battle raged on, word finally came that Henry's forces were approaching from Flanders. The French, already faltering under the weight of

Ælfwynn's defenses, began to break. Clito, seeing the writing on the wall, tried to rally his men for one last push, but it was too late. The combined forces of England, Denmark, Scotland, Wales, and Brittany were too much for him.

The French knights began to retreat, leaving the field littered with their dead. Clito, realizing that the battle was lost, turned his horse and fled, his dream of reclaiming Normandy shattered once again.

Louis, furious but unable to salvage the situation, ordered a general retreat. The French forces, battered and bloodied, withdrew from the battlefield, leaving Ælfwynn's forces victorious.

As the dust settled, Beorhthelm approached Ælfwynn, wiping the blood from his sword. "Well, that was invigorating. I'd almost feel sorry for Clito if he wasn't such a miserable excuse for a human being."

"Don't waste your pity," Ælfwynn replied, her eyes scanning the field. "He'll be back. Men like Clito never know when to quit. But next time, we'll be ready for him—and for Louis."

Beorhthelm grinned. "And what about Henry? He'll be expecting his tribute now that we've held the line."

"He'll get his tribute," Ælfwynn said with a nod. "But first, we'll make sure Normandy is secure. We've won this battle, but the war is far from over. Let's prepare for the next move."

The Gathering Storm

Normandy had always been known for its lush fields and rolling hills, but today, the landscape was marred by the scars of recent battles. The scent of smoke still hung in the air, a reminder that while one battle had been won, the war was far from over. Inside the fortified walls of Rouen, Queen Ælfwynn sat at the head of a long table, surrounded by her most trusted advisors, her gaze fixed on the letter she'd just received from Henry, the Holy Roman Emperor.

"He wants what?" Beorhthelm asked, raising an eyebrow as he peered over her shoulder.

Ælfwynn sighed, folding the letter with a practiced calm that belied the irritation bubbling beneath the surface. "Control over key fortresses in Normandy. Henry's feeling rather bold after we held the line against Louis, and now he's decided that a few strategic fortresses would be a nice addition to his collection."

Beorhthelm chuckled, though his eyes were hard. "Well, he's not exactly subtle, is he? What's next, does he want a crown to go with those fortresses?"

"Only if it comes with a matching throne," Ælfwynn muttered, her voice dripping with sarcasm. "He's testing us. Wants to see how far we're willing to bend before we break."

Beorhthelm crossed his arms, his grin fading. "And are we?"

"Bend, perhaps. Break, never," Ælfwynn replied, her tone resolute. "We need Henry's support, but I'll be damned if I'm handing over half of Normandy to satisfy his greed."

She leaned forward, her fingers drumming on the table. "We'll give him a taste of what he wants—a few fortresses, nothing too significant, but enough to keep him on our side. And while he's busy gloating over his new acquisitions, we'll strengthen our hold on the rest of Normandy."

Beorhthelm grinned. "And when he realizes he's been outmaneuvered?"

Ælfwynn's smile was cold. "He'll be too deep in the fight to back out. Louis is still out there, and Henry knows he needs us as much as we need him. Let him have his fortresses—he'll find they come with more strings attached than he expected."

As Ælfwynn dealt with Henry's demands, news arrived that was as surprising as it was welcome. Louis's disastrous attempt to retake Normandy had not gone unnoticed in his own court. French nobles, always a fickle bunch, were beginning to question the king's leadership. Whispers of dissent echoed through the halls of Paris, and some of Louis's most powerful vassals were beginning to consider their options.

Beorhthelm, ever the bearer of good tidings, delivered the news with a wide grin. "Seems Louis's little escapade in Normandy hasn't exactly won him any friends. Thibaut the Fat is nursing a bruised ego—and a few broken ribs, thanks to our Scots—and Robert of Dreux is sulking like a child who's lost his favorite toy."

"And what about Clito?" Ælfwynn asked, her voice sharp.

"Still licking his wounds somewhere in the French countryside," Beorhthelm replied with a smirk. "But even he's starting to see that backing Louis might not be the path to glory he thought it was."

Ælfwynn leaned back in her chair, considering the possibilities. "If the French court is divided, we could exploit that. Encourage those who are unhappy with Louis's leadership to stir up trouble. The more divided France is, the less likely they are to launch another coordinated attack on Normandy."

Beorhthelm's grin widened. "Nothing like a little chaos to brighten the day."

"Indeed," Ælfwynn said, her eyes gleaming. "Send word to our agents in France. Let them know that we're willing to support any noble who wants to challenge Louis's authority. The more fires we can light in his backyard, the better."

As if dealing with Henry's demands and stirring up trouble in France wasn't enough, a new opportunity—and challenge—arrived from the south. Alfonso of Aragon had sent a delegation, offering an alliance against France. The price? English naval support in his ongoing campaigns against the Moors and the promise of joint control over any lands they could seize from southern France.

Beorhthelm, who had been enjoying the chaos of the day a bit too much, read the proposal aloud with exaggerated flair. "So, Alfonso wants us to sail down to the Mediterranean, help him fight the Moors, and in return, we get a slice of southern France. How generous."

Ælfwynn raised an eyebrow. "Generous, or desperate? He must be seeing cracks in France's armor if he's reaching out to us."

"Or he's hoping to drag us into his mess," Beorhthelm added. "The question is, do we want to be dragged?"

Ælfwynn considered the map spread out before her, tracing the borders of France with her finger. "A campaign in southern France could weaken Louis further—and expand our influence. But it's risky. We're already stretched thin, and sailing to the Mediterranean is no small feat."

Beorhthelm shrugged. "Could be worth it. But we'd have to be careful not to overextend ourselves. And we'd need to ensure that Alfonso's commitment is more than just words on parchment."

Ælfwynn nodded, her mind racing through the possibilities. "We'll send a delegation to Aragon, see what Alfonso's really offering. If it looks like a fair trade, we'll consider it. But I won't commit to anything until we're sure it won't weaken our position here."

Beorhthelm smirked. "Always the cautious one."

"Cautious, but not afraid to strike when the time is right," Ælfwynn corrected, her tone laced with warning. "And speaking of striking, we've got one more problem to deal with."

As if the situation wasn't complicated enough, a missive arrived from Rome that made Ælfwynn's blood boil. The Pope, furious at her continued defiance and the chaos she was sowing in Europe, had called for a Crusade—against England.

Beorhthelm read the letter aloud, his voice dripping with sarcasm. "'Heretical queen,' 'rebellion against the Church,' 'holy war to restore order in Christendom'—the usual papal threats. But this time, he's serious. He's calling for the full might of Europe to descend on us."

Ælfwynn's smile was more a baring of teeth. "A Crusade, is it? The Pope wants to rally Europe against me? I suppose I should be flattered."

Beorhthelm laughed. "Or you could just send him a fruit basket, thank him for the attention, and carry on as usual."

Ælfwynn's eyes narrowed. "We'll need to rally our allies—Henry, Alfonso, Conan of Brittany, and even David of Scotland. If the Pope wants a holy war, we'll give him a war he'll never forget. But first, we need to secure Normandy and deal with the French."

Beorhthelm's expression turned serious. "This won't be like fighting Louis. If the Pope succeeds in rallying Europe against us, we could be facing a war on all fronts."

"And that's why we need to be ready," Ælfwynn replied, her voice steely. "Start preparations. If the Pope wants to turn this into a battle for the soul of Europe, we'll make sure he regrets ever challenging England."

The Sicilian Offer and the Merchant Plot

In the grand hall of Rouen, the air was thick with the scent of intrigue, a mix of musty parchment, candle wax, and the faint odor of too many overambitious men crowded into one room. Queen Ælfwynn, ever the picture of poise under pressure, sat at the head of the table, her fingers drumming a steady rhythm on the armrest of her chair. Her eyes, sharp as ever, scanned the faces of the assembled advisors, emissaries, and one particularly annoying merchant representative who was currently testing the limits of her patience.

"Let me get this straight," Ælfwynn said, her tone dangerously calm. "The merchants are unhappy because the wars are bad for business, and they're threatening to... what, exactly? Overthrow the crown? Raise an army of accountants and bankers to storm the castle?"

The merchant, a rotund man with a face that seemed permanently flushed from a combination of drink and self-importance, cleared his throat nervously. "N-no, Your Majesty. We simply wish to express our concerns. The disruptions to trade, the increased taxes, the—"

Ælfwynn raised a hand, cutting him off. "Concerns duly noted. And promptly ignored. Next."

Beorhthelm, standing by her side as always, barely stifled a grin. "Shall I escort him out, Your Majesty? Perhaps with a polite reminder that threatening the crown is bad for business too?"

"Tempting," Ælfwynn replied, a smirk tugging at her lips. "But let him stay. He might learn something."

The merchant visibly relaxed, though the relief was short-lived as Ælfwynn turned her attention to the next matter at hand.

"Now, what's this I hear about the Emperor Henry proposing a marriage?" Ælfwynn asked, her voice dripping with both amusement and exasperation. "Has he forgotten that I'm already married?"

"Apparently, he's taken an interest in your children," Beorhthelm said, his grin widening. "Thinks marrying his son to your daughter would solidify the alliance. Or maybe your son, if he's feeling particularly ambitious."

Ælfwynn rolled her eyes. "My children are three and five years old. And here I thought I'd at least have a few more years before I had to start worrying about their love lives."

Beorhthelm shrugged. "Henry's not exactly a patient man. He sees an opportunity and grabs it—sometimes a bit too eagerly."

"Indeed," Ælfwynn said, her mind already calculating the potential benefits and pitfalls. "A marriage alliance could be useful, but I'm not about to hand over my children as bargaining chips. We'll negotiate—promise him something for the future, perhaps. But for now, he'll have to settle for fortresses, not family."

"Shame," Beorhthelm said with mock disappointment. "I was looking forward to the wedding feast."

As the discussion shifted, the doors to the hall swung open to admit a delegation from Sicily, their leader a sharp-eyed man with a flair for the dramatic—a necessary trait when serving Roger, King of Sicily, a man who seemed to treat politics like a particularly dangerous game of chess.

"Your Majesty," the Sicilian envoy began with a deep bow, "King Roger sends his warmest regards and an offer of alliance. He proposes a joint campaign against the Pope's Italian territories, an effort to secure both our kingdoms against the Vatican's overreach."

Ælfwynn leaned back in her chair, considering the offer. "Have we been here before? Let me guess—Roger wants to drag us into a war in Italy while he reaps the benefits?"

The envoy smiled thinly. "Your Majesty is as astute as ever. But I assure you, the benefits would be mutual. Sicily's navy is formidable, and with English support, we could dominate the Mediterranean."

"Dominate the Mediterranean," Ælfwynn repeated, her tone heavy with

THE SICILIAN OFFER AND THE MERCHANT PLOT

sarcasm. "While Normandy, Flanders, and England burn? You'll forgive me if I don't leap at the chance to stretch my forces even thinner."

The envoy's smile faltered. "Of course, Your Majesty. But consider the opportunity—if we weaken the Pope's hold on Italy, we could force him to abandon his plans for a Crusade against England."

"And if the Pope doesn't back down?" Ælfwynn asked, her voice sharp. "Then we're left fighting on two fronts, with no guarantee of victory."

Beorhthelm, who had been listening with interest, finally spoke up. "It's a gamble, Your Majesty. But if we play it right, we could turn the Pope's own game against him. We'd need to ensure that Roger is fully committed—and that we're not left holding the bag if things go south."

Ælfwynn nodded slowly. "We'll send a delegation to Sicily, see if Roger's as serious as he claims. But we're not committing to anything until we're sure it won't leave us vulnerable. If Roger wants an alliance, he'll have to prove he's worth the risk."

As the Sicilian envoy took his leave, the merchant representative, who had been stewing in silence, finally found his voice again. "Your Majesty, with all due respect, the merchants of England cannot continue to shoulder the burden of these wars. We need relief—lower taxes, fewer disruptions to trade—or you'll find yourself facing unrest in the cities."

Ælfwynn's eyes narrowed. "Unrest? Is that a threat, merchant?"

The man blanched. "N-no, Your Majesty. Simply a warning. The merchant class is powerful, and if we were to... withdraw our support..."

Beorhthelm, unable to resist, chimed in. "Withdraw your support? As in, stop paying taxes? Stop funding the crown?"

The merchant nodded, albeit reluctantly. "If things don't improve, yes."

Ælfwynn's smile was cold, calculating. "Then allow me to remind you, good merchant, that the crown's protection is what allows your trade to flourish in the first place. Withdraw your support, and you'll find your ships undefended, your goods seized by pirates, and your profits dwindling to nothing."

The merchant swallowed hard, realizing he had overplayed his hand. "Your Majesty, I—"

Ælfwynn raised a hand to silence him. "However, I am not unreasonable. I understand the burdens you face, and I am willing to make adjustments—provided you remember where your loyalty lies."

The merchant's relief was palpable. "Of course, Your Majesty. We are loyal to the crown."

"Good," Ælfwynn said with a nod. "Then let's find a solution that benefits both of us. Lower taxes on certain goods, perhaps, in exchange for increased funding for the war effort. After all, it's in your best interest to ensure that England remains strong."

The merchant bowed deeply. "Thank you, Your Majesty. We will gladly continue to support the crown."

As the merchant scurried out of the hall, Beorhthelm shook his head, chuckling. "You know, I almost miss the days when our enemies wore armor and carried swords. At least you could see them coming."

Ælfwynn smiled, though there was a hardness to it. "Politics, Beorhthelm. It's the deadliest game of all."

How to Break a Kingdom (And Make It Look Like an Accident)

The war room in Rouen was buzzing with the sound of crackling fire and the murmur of hushed voices. Maps and letters were strewn across the table, some bearing the elegant scripts of dukes and counts, others the rougher hand of soldiers' dispatches. Ælfwynn sat at the head of the table, her expression a careful mix of amusement and calculation, as she sifted through the latest reports.

"Henry is at it again," Beorhthelm announced as he entered the room, holding yet another letter from the Holy Roman Emperor. "He's pushing hard for that marriage alliance. Says he'll 'withdraw his support' if we don't agree."

Ælfwynn rolled her eyes, her voice dripping with sarcasm. "Of course he will. And what, pray tell, would he do without our lovely Normandy to keep him entertained? I suppose he could go back to counting sheep—or fortresses—but I doubt it would hold his interest for long."

Beorhthelm chuckled, handing her the letter. "He's persistent, I'll give him that. What's the plan, Your Majesty?"

Ælfwynn took the letter, scanning it quickly before setting it aside with a smirk. "Henry's playing a dangerous game. He wants a royal marriage to secure his grip on Normandy and beyond, but he's forgetting that I don't hand over my children like they're pieces on a chessboard. We'll stall him—promise him we'll consider it when the children are older. By then, who knows? He might find someone else's offspring more to his liking."

"Smart," Beorhthelm agreed. "Keeps him on our side without giving away too much. And speaking of giving away too much—what's the word from Sicily?"

Ælfwynn had sent a delegation to Sicily, tasked with negotiating the terms of the alliance Roger had proposed. But the situation in Italy was proving more complicated than she'd anticipated. The Pope's influence still lingered, and while Roger was eager to strike at the Vatican's heart, the risks were high.

Beorhthelm's grin faded as he relayed the news. "Roger's serious about the campaign, but he's also got a mess on his hands. The Pope's still got supporters in Italy, and they're not going down without a fight. If we commit troops, we're in for a long, bloody war."

Ælfwynn sighed, tapping her fingers on the table. "A war in Italy would stretch us thin, especially with Henry breathing down our necks and Louis lurking in the background. But if we pull back, we risk losing Sicily as an ally—and the chance to weaken the Pope where it hurts."

Beorhthelm leaned in, his tone more serious. "We need to make a choice, Your Majesty. Either we go all in with Roger, or we keep our focus here and let Sicily fend for itself. But half measures won't do."

Ælfwynn nodded, her mind racing. "We'll send Roger some naval support—enough to keep him in the game without overcommitting our forces. If he can prove his worth in the initial battles, we'll reconsider. But for now, our focus stays on Normandy and France."

Just as Ælfwynn was beginning to feel like she had a handle on things, a new problem emerged from the south. The Pope, ever the meddler, had caught wind of her budding alliance with Alfonso of Aragon and wasn't pleased. In an effort to disrupt their plans, the Pope sent envoys to Spain, hoping to drive a wedge between the two rulers.

Beorhthelm delivered the news with a wry grin. "The Pope's playing his cards, trying to turn Alfonso against us. He's offering all sorts of religious incentives—blessings, indulgences, the whole lot."

Ælfwynn snorted, unimpressed. "Typical. The Pope thinks he can bribe his way out of anything. But Alfonso's a pragmatist—he won't abandon our alliance just because the Pope waves a few holy relics in his face."

"Still," Beorhthelm cautioned, "we should keep an eye on things. If the Pope gets too cozy with Alfonso, we could be in for trouble."

"We'll keep a close watch," Ælfwynn agreed, her tone firm. "But for now, we press ahead. Alfonso needs us as much as we need him, and if we can keep him on our side, it'll only strengthen our position against France."

Back in France, the Pope's call for a Crusade against England was floundering. Support was lacking, and Louis's authority was waning after his recent failures in Normandy. Ælfwynn saw an opportunity to press the French, to drive deeper into their territory and force Louis's vassals to reconsider their loyalties.

Beorhthelm, sensing her thoughts, leaned closer. "You're thinking of taking the fight to them, aren't you?"

Ælfwynn leaned over the map of France, a wolfish grin tugging at the corners of her mouth. "Divide and conquer," she murmured, tracing her fingers along the borders of France. "It's what the Romans did, and look how well that turned out—until it didn't, of course."

Beorhthelm chuckled. "Good thing we're not Roman. So, we're really going to do it, then? Conquer France? Ambitious, I must say."

Ælfwynn looked up, her eyes gleaming with a mix of mischief and deadly intent. "Ambitious, yes. Impossible? No. But let's not get ahead of ourselves. We're not going to march in with banners waving and expect the French to roll over. That's not how this works."

Beorhthelm nodded, leaning in closer. "Right, so what's the plan? A grand parade through Paris?"

Ælfwynn's smile was sharp. "Not quite. Think less parade, more slow-burning fuse. We're going to break France, piece by piece, and make sure they don't even realize it's happening until it's too late."

Step 1: Divide and Conquer

Ælfwynn's first move in her grand plan was to fracture the French nobility from within, to make sure Louis VI couldn't so much as sneeze without his vassals debating the merits of offering him a handkerchief. But, of course, she wasn't going to spell this out to anyone but her most trusted advisors. After all, secrets were best kept in the dark, and false moves were part of the dance.

"We'll start with the discontented lords," Ælfwynn said, her tone light but her meaning anything but. "We'll offer them exactly what they want—land, titles, power. And if they think we're sincere, well, that's their problem, not ours."

Beorhthelm raised an eyebrow. "And if they get cold feet?"

Ælfwynn shrugged, a smile playing on her lips. "Then we'll just have to warm them up. A little fire here, a little rumor there. Nothing too overt, of course. Wouldn't want Louis to catch on before we've had our fun."

The plan was to keep Louis distracted, paranoid, and always a step behind. Ælfwynn's envoys would approach the most restless of the French lords, promising them the moon if they played their cards right. And if a few of them got a little too ambitious and tried to play both sides—well, that's what false promises were for.

Step 2: Fortify and Fabricate

While the French nobles were busy sharpening their knives—hopefully in each other's backs—Ælfwynn had another move in mind. Normandy would become an impenetrable fortress, a thorn in Louis's side that he couldn't ignore but also couldn't remove without bleeding himself dry.

"We'll fortify Normandy," Ælfwynn continued, her tone deceptively casual. "Make sure Louis knows that any attempt to take it back will be a slow, painful disaster. But we'll let him think he's got a chance. Everyone loves a good siege—until they're the ones starving."

"Nothing like a little hope to crush a man's spirit," Beorhthelm quipped.

"Exactly," Ælfwynn agreed. "We'll let him bash his head against our walls while we quietly slip through the cracks elsewhere. And while he's busy trying to knock down doors, we'll be building a few of our own—inside France."

The idea was simple: let Louis waste his resources on a fruitless siege, all the while Ælfwynn's forces would be taking key fortresses within France, places Louis would never expect her to strike. But these fortresses wouldn't just be military assets; they'd be breeding grounds for dissent, safe havens for discontented nobles to rally around, all under the illusion that they were still in control.

Step 3: Psychological Warfare

But what was a war without a bit of psychological torment? Ælfwynn wasn't content with just outmaneuvering Louis—she wanted him to know he was being outmaneuvered, but only when it was too late to do anything about it.

"We'll feed him false information," Ælfwynn said, a glint of mischief in her eyes. "Let him think he's outsmarted us, that he's got us figured out. And when he moves his pieces, thinking he's caught us in a trap, he'll find it's his own foot in the snare."

"Deception is a dish best served with a side of irony," Beorhthelm added, clearly enjoying the prospect.

"And we'll spread rumors," Ælfwynn continued, her mind already racing through the possibilities. "Let the French soldiers believe their king has abandoned them, that their fortresses are doomed, that surrender is the only option. Fear is a powerful weapon, and we'll make sure they're well-armed with it."

False flags, fake retreats, and whispered lies in the dark—all designed to make Louis question every move he made, to make his soldiers second-guess their orders, to turn every victory into a Pyrrhic one. The more Louis fought, the more he'd lose, until finally, he wouldn't even realize he'd already been defeated.

Step 4: The Alliances

Of course, Ælfwynn wasn't so arrogant as to think she could conquer France alone. She needed allies, and she needed them to play their part without knowing exactly what part they were playing.

"Henry thinks he's getting a marriage alliance," Ælfwynn mused, her voice low. "And maybe he is—eventually. But for now, we'll dangle the possibility just out of reach, keep him interested but never satisfied."

"Keep him close but not too close," Beorhthelm said, nodding. "A hungry dog is more eager to please."

"And Roger of Sicily?" Ælfwynn continued, ignoring Beorhthelm's metaphor. "We'll give him just enough support to keep the Pope busy in Italy. But we won't commit too much—we can't afford to get bogged down there. If Roger succeeds, all the better. If not, well, Sicily's a long way from Normandy."

"Alfonso in Spain's another matter," Beorhthelm pointed out. "The Pope's trying to woo him, but Alfonso's not stupid. He knows we're the better bet if he wants southern France."

"Which is why we'll keep him on a tight leash," Ælfwynn said with a sly smile. "Promise him lands, but only if he delivers first. And make sure he knows the Pope's blessings won't fill his coffers."

The idea was to keep each of her allies focused on their own interests, while subtly guiding them toward hers. Henry, Roger, and Alfonso would all be too busy fighting their own battles to realize that Ælfwynn was the one winning the war. And when the dust settled, they'd be too indebted to her to object when she took the lion's share.

Step 5: The Final Push

With the groundwork laid, Ælfwynn's plan would culminate in a coordinated strike, one that would see her forces march deeper into France while Louis VI was still scrambling to keep his kingdom together. It would be a slow, steady advance, one that gave the appearance of inevitability—because that was the most terrifying enemy of all.

"Once the French lords have turned on each other, and Louis is running out of options, we'll make our move," Ælfwynn said, her voice calm but with a dangerous edge. "We'll push into the heart of France, take Paris if we can, or at least surround it. And all the while, we'll let Louis think he's still got a chance—until he doesn't."

Beorhthelm grinned, the anticipation almost too much to bear. "And then?"

Ælfwynn's smile was cold, calculated. "And then we'll make sure everyone knows who really holds the power in France. Louis will be a king in name only, if he's even that. And as for the Pope—well, I'm sure he'll find new ways to amuse himself once he realizes Europe isn't so eager to march to his tune."

It was a monumental plan, ambitious to the point of madness, but it was also methodical, deliberate, and—if all went well—utterly devastating to France. Ælfwynn had no illusions about the risks, but she also had no intention of playing it safe. France was a prize worth risking everything for, and she intended to claim it, one step at a time.

The Best Laid Plans...

War has a way of taking the best-laid plans and throwing them out the window—or, in Ælfwynn's case, out the highest tower of Rouen, where they splattered all over the cobblestones below. But if there was one thing Ælfwynn excelled at, it was thinking on her feet—or as Beorhthelm liked to say, "dancing on a tightrope with a sword in one hand and a smile on your face."

The grand plan to conquer France was ambitious, yes, but it wasn't without its hiccups—hiccups that occasionally felt more like violent spasms. Still, Ælfwynn wasn't about to let a few setbacks ruin her fun. After all, if you can't laugh in the face of disaster, what's the point of being a queen?

Ælfwynn's strategy of dividing the French nobility met with early success—at least, at first. Several discontented lords, eager for the promises of land and power, whispered their support and sent secret messengers to pledge allegiance to the English queen. For a brief moment, it seemed like everything was going according to plan.

But, as any good strategist knows, there's always a snake in the grass—or, in this case, a French duke named Guillaume of Poitou. The man had played his part perfectly, feigning discontent with Louis's rule and pledging his support to Ælfwynn. But just as her forces were preparing to strike, Guillaume revealed his true colors—by stabbing Ælfwynn's envoy in the back and rallying his troops for a surprise attack on her allies in Anjou.

"Well," Ælfwynn remarked dryly as she received the news, "it seems Guillaume enjoys a good plot twist. Shame he won't live long enough to write another one."

THE BEST LAID PLANS...

The betrayal was a blow, but Ælfwynn wasn't one to be caught flat-footed. She immediately ordered her forces in Normandy to shift southward, launching a counterattack that caught Guillaume's troops off guard. The battle was bloody and brutal, but by the time the dust settled, Anjou was firmly under Ælfwynn's control—and Guillaume's head was firmly separated from his shoulders.

"Let that be a lesson to any other would-be dramatists," Beorhthelm quipped, wiping blood from his sword. "Next time, stick to poetry."

Meanwhile, in Normandy, Louis made his move, just as Ælfwynn had anticipated. Convinced that retaking Normandy was the key to breaking Ælfwynn's momentum, Louis threw everything he had at the region. He laid siege to Rouen, hoping to starve the city into submission.

But Ælfwynn, ever the master of misdirection, had a few surprises of her own. First, she had stocked Rouen with enough supplies to outlast the Crusades themselves, a fact that became painfully clear to Louis after months of fruitless siege.

"This city's got more bread than a baker's guild," Beorhthelm noted, as they watched the French army grow increasingly desperate from the walls. "And I think they're starting to realize it."

As Louis's men grew hungrier and more demoralized, Ælfwynn ordered her forces to stage a series of lightning raids on the French supply lines. The French soldiers, already tired and underfed, were caught off guard and suffered heavy losses.

"Let them eat cake," Ælfwynn said with a grin as the French retreated, tails between their legs. "Oh, wait—they can't. We've got all the flour."

Ælfwynn's psychological warfare tactics worked wonders in some regions—less so in others. In Brittany, her agents succeeded in spreading rumors that Louis was planning to seize land from his own vassals to fund the war. The Breton lords, never ones to shy away from a good rebellion, took the bait and turned on Louis, declaring their independence and swearing fealty to Ælfwynn.

Brittany fell quickly, and with it came control of the valuable ports along the coast. Ælfwynn was thrilled, though not as thrilled as the Bretons, who celebrated their newfound freedom by drinking themselves into oblivion.

"Can't argue with results," Beorhthelm observed as they watched the Breton nobles stagger out of their newly acquired manors. "Even if they are too drunk to remember who they swore loyalty to."

In the south, however, things weren't quite as smooth. The whispers that Louis had abandoned his people fell on deaf ears in regions like Aquitaine and Provence, where the local lords were more interested in keeping their lands than gambling on a distant English queen. Ælfwynn's agents there were met with suspicion, and in some cases, outright hostility.

"Can't win them all," Ælfwynn remarked, unfazed. "But we'll see how loyal they are when their neighbors start turning up with English banners."

As the campaign dragged on, Ælfwynn's forces pushed deeper into France. The regions of Normandy, Anjou, Brittany, and Maine were now firmly under her control, and her troops were pressing into the heart of the kingdom. The strategy of slow, steady advancement was working—mostly.

In the west, her forces managed to take control of Poitou and Touraine, despite the earlier betrayal by Guillaume of Poitou. The local lords, having seen what happened to their treacherous neighbor, were more than happy to swear allegiance to Ælfwynn rather than face the same fate.

However, in the east, progress was slower. The regions of Champagne and Burgundy remained loyal to Louis, bolstered by fresh troops from the Holy Roman Empire—a not-so-subtle reminder from Henry that his patience with Ælfwynn's delays was wearing thin.

"Henry's getting antsy," Beorhthelm noted, watching the latest dispatches come in. "And it looks like Louis is digging in for a long fight."

"Let him," Ælfwynn replied with a cold smile. "We've taken enough ground to keep them on the defensive. Let them waste their resources trying to hold on to what's left. We'll wear them down, one fortress at a time."

By the time the year drew to a close, Ælfwynn's grand plan had seen both triumphs and setbacks. Normandy, Anjou, Brittany, Maine, Poitou, and Touraine were firmly under her control, while other regions remained stubbornly resistant. Louis, battered but not beaten, had managed to rally what remained of his loyalists in the east, and the war showed no signs of ending soon.

But Ælfwynn was undeterred. The more the French resisted, the more determined she became. There were still pieces on the board, and she intended to move them until France was hers, one way or another.

"Not bad for a year's work," Beorhthelm commented, surveying the map with a satisfied grin.

"Not bad at all," Ælfwynn agreed. "But we're not done yet. Not by a long shot."

Of Kings, Popes, and Rebellious Bretons

The summer sun streamed through the tall, stained glass windows of the grand hall in Château de Nantes, casting colorful patterns on the floor and walls. This was supposed to be a simple ceremony—a routine audience with the local nobility to reaffirm their loyalty. Instead, it had turned into a spectacle of Breton stubbornness, complete with an ill-advised attempt at rebellion, a poorly timed insult, and a botched assassination attempt.

"Your Majesty," one of the Breton lords, a man with a face like a dried prune and an attitude to match, was currently attempting to out-scowl a gargoyle, "we feel that your demands are... excessive. The taxes, the levies, the—"

"Oh, do get on with it," Ælfwynn interrupted, barely masking her boredom. "You've been whining for ten minutes, and I've yet to hear anything that remotely resembles a point."

The Breton lord, not accustomed to being interrupted—especially not by a woman, let alone a queen—spluttered in indignation. "The point, Your Majesty, is that we Bretons are not accustomed to such heavy-handed rule! We are independent, proud—"

"Proud? Of what, exactly?" Ælfwynn's tone was sweet as honey, but there was steel beneath it. "Proud of getting thoroughly trounced by the French for centuries? Proud of being little more than a nuisance on the western edge of Christendom?"

The man's face turned a delightful shade of purple. "We demand—"

"No, I think we've had enough of your demands," Ælfwynn cut him off, her smile never wavering. "You see, I'm feeling rather generous today. You can either accept my terms and enjoy the many benefits of being part of my kingdom—or you can continue to play at rebellion and find out just how much patience I don't have."

Before the Breton lord could respond, there was a sudden, sharp sound—the unmistakable twang of a crossbow string. It was followed by a thunk as a bolt embedded itself in the wooden throne where Ælfwynn had been sitting just moments before.

"Good aim," Beorhthelm remarked casually as he stepped in front of Ælfwynn, drawing his sword. "Shame about the timing."

The would-be assassin, a young man barely out of his teens, looked as though he'd just realized the terrible mistake he'd made. He tried to flee, but was promptly tackled by two guards who appeared almost disappointed by how easy it was.

Ælfwynn glanced at the crossbow bolt with mild interest, then turned back to the assembly. "And here I thought Bretons were supposed to be good at this sort of thing. Was that really the best you could do?"

The hall fell deathly silent. The assembled lords exchanged nervous glances, each trying to gauge how much trouble they were in and who among them might be next.

Ælfwynn let the silence stretch for a moment before she spoke again, her tone icy. "Let this be a lesson to all of you. I'm willing to forgive a lot—stupidity, for instance—but treason is where I draw the line. And assassination attempts? Well, that's just rude."

The offending lord opened his mouth to protest, but thought better of it when Beorhthelm took a step closer, his sword glinting in the sunlight. The guards dragged the assassin away, and the rest of the lords seemed to decide that perhaps loyalty wasn't such a bad idea after all.

"Now that we've got that settled," Ælfwynn said, her smile returning, "shall we continue?"

Later that evening, as Ælfwynn reclined in a lavish chamber with a goblet of wine, she couldn't help but marvel at the sheer audacity of her life. Here she was, not just holding Brittany but facing down an entire kingdom—and, as if that weren't enough, dealing with rebellious Bretons, scheming Popes, and an emperor who seemed to think that the sun rose and set at his command.

And speaking of imperial arrogance, a letter from Roger of Sicily had arrived that afternoon, its contents predictably dramatic. Roger, it seemed, had gotten himself into a bit of a mess in Italy, and he was now calling on Ælfwynn for more substantial military support. His plea was laden with the usual Sicilian flair—descriptions of brutal battles, the Pope's treachery, and how only Ælfwynn's intervention could save the day.

Beorhthelm, lounging in a chair opposite her, looked up from the letter he was reading with a bemused expression. "Roger's gotten himself into a real pickle, hasn't he?"

"I'd say it's more of a full-blown Sicilian stew," Ælfwynn replied, sipping her wine. "And now he's asking us to send more troops, or else he'll abandon the alliance."

"Typical," Beorhthelm said with a sigh. "So, do we send help, or let him simmer in his own juices?"

Ælfwynn considered it for a moment. Roger was a valuable ally, but Italy was a long way from Normandy, and she couldn't afford to weaken her forces here, especially with Henry breathing down her neck and Louis still lurking.

"We'll send him a token force, again," she decided, "enough to keep him in the game but not enough to bleed us dry. If Roger wants to play the hero, he can do it on his own terms. We'll just make sure he remembers who saved him when the time comes."

As if on cue, another letter arrived, this one bearing the seal of Henry. Ælfwynn recognized the handwriting immediately—bold, authoritative, and, unsurprisingly, annoyed. The emperor was growing impatient with Ælfwynn's delays in agreeing to the marriage alliance, and his letter made it clear that his patience was wearing thin.

"Henry's at it again," Beorhthelm remarked, handing her the letter with a grin. "He's demanding an answer, or else he might just take matters into his own hands."

Ælfwynn skimmed the letter, her eyes narrowing. "He's threatening to attack one of our newly conquered regions if we don't agree to the marriage alliance. Typical Henry—thinks he can bully me into submission."

Beorhthelm chuckled. "The man's got nerve, I'll give him that."

Ælfwynn sighed, setting the letter aside. "We'll respond, but not with what he wants. We'll promise to consider the marriage—eventually. But first, he needs to back off and let us finish what we started here in France. If he wants to play the waiting game, let him. He's not going anywhere, and neither are we."

And then there was the Pope, who had apparently decided that Ælfwynn's successes were just too much to bear. Word had arrived that the Pope was calling for a renewed Crusade against her, this time (is it the third time now?) with more fervor and support from across Europe. It seemed the Holy Father was getting desperate.

"Isn't it flattering," Ælfwynn mused, "how much attention we're getting from Rome?"

Beorhthelm rolled his eyes. "Flattering? More like annoying. The Pope's pulling out all the stops this time. We've got reports of knights gathering from all over—Germany, Spain, even Italy."

"And yet," Ælfwynn noted, "no mention of France."

Beorhthelm grinned. "Because they're too busy getting their teeth kicked in here."

Ælfwynn laughed. "Let them come. We'll be ready for them. And if the Pope thinks he can rally Europe against us, he's going to be in for a very rude awakening."

Just as Ælfwynn was beginning to feel that she had everything under control—or as close to control as one could get in the middle of a war—a messenger arrived with more troubling news. Discontent was brewing back in England, where a group of powerful nobles, unhappy with her focus on France, were plotting to overthrow her.

"Well, isn't that just the cherry on top," Ælfwynn muttered, rubbing her temples.

Beorhthelm frowned. "You could go back to England, deal with them personally."

Ælfwynn shook her head. "No. That's what they want. They want me to abandon France, to leave it vulnerable. I'll send word to our loyalists—tell them to crush the rebellion before it gains any traction. We've come too far to turn back now."

Beorhthelm nodded. "And if the nobles get too uppity?"

Ælfwynn's smile was razor-sharp. "Then we remind them why it's not a good idea to cross a queen who's taken on France and won."

The Long Game

It was early morning in the vineyards of Anjou, the kind of morning that made you almost forget there was a war on. The sun was just beginning to rise, casting a soft golden light over the fields, and the scent of ripening grapes hung in the air. If Ælfwynn squinted, she could almost imagine she was back in England, enjoying a moment of peace. Almost.

But peace was a luxury she couldn't afford. Not with rebels brewing in England, the Pope sharpening his holy sword, and Paris looming like a prize just out of reach. Still, if she was going to plot the downfall of a kingdom, she might as well do it somewhere scenic.

She leaned back against a stone wall, taking a sip of wine from a goblet that had definitely not been intended for use at this hour, and considered her options. The vineyard owner—who was somewhere between flattered and terrified that the Queen of England had chosen his land as a temporary headquarters—stood awkwardly nearby, unsure whether he should offer her more wine or run for the hills.

"I always thought war would be more glamorous," Beorhthelm said, breaking the silence as he picked a grape and popped it into his mouth. "Turns out it's mostly about waiting around and trying not to get killed."

"You say that like it's a bad thing," Ælfwynn replied, her tone as dry as the wine. "If you're not waiting, you're probably already dead."

Beorhthelm shrugged. "Fair point. So, what's the plan, Your Majesty? How do we take down Paris when the whole world's trying to take us down first?"

Ælfwynn's first move was to keep her enemies guessing. While Louis was holed up in Paris, paranoid and seeing traitors in every shadow, she turned her attention south. Aquitaine and Provence were key to weakening Louis's support base, and by securing these regions, she could cut off vital supplies to the French capital.

But, of course, nothing was ever simple. The local lords in Aquitaine and Provence were fiercely independent, more interested in their own power than in playing second fiddle to a distant king—or queen. And then there was the Pope, who, like an overly zealous shepherd, was determined to keep his flock in line.

Ælfwynn dispatched envoys to the southern lords, offering them autonomy in exchange for loyalty. She knew better than to try and force them into submission—after all, it was easier to lure a wolf with a bone than to chain it to a post. The negotiations were delicate, with more than a few backhanded compliments and thinly veiled threats exchanged over goblets of wine.

But the real genius of Ælfwynn's plan lay in the deception. While she appeared to be focusing her efforts on the south, she secretly moved her main forces closer to Paris, hiding her true intentions behind a smokescreen of diplomatic wrangling and minor skirmishes.

"Let the Pope think we're chasing shadows," she said, her smile like a blade. "Meanwhile, we'll carve our path to Paris one step at a time."

Of course, not everyone was so easily appeased. The Bretons, never ones to do anything the easy way, had decided that now was the perfect time to stir up trouble. Ælfwynn had already dealt with one rebellion, but it seemed that the lesson hadn't quite sunk in.

This time, the rebellion was more organized, more dangerous. It wasn't just a handful of disgruntled lords—it was a coordinated effort, with the backing of a few particularly stubborn barons who still believed in Breton independence.

"Well, isn't this charming," Ælfwynn remarked when she heard the news. "Our dear Bretons have decided they'd rather not play nice after all."

Beorhthelm smirked. "Can't say I'm surprised. They've always had a flair for the dramatic."

Ælfwynn's response was swift and brutal. She sent in her most loyal commanders, men who knew how to crush a rebellion without getting bogged down in the details. A few strategic executions, a couple of villages burned as a reminder, and suddenly the Bretons were much more agreeable.

But Ælfwynn also knew that you couldn't rule by fear alone—at least, not without exhausting yourself. So, after the rebellion was quashed, she held a grand feast in Nantes, inviting the remaining Breton lords to drink, eat, and remember who held the power. The wine flowed freely, and by the end of the night, most of them were too drunk to remember why they'd ever been angry in the first place.

"Wine works wonders," Ælfwynn mused as she watched the drunken lords stumble out of the hall. "If only it worked on Popes."

Speaking of troublesome allies, there was still the matter of Henry. The Holy Roman Emperor was getting impatient—his letters had become increasingly insistent, demanding that Ælfwynn honor the marriage alliance or face the consequences.

"Honestly, the man's worse than a nagging mother-in-law," Ælfwynn muttered as she read the latest letter. "He wants a marriage, but I'm not about to let him put a leash on my children."

Beorhthelm, leaning casually against the doorframe, raised an eyebrow. "So, what's the plan? Agree to the marriage and hope he doesn't notice we're stalling?"

"Something like that," Ælfwynn replied with a smirk. "We'll promise him a marriage, but only after Paris falls. If he's so eager to tie the knot, he'll have to help us first."

It was a clever move, one that bought her time and secured Henry's military support for the final push toward Paris. And if he got too demanding? Well, there were plenty of other ways to delay a wedding.

Meanwhile, the Pope, ever the thorn in her side, had renewed his call for a Crusade against Ælfwynn. Knights from across Europe were gathering, ready to march on Normandy and crush the heretical queen who dared to defy Rome.

But Ælfwynn wasn't about to let the Pope dictate the terms of this war. She devised a cunning plan to stage a false retreat from Normandy, spreading rumors of internal strife and inviting the Crusaders to strike while they thought her forces were in disarray.

"We'll let them come," Ælfwynn said with a wicked grin. "And when they think they've won, we'll spring the trap. Nothing like a good massacre to keep the Pope busy."

The plan worked like a charm. The Crusaders, emboldened by the rumors, marched straight into the trap Ælfwynn had laid for them. Her forces, hidden in the dense forests of Normandy, ambushed the Crusaders with a ferocity that left few survivors. The Pope's grand offensive was turned into a bloody rout, and Ælfwynn's reputation as a fearsome warrior queen grew even stronger.

While all this was happening, Ælfwynn continued her efforts to destabilize Louis from within. She reached out to the most discontented of the French nobility, offering them generous terms if they switched sides. The promise of land, titles, and autonomy was tempting, and more than a few nobles found themselves reconsidering their loyalty to the increasingly paranoid and isolated king.

"Louis is like a ship in a storm," Ælfwynn remarked to Beorhthelm as they watched the latest reports come in. "And we're the waves, battering him from all sides."

By the time Ælfwynn's envoys were done, several key regions—Champagne, Blois, and parts of Burgundy—had either declared neutrality or quietly pledged allegiance to her. Paris, once the heart of a powerful kingdom, was now surrounded by a web of betrayal and fear.

After months of maneuvering, deception, and more than a few close calls, Ælfwynn was finally ready to make her move on Paris. The city was weakened, its defenders demoralized, and its king increasingly isolated. The southern lords were either neutralized or bought off, the Bretons subdued, and the Pope's forces shattered. Even Henry was on her side, at least for the moment.

It had been a long, bloody road, but Paris was now within her grasp. All that remained was the final push—a push that would decide the fate of France, and perhaps all of Europe.

As she gazed out over the vineyards of Anjou, Ælfwynn allowed herself a rare moment of satisfaction. The pieces were in place, the trap was set, and the final act of this bloody play was about to begin.

"Paris will fall," she whispered to herself, a smile playing on her lips. "And when it does, the world will know that Ælfwynn of England is a force to be reckoned with."

The Breaking of Paris

The smell of smoke and the clang of steel filled the air, mingling with the scent of wet earth after a summer rain. But this wasn't some poetic battlefield—this was the garden of a once-grand Parisian estate, now trampled into mud by a thousand boots. Ælfwynn stood in the center of the garden, surveying the wreckage with a mixture of satisfaction and irritation.

"Funny," she remarked, twirling a crushed rose between her fingers, "I always imagined taking Paris would be a bit more... elegant. But I suppose even the City of Light has its dirty laundry."

Beorhthelm, standing beside her with his arms crossed, glanced around at the disheveled remains of what had once been a finely manicured lawn. "It's not exactly a royal reception, is it?"

"No," Ælfwynn agreed, tossing the rose aside, "but it's ours."

Paris had finally fallen. After months of siege, deception, and more blood than she cared to think about, the city had broken beneath the weight of her armies. Louis VI had fled like a rat abandoning a sinking ship, leaving his capital—and with it, his crown—behind.

It hadn't been easy. The city's defenses had proved stronger than anticipated, and the siege had dragged on far longer than anyone had hoped. There had been moments when even Ælfwynn had wondered if she'd have to call it off, cut her losses, and find another way. But she'd pressed on, knowing that Paris was the key to controlling France—and she was nothing if not persistent.

The final assault had come at dawn, when the defenders were at their weakest. Ælfwynn's forces had stormed the walls, cutting down anyone who stood in their way. By midday, the city was hers.

"Do you think they'll write songs about this?" Beorhthelm asked, watching as a group of soldiers dragged a battered French banner through the mud.

"Only if they like their songs grim," Ælfwynn replied, a hint of a smile on her lips. "But let's not get ahead of ourselves. We've taken Paris, but holding it is another matter."

"True," Beorhthelm acknowledged. "But with Paris under our control, the rest of France will fall in line. It's just a matter of time."

"And blood," Ælfwynn added, her tone darkening. "There's always more blood."

The next few days were a blur of victories and celebrations. With Paris in her hands, Ælfwynn was practically the ruler of France. The remaining French nobles, those who hadn't already switched sides, were quick to swear fealty, eager to avoid the fate of their fallen king. The Pope, too, sent a message— though it was less a blessing and more of a thinly veiled threat. But for now, Ælfwynn was in no mood to worry about Rome.

The coronation ceremony took place in Notre-Dame, the once-proud cathedral now filled with the banners of England. Ælfwynn ascended the steps of the altar, a crown that had once belonged to a French king now resting on her head. She felt a surge of satisfaction as she looked out over the assembled lords and ladies, all of whom now knelt before her.

"Long live Queen Ælfwynn!" the crowd chanted, their voices echoing through the vast space.

Ælfwynn raised a hand, silencing them. "Thank you," she said, her voice carrying the authority of a queen who had fought for every inch of her power. "But remember—titles mean nothing without the strength to back them up. I have taken France, but I have no intention of resting on my laurels. There is still much to be done."

The lords and ladies nodded, their faces a mix of fear and respect. They knew better than to question her now. Paris was hers, and with it, the future of France.

But even as Ælfwynn savored her victory, a dark cloud loomed on the horizon. Word had arrived from England—troublesome word, the kind that made her blood boil and her heart ache.

The lords in England, it seemed, had taken her extended absence as an opportunity to air their grievances. A full-scale rebellion had broken out, led by a coalition of powerful nobles who believed they could seize the throne while Ælfwynn was preoccupied with her conquests in France.

"The nerve," Ælfwynn muttered, pacing the floor of her newly claimed Parisian palace. "I leave them for a few years—give or take—and they decide they'd rather have a civil war than a queen."

Beorhthelm watched her pace, a wry smile on his face. "You did make it look easy. Maybe they thought they could do the same."

"They're welcome to try," Ælfwynn shot back, her eyes blazing. "But they'll find that taking a throne from me is a lot harder than it looks."

But it wasn't just the rebellion that troubled her. News had also arrived about her children—her young son and daughter, left behind in England when she had set out on her campaign. They were safe, for now, but the thought of them caught in the middle of a war back home made her stomach twist.

"It's time to go back," she said at last, her voice firm. "Paris is ours, but England is my home. I can't let it fall to pieces while I'm here playing conqueror."

Beorhthelm nodded, his expression serious. "And what of France? Will you leave it to the wolves?"

Ælfwynn shook her head. "No. I'll leave it in capable hands—those who have proven their loyalty. But England comes first. Always."

The day Ælfwynn departed Paris, the city was still reeling from the impact of her conquest. Streets that had once echoed with French voices now buzzed with the sounds of English soldiers, merchants, and bureaucrats. The city's residents were slowly adjusting to their new reality, though not without some grumbling.

As she prepared to board the ship that would take her back to England, Ælfwynn took one last look at the city she had fought so hard to claim. Paris had been a challenge, but it had also been a victory—a victory that had secured her place as one of the most powerful rulers in Europe.

"Goodbye, Paris," she whispered, a rare touch of sentiment in her voice.

"Try not to get yourself conquered while I'm gone."

Beorhthelm, ever the pragmatist, was already going over the logistics of the return journey. "We'll need to move quickly," he said. "The rebellion's gaining ground. If we don't crush it soon, it could spread."

"We will," Ælfwynn replied, her tone deadly serious. "And when I'm done, those lords will wish they'd never even thought of defying me."

As the ship set sail, Ælfwynn turned her thoughts to England. The rebellion would be put down, her throne secured, and her children reunited with their mother. And once that was done, who knew? Perhaps Paris would still be waiting for her return, ripe for another challenge.

The Queen Who Dances on Thrones

The wind howled through the ancient oaks of Winchester, their gnarled branches clawing at the stormy sky as if in protest. Beneath them, the ground was soaked with the blood of traitors and loyalists alike, a fitting tribute to the bloody mess that England had become in Ælfwynn's absence. But this wasn't some grand battlefield with banners waving and armies clashing—no, this was the aftermath. The kind of silence that follows a storm, where the only sound is the groan of the dying and the shuffle of boots across the wet earth.

Ælfwynn stood in the shadow of her family's castle, her face set in stone as she surveyed the wreckage. The rebellion had been swift and brutal, but so had her response. She'd left a trail of ruined castles and headless lords across the countryside, but in the end, the rebels had gotten their claws into the one thing she hadn't anticipated: her children.

"I leave for six years," Ælfwynn muttered, her voice carrying the sharp edge of disbelief, "and they think they can take everything from me—including my own flesh and blood."

Beorhthelm, the old man who had somehow managed to stay by her side through the entire blood-soaked ordeal, glanced over at her with a look that was equal parts concern and exasperation. "You know, most queens would've considered delegating a rebellion like this. Maybe send a few trusted generals, let them handle the dirty work."

"I'm not most queens," Ælfwynn replied flatly. "And if I'd left this to some general, I'd be mourning more than a few lords and a ruined garden."

That much was true. The rebellion had been more organized than she'd expected, with some of the most powerful nobles in England leading the charge. They'd struck at her weakest points, hoping to force her to abandon France and come crawling back to England in disgrace. But instead of crawling, Ælfwynn had returned like a storm, sweeping through the rebel forces with a fury that left entire towns trembling in her wake.

But the rebels had known how to hit her where it hurt. They'd taken her children—her son and daughter, barely old enough to understand the world they were born into—and hidden them away like pawns in a game of chess. Ælfwynn had found out too late, when the bloodied messenger had delivered the news at the gates of Canterbury.

"They're safe," the messenger had gasped, his voice a mix of fear and hope. "For now. But the lords demand your surrender—give up the crown, and they'll return your children unharmed."

Ælfwynn had stared at him for a long moment, her face unreadable. Then, with a calmness that was almost chilling, she'd simply said, "Find me the names of every lord involved in this. We'll see how long they keep their nerve."

The days that followed were a blur of negotiations, ambushes, and swift, merciless justice. Ælfwynn had played the game like a seasoned gambler, bluffing when necessary, but never showing her hand too soon. She'd offered terms to some, promises to others, but behind it all, she'd been weaving a trap.

One by one, the rebel lords had fallen—some by the sword, others by their own greed and ambition. And in the end, it was a desperate noble, caught between a rock and the wrath of Ælfwynn, who'd betrayed the location of her children.

When Ælfwynn had finally stormed the fortress where they were being held, there had been no mercy left in her. The few rebels who hadn't fled at the sight of her banners were cut down without a second thought. She'd found her children locked in a tower, frightened but unharmed, and as she embraced them, the iron mask she wore cracked just for a moment.

"Never again," she'd whispered to them, her voice breaking as she held them close. "No one will ever take you from me again."

But victory had come at a heavy price. The rebellion had gutted the English nobility, leaving the country fractured and bleeding. Many of the old families were either dead or disgraced, and those who remained were wary, fearful of what their queen might do next.

As Ælfwynn returned to her throne in London, the weight of it all settled on her shoulders. She was now the undisputed ruler of both England and France, a queen who had conquered nations and crushed rebellions with her own hands. But she was also a mother who had nearly lost everything that mattered to her.

The wind swept through the halls of Winchester Castle, carrying with it the whispers of history. Ælfwynn, Queen of England, Queen of France, conqueror of kings, and general thorn in the side of everyone who ever underestimated her, stood by the tall windows, looking out over the rolling hills of her homeland. She couldn't help but feel a pang of irony in the fact that after all the wars, rebellions, and power plays, she was right back where she'd started. But this time, she was the one sitting on the throne—and what a journey it had been to get there.

She thought back to the beginning, to the days when she had been just another noblewoman with a sharp tongue and sharper wits. The kings she'd annoyed, the Popes she'd infuriated, the nobles she'd outmaneuvered—it was a wonder she was still standing, let alone ruling over two of the most powerful kingdoms in Europe.

"So, this is what victory feels like," she mused aloud, her tone as dry as the wine she swirled in her goblet. "It's a bit less satisfying when there's no one left to gloat over."

Beorhthelm, who had long ago learned that quiet contemplation was the best way to survive one of Ælfwynn's rare reflective moods, simply nodded from his place by the fireplace. "You could always write a letter to the Pope," he suggested with a smirk. "I'm sure he'd appreciate a reminder of how much he despises you."

Ælfwynn chuckled, though there was a hint of weariness in her laugh. "The Pope has enough on his plate without me rubbing salt in the wound. Besides, what's the point? I've already won. Twice, if you count France."

She let her thoughts drift back to Paris, to the day she'd taken the city and finally broken the back of Louis's resistance. It had been a hard-fought victory, one that had cost her dearly, but it had also solidified her place in history. And yet, even as she'd stood in Notre-Dame, the crown of France on her head, she'd known that the real battle was still to come.

The battle for England—her home, her heart, and the one place she couldn't bear to lose.

She took another sip of wine, savoring the taste of it, and allowed herself to think of her children. They were safe now, tucked away in the very castle where she herself had been raised, surrounded by loyal guards and servants. But the memory of their capture, the fear that had gripped her when she'd realized they were in danger, still lingered like a shadow at the edge of her mind.

"You know," she said, turning to Beorhthelm with a wry smile, "I never intended for any of this to happen. I just wanted to annoy a few kings, maybe stir up some trouble. I never thought I'd end up ruling half of Europe."

Beorhthelm grinned. "And yet, here you are. The queen who danced on thrones."

Ælfwynn laughed, a genuine, full-throated laugh that echoed through the chamber. "Danced, trampled, whatever you want to call it. But I suppose that's the way of things, isn't it? You start out with a plan, and before you know it, you're standing on top of the world, wondering how you got there."

"Must be lonely at the top," Beorhthelm remarked, though there was a knowing glint in his eye.

"Lonely?" Ælfwynn snorted. "Hardly. I've got a kingdom full of people to keep me company. Granted, most of them would love to see me dead, but that's part of the charm."

They both fell silent for a moment, the fire crackling softly in the hearth. Outside, the first signs of dusk were beginning to settle over the landscape, painting the world in shades of gold and amber. Ælfwynn watched as the sun dipped lower on the horizon, feeling a rare sense of peace wash over her.

She had won. Not just the battles, not just the wars, but the game itself. She had outmaneuvered kings and Popes, crushed rebellions, and secured her legacy as one of the most formidable rulers in history. But more than that, she had kept her family safe, her children protected, and her kingdoms strong.

As the last rays of sunlight slipped away, Ælfwynn turned away from the window, setting down her goblet and straightening her shoulders. There would be more challenges ahead—there always were—but she was ready for them. She had faced down the greatest powers in Europe and emerged victorious. What was one more fight?

"Well," she said with a final, satisfied grin, "if they thought they were rid of me, they're in for a nasty surprise."

Beorhthelm raised his goblet in a mock toast. "To Ælfwynn, Queen of Everything Worth Having."

"To Ælfwynn," she echoed, her eyes gleaming with the fire of a thousand victories. "And to whatever poor fool thinks they can take it all away."

THE END (FOR NOW)

Printed in Great Britain
by Amazon